THE ACCIDENTAL PILGRIM

The Accidental Pilgrim

A NOVEL BY

Stephen Kitsakos

ASD PUBLISHING

THE ACCIDENTAL PILGRIM
Copyright © 2014 by Stephen Kitsakos. All rights reserved.
www.stephenkitsakos.com

All persons and places described in this novel are fictitious. Any similarity to persons alive or dead is purely coincidental.

No part of this publication may be reproduced or transmitted in any form or by any means electronic or mechanical, including photocopying, recording, or by any information storage and retrieval system without the written permission of the publisher except in the case of brief quotations embodied in articles and reviews.

Published by ASD Publishing
ISBN: 9780996102919

Manufactured in the United States of America

For My Father, Spero Kitsakos
(1925-2014)

Israeli Archeologists Rush to Excavate 'Jesus Boat' From Sea of Galilee

February 26, 1986 from the Los Angeles Times

SEA OF GALILEE, Israel – An ancient craft described by the excited Israeli press as the "Jesus Boat" has inspired one of the most unusual archeological excavations ever in a land known for biblical discoveries. "I've never seen anything like this," marine archeologist Kurt Raveh said as he watched a group of volunteers race nature to dig the remarkably well-preserved boat out of the muck in which it has been buried for possibly 2,000 years. It appears from weights inside that the boat was used for fishing. The discovery was made by two brothers, members of Kibbutz Ginosar, a lake-side collective farm that has branched out into the tourist business, after they spotted a piece of the boat sticking up out of the mud during an extensive drought.

CHAPTER ONE

Galilee, Israel - September, 2014

It was hard for Simon Strongin to imagine life without Rose. They had been married for close to forty-eight years and, from the very beginning, she was the one who was the great planner, the tireless organizer. Now Simon was forced to step into her shoes, follow her directions, make sure he carried through what he needed to.

He stood on the long dock adjacent to the Grand Tiberias Hotel holding a decorated wooden box. In front of him was the 28-foot Sea Ray Sundancer he had arranged for hire a few weeks ago. He could tell it was spacious enough to accommodate everybody comfortably, but perhaps a little too stylish for its purpose. The boat had been fitted nicely with a doublewide helm seat and fold-down sun pad in the bow, plus further seating towards the rear. The interior was a ridiculous waste of space for he and his three grown children. They were there for one reason only, and there was no way they would spend any significant time downstairs with the wet bar and custom-fitted kitchen.

In front of him was a magnificent view of the astonishing lake spread out beyond, overlapping sapphire and teal, mysterious and refreshing. Sourced by the River Jordan, it had been called many names: Kinneret, Gennesaret, Lake Tiberias, and the Sea of Galilee.

It was here against the shore of these waters that Jesus recruited his provincial fishers of men, walked atop the lake's crystal waves and calmed a nasty storm. The miracles that had occurred within a twenty-mile radius of the hotel had been chronicled, edited, argued about, interpreted and sneered at for two thousand years. But one fact was undeniable. The waters were narcotic and the lake's position from the coastal city of Tiberias afforded panoramic vistas of the small towns that dotted the shoreline oddly juxtaposed with resorts, kibbutzes, anachronistic factories and the enigmatic Mount Tabgha lurking afar.

Simon had arrived in Israel the day before, accompanied by his two daughters. He had been second-guessing himself about taking the trip ever since he read his wife Rose's instructions. But when the young porter escorted him into the dark hotel room and opened the heavy, damask drapes, he knew this was the right decision.

"I was here once before you know. Forty years ago. In 1974," Simon told the porter, "with my wife Rose and my two young daughters. Athens to Tel Aviv to Haifa. Then here. It didn't look like the world we knew. We took a bus the first time to the Galilee. This time we hired a car."

"It is beautiful place, Mr. Strongin," the tanned, wavy-haired man responded kindly in English with a noticeable trace of an accent, "I came Israel from Uzbekistan to Petah Tikah with my wife and kids," the "k" in kids sounding more like a small ball of phlegm stuck in his throat. "We find work here in Tiberias. We get pilgrims from all over. If you need assist, please ask for Arkin."

Simon assessed the young man for a moment, "Well, actually I do have something I'd like to ask. A request. Or perhaps a favor. For my family." He folded a large bill into the porter's hand and closed it. Arkin looked at him curiously when he explained what he wanted done, but assented and then gently bowed before he left Simon alone staring out of the single-paned, floor-to-ceiling windows where the smooth, undulating water of the fresh water lake had spread out.

Then he opened the smaller of the two cases he had brought with him from Toronto, a lightweight expandable hand luggage, and lifted out the contents. It was a box of inlaid wood, about the size of a small shoebox, cherry-colored with delineated golden strips. The package had been wrapped in a series of felt cloths. It contained the remains of Rose, cremated almost one year ago. She had left specific instructions that they be scattered in the lake by her husband and three children, distributed into the vastness of that preternatural water.

"Daddy, Daddy are you in there? It's Barbara," announced the gentle voice of a woman who jiggled the door handle a few times. Again another knock.

"Sorry honey. I didn't hear," his voice cracked a little.

"You must still be exhausted," the well-dressed woman answered. She came into the room dropping her large crushed leather satchel on the floor. "We only flew into Tel Aviv yesterday, and today was a long drive. You're seventy-one now, not twenty-one."

He rubbed his eyes. Even though they were watery with age, they sparkled the brightest blue. "Are you and Sharon settled in your room yet," he asked referring to his older daughter, a respected psychiatrist with a thriving practice in Montreal.

Barbara, the middle child, was an unmarried attorney, Canadian-born but admitted to the bar in New York and working in a practice that specialized in environmental law. Forty-five and now slightly overweight, she had no complete recollection of her visit to Israel when she was barely seven, but she had returned years later to visit an Israeli exchange student she met the summer she floated between her sophomore and junior years at McGill University. It was there, at a kibbutz outside Netanya, that she had sex for the first time with a young Swedish boy who was traveling with a school group.

"Yes, she's just cleaning up and changing. We're going to the bus station together to meet Nathan, and then we can go eat."

"Was it really forty years ago? You and Sharon were babies," he reminded her. "It didn't look like the world we knew. After we had been here for a few days, I said to your mother 'look at this place! I think I could believe in this planet and this God,'" he chuckled. "But then on the day we were to return home your mother went missing."

Barbara looked up at him lightly and smiled. She had heard this story many times before and over the years she'd had odd remembrances of her mother's disappearance. When she did turn up eventually they were late getting to the airport and missed their flight home. TWA 841. Blown up in midair over the Mediterranean. All of them dead from a bomb in the luggage.

She looked at her watch, "Daddy, I'll leave you to get ready and then when we get back from the bus with Nathan I'll collect you and we can all head down to dinner. I'm sure he will be on his best behavior, cranky as he will be from traveling."

"Your brother never had a sense of seemliness. As a boy I could tolerate his being changeable, but as a man, he's a sourpuss," Simon responded. "Now he doesn't even telephone."

"He's busy, Daddy. Musicians have complicated schedules."

"And this is my fault?" he retorted tunefully. "He said I didn't do enough to change her mind and keep her alive. But she knew what she wanted. Your mother was a scientist. She listened to her body. She understood the power of mitosis – both the good cells and the bad ones."

Barbara answered gently, "Daddy, come on. He lived with her through her breakdown when he was just a boy. He had no idea what was going on. Or how to help. You were the one who couldn't deal with it. So when she got sick again it was natural for him to think it was your turn to make her well."

"Your mother and I always struggled to be present to each other. But I could not help her back then. I thought she was a different person. Perhaps I was. In any event your brother has always been resentful of this."

"We need to move forward. Okay?" she added as benevolently as she could. "Maybe this meeting will be propitious? Sharon's still so anxious about another confrontation between the two of you."

"Anxious? She's a doctor. She can prescribe something for herself. And she needs to do something about those cigarettes," Simon stated pragmatically.

"She'll quit when she's ready. She's always been high-strung. We're all a little *meshuga*. It's coded in our genes. Let's not argue. We can't really have any more arguments."

"Arguments? About what?" he asked unconvincingly.

"The secrets. *Her* secrets," Barbara reminded him a little more bluntly than he was accustomed to but she, too, was tired and anxious.

"At the end of her life your mother had no secrets from me," he said.

Barbara walked over to the long windows, now reflecting shadow and light both inside and outside. She could see the distorted outline of her face in the reflected glass.

"Look," Simon paused and then continued deliberately, "I'm sorry that you three had to travel all this way. But coming back here was your mother's idea, after all."

~~~

A few hours later the three siblings had all gathered in the small waiting area outside the Grand Tiberias Hotel restaurant and agreed they would keep the lid on. Barbara and Sharon had picked up their brother from the Tiberias Central Bus Station, a modern monstrosity with upright red stanchions looking like cattle stalls, and driven him back along the scenic route to the hotel. There was a honky-tonk feel to the town – a bit like a Middle Eastern take on the Atlantic City boardwalk – loud signs, restaurant hawkers advertising "St. Peter's Fish" and crass souvenir shops. Though Simon had booked them all into a first class hotel, it was hard to avoid the vulgar commercialism.

Sharon's apprehension was obvious and she inhaled loudly and fiercely on a cigarette.

"Another one?" her sister asked, "Sharon please don't let Daddy see you."

"I'm just uneasy about tonight, about tomorrow. Nathan wasn't exactly charming at the bus terminal."

"Well he's been traveling for a day now. Hasn't seen his father in almost a year. What do you expect?"

Barbara, the middle child, had always taken the role of mediator, bartering and brokering her siblings' relationships and interceding for her parents. She was suited to be a diplomat but instead found herself defending large polluters. They both required similar skills.

She studied her older sister for a moment. She knew Sharon was always a bit high strung, carrying her wounds deeply. Though they were only fifteen months apart, they could not have been more different. Sharon had negotiated an adolescence filled with nervous tics and twitches. But this had eventually been set off by an alluring beauty, inherited from her mother. By the time she had moved beyond the awkwardness of adolescence, she had ripened with full rich lips, high cheekbones, piercing blue-green eyes and a fit body proportioned the way most men wanted their women. Thin and large breasted, in many ways she was the child who most resembled Rose.

Barbara, on the other hand, always struggled with her appearance, more comfortable wearing sweatpants than any tight clothing that might exaggerate her shape. She was the one who had introduced Sharon to her eventual husband, a French-Canadian classmate from law school. But he bullied her sister, and though the union had produced one child, a daughter Michelle who was now at a private school, the marriage had not lasted.

Now she spotted her brother exiting the elevator and it broke her gaze, "Oh there's Nathan now. We're over here Nate," she waved her two arms, like an umpire calling a play.

Dressed casually and comfortably in a button-down powder blue linen shirt and white denim pants, he walked towards them without any urgency. Even as a boy Nathan had an eye for presenting himself well to the world. This evening was no exception. And though he really was tired, he assumed a handsome, expressive face with deep, walnut-colored eyes, a full head of sandy brown hair, parted in the middle, and a well-formed body that had just a slight hint of belly fat.

At forty, he was six years younger than Barbara and a little more than eight years younger than Sharon; he truly played the role of pampered baby brother. But it was his mother Rose, the scientist, who influenced his outlook, shaped his perspective and imbued him with a sense of privilege that sometimes suggested arrogance rather than expose insecurity.

In his left hand he held a black, chrome-plated clarinet case, forged from heavy-duty aluminum. It was an appendage that rarely left his side. He certainly wouldn't leave it unguarded in a foreign hotel room. Every ritual required some music and, in this case, as with all the other preparation, his father communicated to him that it had been specified.

"You look well," Sharon said to him, "Did you get any rest?"

"I'm still feeling the effects of my Boeing cocktail," he snickered, "an Ambien and then a half dose of an Ativan, knocked down with a couple of glasses of whatever swill they were pouring on the plane."

"Did you take any *nice* pills though?" Barbara interjected. "Given all that he needs to do, Daddy is being quite measured and tomorrow is not going to be easy for him."

"Oh, and it's going to be a picnic for us?" he shot back. "Where is he anyway?"

"He's meeting us down here by the restaurant," she answered.

"Don't you think it's senseless? Just a bit. Don't you ever question what he does?"

Barbara answered quickly, "I don't ask him questions. After what he's been through."

"What *he's* been through? Simon is the family terrorist. Well, now he's in the right location for that. Odd for an atheist, no?"

"But your father nonetheless," Barbara interjected. Sharon stayed silent.

"Okay," he withdrew, "so I flew in for her sake though you know I really hate to fly."

This was an undeniable irony because Nathan had been employed as a member of the Toronto Symphony Orchestra for the past ten years flying regularly across Canada.

"Nobody knew how sick she was Nathan. She wouldn't even tell Daddy." Barbara said, "She refused any treatment. What could he do?"

"Simon wasn't there for her the first time she got sick," he said cutting her off, "and he wasn't there when she got sick again, Barbara. You know that. You were practically commuting between New York and Houston defending those BP fuck-ups. I had a concert schedule I was committed to and Sharon had her own family issues." He rambled on as if someone had pulled the cap off a bottle of fizzy water.

"So he just pretended he had no control over what was happening. He thought she was having another breakdown. Only this time it wasn't an 'out-of-body experience.' It was happening *in* her body," Nathan continued.

"This is what happens when patients succumb to obsession," Sharon began to explain, and Nathan turned on her quickly.

"Patients? You mean your mother and the business you're in. But I'm talking recent history. I'm not going back to when I was a pimply, insecure twelve-year old and my mother popped pills and decided to have imaginary conversations with Jesus. It was Simon's abandoning her that I needed to work through, and when I had finally found a way to dissolve the anger, he does the same thing to her again. When she's an old woman. Broken and sick."

"Scientists have irrational beliefs all the time," Barbara said, "and he didn't abandon her Nathan. You know that." She tried to clear it up for the umpteenth time. "He just went back to Halifax. He was wounded, too hurt that she wouldn't do anything to help herself get better. He thought it was selfish."

Nathan jumped in, "Why is it that each of us is brought up in the same house, eating the same food, carrying the same DNA, living through the same events, thinks back and, instead of comfortable consensus, recalls everything so differently?"

"Keep your voice down. He'll be here any second," Barbara cautioned him.

"Look, I'm just frazzled from traveling. From working. And I replay everything over and over in my mind. It's all pointless. You're my sisters and we're all here now to tie up a very sad loose end."

"Let's just make the best of this, baby brother," Barbara agreed, "there's an elegance, of sorts, to all this preparation."

"Sounds to me more like some sort of re-creation," Sharon piped in.

"Just more drama," Nathan mumbled to himself.

And then Simon was standing there, his arms folded, wearing charcoal slacks and a casual shirt, his thick, white hair combed back but still showing subtle hints of black. The high forehead and receding hairline revealed small freckled brown spots of age, and though he had begun to shrink slightly after he had turned sixty, he still projected a strong sense of physical adequacy. His shoulders and chest were developed and, even at a height less than six feet, he seemed taller. Rose, a few inches higher, had always worn flat shoes, and both Sharon and Nathan followed their mother's rangy stature.

"My children are all here," he declared loudly.

When father and son saw each other there was a brief almost imperceptible moment of awkwardness and then Simon offered his arms and his son went right into them.

"Daddy," he said, "I'm very happy to see you. You look well and very handsome." It was a strategic gambit. Simon kissed him on both of his cheeks.

"Hello, Daddy. We're all starved and I need a drink badly," Sharon broke in and started to walk to a table in the dining room. Barbara followed her, slightly behind. From the way she walked it was clear that Barbara was definitely her father's daughter. Their comportment had roots in the same familial structure.

Simon walked next to Nathan, taking his arm, "I'm glad to see you here son. It has been awhile. May I ask you how Ricky is doing?"

"He's fine. He drove me to the airport yesterday and says he will pick me up too. He has a new car and is obsessed with it. I heard him screaming at a bird the other day for pooping on the hood." They all laughed. Ricky had accompanied Nathan many times to see Rose during her illness.

"Well, please extend my regards to him. I haven't of course seen him either for quite a while. I've always admired him."

Nathan saw Ricky as much as possible, but only when the two of them had inhabited Toronto at the same time. A punishing concert schedule, both in Toronto and in a six-city

North American tour, had left him with little time for anything else. Ricky did "creative" for a large ad agency and was constantly on the go. Still, the spontaneity and the uncertainty of the relationship were more appealing to Nathan than the idea of anything lasting or permanent. Besides, Ricky, ten years his junior, liked it that way.

They had met filming a TV commercial for the pharmaceutical company AstraZeneca. Nathan had been hired as a freelance musician to record the commercial's music for which Ricky had written the copy and the first time Ricky saw him he thought, "This boy can really play a horn." Coffee led to a date and then another. Though they did not have a live-together relationship, when they were both in Toronto they stayed at Nathan's spacious condominium in the Woodbine Heights of East York.

Simon grasped his daughters' hands and sat them in their chairs at the table, "Meanwhile, my beautiful daughters are dressed to kill tonight, no?"

The two of them giggled. They both had chosen black, sleeveless dresses. Barbara's long auburn hair was tied back, and Sharon's, which had been through a myriad of colors and blends over the years, was cut short and frosted.

The table was adjacent to a wall of two-story clear glass windows that overlooked the water. Lights flickered in the distance beyond the small, private beach dotted with palm and eucalyptus trees. The harp-shaped lake was easily discernible.

Nathan, who had never been to Israel before, took in the view, "So this is the place where they demand miracles," unsure of whether he was being sarcastic or not.

Simon didn't miss a beat, "Look at it this way. My children are all here together. Gathered in the same place at the same time. This, itself, is a miracle."

Hours later they all had drunk much more than they should have. By the time the third bottle had arrived, a Cabernet from an upper Galilee reserve, Simon was making another observation about the American evangelicals who were interspersed throughout the dining room.

"Such arrogance. To think that God listens directly to them," he said a bit too loudly. There were others still eating in the multi-leveled dining room, but it was towards the end of the evening, and the staff seemed to be pushing to close up and go home.

"A tornado touches down in the middle of America," the older man went on. "It picks its target randomly. We all know that. Blows through a neighborhood, a street, a shopping center, and destroys what's in its path. Kills children sitting at their desks in the schoolhouse. And when it's all over some born-again says, 'I prayed that God would spare me and *he* listened.' What about the dead people? Didn't they pray too? Such impudence."

"Daddy, they're taught to think that way," Barbara offered. "And it gives them something to believe in."

"They're taught to be narcissists you mean. It's *chutzpah* in the worst form. And they're everywhere around here. These so-called pilgrims. Climbing every rock, touching every stone, smelling every tree in a fifty-mile radius because Jesus might have smelled it."

"Hello? And Jews aren't narcissists, too?" Nathan chirped in. "Ever read the history of our people?"

"This family produces only reluctant Jews. We are always uncertain. You never knew your grandfather. He had the brains to get out of Europe, wound up in Canada and avoided associating with any other Jew. Your grandmother was more always comfortable with the *goyim* and I don't think she ever made a Jewish friend. We've always been ill-at-ease about our history. Our religion. And your mother? When we met she already distrusted anything that couldn't be explained by a theory or formula or mathematical proof. This from a girl whose family was strictly *kashrut*, who bristled at the thought their only daughter would date the unorthodox. This is why the deliberation and writing out of her instructions is so extraordinary to me." He stumbled on the last few words, the weight and emotion of them forcing the pitch of his voice higher. Barbara put her hand on top of his and began to massage it. Sharon and Nathan stayed silent.

A moment later Simon continued, "Well, we have a big day tomorrow. It's time for all of us to go to bed."

They all stood up and Simon reached out to hug them. First Barbara, then Sharon and finally, Nathan. "Son, I'll see you in the morning."

Nathan nodded his head gently and then turned quickly, exiting into the lounge and headed towards the elevators, his room and the bed that awaited him.

CHAPTER TWO

Galilee, Israel - September, 2014

By eleven o'clock the next morning the Strongin daughters were gathered on the private dock that serviced the hotel and its clients. Both of the women boarded the boat first, wearing large sun-hats and fashionable sunglasses.

"I just hope Nathan will be on time. He has to drive this boat wherever we are going," Sharon said gloomily. But as soon as the words came out she spotted him about twenty yards away, coming out of the rear doors to the hotel that flanked the pier. He held the clarinet case in one hand and the other held an I-Phone pressed against his left ear. He had forgotten to put the phone on vibrate and the sound of the ringtone had startled him. The first melodic phrase of the Beethoven Ninth. He looked down on saw Ricky's name and the photo of him he had captured.

"What time is it there?" Ricky laughed. "I hope it's morning."

"It's ten o'clock and I'm on the way to meet the girls. My God, you're up late. You haven't been to bed yet?" he yawned.

"How did the reunion go?"

"It wasn't as bad as I thought it would be. My sisters are great buffers, but Simon was firmly in control."

"And today? You're still going through with the ceremony?"

"Yes. Shortly. I guess that's what you'd call it though, frankly. I'm not certain of the details. My father has kept this whole affair tightly wrapped." He had secured the phone between his neck and his left shoulder and waved to Sharon with his right hand.

"Mama was the one who was always more cryptic," he added.

After a beat Ricky asked, "How are your sisters holding up? This must be hard for them."

Nathan looked out at the busy activity on the hotel's esplanade noticing a swarthy, but handsome waiter with thick eyebrows, who had been serving coffee to the guests sitting at tables outside.

"Well, Barbara always takes Simon's side. And Sharon keeps things bottled up. That's probably why she likes to work with the emotionally handicapped."

"Ouch," Ricky shot back.

"Oh come on, you know she's always been a bit uptight. Though they're close in age, Barbara was a lot bossier than Sharon when we were growing up. She took on a lot of mommy duties. Rose was often too self-absorbed," and then, "I miss her so much."

He went on, "Simon's rented a boat and we are taking it up north. It's some kind of fishing vessel, I think. Let's hope it has a motor," he laughed. "He made arrangements with, get this, a company called "Jesus-Sailed-These-Waters" dot com. They're handing it off to us at the hotel's dock and it's ours for the day. One thing I can say for Simon is he has always been efficiently Germanic."

"All those years fishing on Lake Ontario with Daddy will pay off," Ricky chuckled.

"Actually, Mama was the one who was the boating enthusiast. Of course, being a marine biologist, she was often on the water anyway. Even as a boy I was very comfortable in the boat. We had a 198 C V Cuddy. A Chapparal. Both for excursions and Mama's work when we lived in Hamilton."

"Oh, I wish I would have known you then," Ricky sighed. "Handsome buck lying back with a Panama hat on your stomach playing the clarinet. Or were you just steering the big wheel with your manly arms?"

"Shut up, you silly queer. It was none of those," Nathan shot back. "I never looked at being on the water as something that was butch. Besides it was all a family affair anyway. Simon being in the salmon business."

"But I thought that was pink salmon being processed into a can. I didn't know he was a fisherman."

"That's how they met. On a boat. She was a grad student in St. John studying underwater acoustical communication."

"Huh?" Ricky was confused.

"You know, talking to things under the water. And seeing how loud noises affect what's living down there."

"And Simon was a townie?"

"Something like that," he answered his boyfriend. "They had a complicated history. I'll call you later. Go to bed now."

And then he was at the foot of the dock and climbing aboard the Sundancer.

"Oh good. You're here." Barbara hugged him tightly. "Did you see Daddy at all this morning?"

"No," he said as he walked towards the control panel, placing the clarinet case down under the fold-out seat, "but it is ten o'clock, and I am where I am supposed to be. This is a pretty slick craft, no sis?"

He looked out and saw his father walking towards them now, holding tightly onto the cherry-colored box he had brought with him from Toronto. When Simon arrived, he stood on the long dock looking up at the boat.

"I'd asked the porter, Arkin, to make sure the boat had docked and was provisioned with a bottle of wine and a light lunch of *tabouleh, haloumi* cheese and local olives," he shouted as he ascended the steps up to the swanky boat. These had all been specified with his late wife's instructions and he wanted to comply exactly. In the zippered pocket of his jacket he had secured some documents, including a sealed envelope. A letter from Rose to her children. To be given to them after Simon had carried out her final instructions.

"Give me your hand, Daddy," Barbara said. "I'll help you."

"Oh, stop fussing. I can get up there myself," he answered.

"Well then, come and sit by Shar and me," she requested. The two women had already set up a few fold-out deck chairs, arranged so they could all sit together, but Simon wasn't interested. Instead he looked around the boat, waved hello to Nathan, and then proceeded to the rear to sit by himself. He walked as far as he could and then sat down, placing the wooden box on the seat next to him.

Nathan pulled the anchor line and detached the stabilizing ropes, turned the ignition key, and then, effortlessly took the wheel of the Sundancer, guiding it away from the hotel pier and slowly pushing away from the dock.

~~~

The sky was cloudless as the Strongins headed into the midday sun. By boat it was a short distance to Ginosar, the small kibbutz, which lay about nine miles north of Tiberias, hugging the western side of the Galilee and following the coastal road. It was there in 1974 that Simon and Rose had taken their two daughters, the summer when Rose went missing on the beach and they had missed that fateful flight.

But forty years had changed many things in Israel. The lake had risen and fallen: seesaw diplomacy between Israelis and

Arabs, immigration, commercialization and sectarian disputes all had impacted the physical and psychological landscape.

Ginosar, where Rose had been invited by Dr. Noah Chazon, an Israeli scientist who was doing archaeological research in the ancient villages and towns that dotted the Galilee's western shore, was now a tourist destination complete with its own guesthouse for visitors and a restaurant surrounded by silvery smooth eucalyptus trees and colorful bougainvillea. And on the grounds of the kibbutz was the Yigal Allon Center, a museum built by the kibbutzniks to tell the history of the Galilee. The centerpiece of that museum was the remains of an ancient fishing boat that had been discovered in the shallow waters of the Sea of Galilee some twenty-eight years ago.

An extraordinary archaeological find, the boat had been dated to the first century and believed to have been the oldest surviving craft of its kind, perhaps 2,000 years old, and defying the mysteries of scientific preservation. The Israeli media referred to it as the "Jesus Boat" and the Strongins were headed there on that warm afternoon, though only Simon knew the real purpose at the time they boarded and headed out.

There were already other boats out on the crystal water, a combination of leisure craft, ski and banana boats, kayaks, sailboats and fishing vessels. As soon as Nathan pulled away from the hotel's shore, past the mediocre eateries and open-air cafes, they were out in the easily navigable, transparent waters. Surrounded by the rich vegetation of the fertile land that draped the Galilee, the abundant hills, valleys and gorges were a distinct contrast to the dark black pebble beach, remnants of lava rocks that looked unfriendly among the fields of bananas, dates and mangoes that rose just beyond the western perimeter of the lake.

Sharon walked over to Nathan at the wheel. "It's all quite beautiful," she said loudly, "but look over there! That's what I'd call a party boat." The wind and the spray made conversation at a normal audible level difficult.

"Which one?" Nathan shouted holding the wheel steady.

"Starboard. White fiberglass. With the bikini girls swinging their hips. You think that's orange juice they're drinking?" she giggled. "Well, we had our share of party boats back on the St. Laurent during college," she hollered over to her sister. "Remember those were the days, Barbie?"

"Yeah. Girls just gotta have rum," Nathan chimed in but he could see that Barbara's mind was someplace else.

"When are we popping a cork anyway?" Sharon wanted to know. "I'm getting thirsty."

"Didn't you have enough last night?" he asked.

She turned away from him quickly, looking towards the back of the boat where her father was sitting. "What's Daddy doing back there anyway?" she inquired.

They both noticed that their father had reached into his jacket pocket pulling out a silver necklace. Attached to it was a clamshell of polished agate. He was studying it carefully. Sharon recognized it right away. Her mother had worn it around her neck, almost up until the very end. It was one of the few things Simon had kept for himself after she and Barbara had helped him clean out Rose's closets and drawers, unbearably sad but necessary. That day he urged his daughters to take whatever they wanted to, remembrances of their mother to be cherished or discreetly placed in a drawer or on a closet shelf. But the silver pendant was something he pocketed immediately.

"He's just sitting quietly," she told Nathan, answering her own question. "I think he's talking to himself."

And Simon was indeed talking to Rose. Since the day she had grasped his hand as tightly as she could and he watched her pass on. Today was no different. "Funny how the things that happened last month or even last week are murky," he said audibly, "but not the first time I saw you, Rose."

CHAPTER THREE

Atlantic Maritimes, Canada - August, 1963

The tall, attractive woman with the long, straight blonde hair held in place by two white plastic clips, stood on the deck of the ferry that transported people and cars from St. John to Digby. It was the summer of 1963 and Rose Marian Fonseca from Park Slope, Brooklyn had arrived a few days earlier in St. John, New Brunswick. She brought with her a Bachelor of Science degree in Biology, summa cum laude, from Brooklyn College, three large suitcases, one of which was heavy with books, two fitted cotton sheets, a green woolen blanket, a feather pillow and a Fred Fowler Company Caliper — a graduation gift from her father and mother. Her grandmother Fanny, who had lived in her house with her since becoming a widow ten years earlier, had bankrolled her travel and provided an ample purse for expenses over the next three years.

It had been a small ordeal to get out of the sweltering New York City heat to the cooler Bay of Fundy, but she bravely pressed on enduring the Greyhound bus ride from the Port Authority to Montreal where she spent the night at a small, uncomfortable hotel near the bus station. The next day she made her way to the Montreal Central Station, where she boarded the overnight train to Moncton, New Brunswick, traveling up the south bank of the St. Lawrence. She had a comfortable seat with nobody next to her, was able to sleep for a while and took a decent enough meal in the train's dining car. At Moncton she transferred to the bus station and boarded a bus for St. John and then, finally, a taxi took her to the campus at the University of New Brunswick where she was welcomed warmly as an "international" student. This was something she always snickered about as she joined a class of probers and researchers whose English carried heavy traces of foreign accents. But nothing mattered more to her than being offered, and having accepted, a fellowship to study marine biology, a field as new to her as her microscope.

Rose had been preparing to be a doctor, encouraged by her father, David, the son of Sephardic Jewish immigrants who had arrived in New York just before the Johnson-Reed Act pushed itself forward to preserve the virtues of American homogeneity. David's own father, Asher, claimed he could trace the Fonseca lineage back to the Spanish Inquisition, but why bother? He was in America now and they were all American Jews. Besides, David had no interest in family ancestry. He fancied himself a "numbers" man and he had been swept up into college under the GI Bill earning an accounting degree and designing for himself a comfortable middle-class life for his wife, daughter and mother-in-law. But then again his generation had been seized by the dream of an upwardly mobile life, and consequently, he was eager to see his only daughter become a doctor for as long as she could remember.

Obediently, Rose began to study biology, a subject that had at least intrigued her. But by her second year at college she began to see that her true calling was in research, and not in the care and healing of other humans. She told her father she had been intrigued by Rachel Carson's *Silent Spring*, a text she admitted was as rich and influential to her as the Old Testament was to him. Naturally, he and her mother were distressed. The Fonseca house was a traditional one and though David Fonseca considered himself a progressive, he never challenged his strict Jewish upbringing. He expected his daughter to continue a custom that had been handed down to her. Though he had glimpses in the past of his daughter's benign dissidence, scientist or not, he expected her to be a good Jew.

All around him were signs of revolt and upheaval: the Viet Cong and U.S. armed forces traded victories and losses, firemen were hosing down black women in the South, hippies injected drugs into their veins and New York had just ended a one hundred fourteen day newspaper strike. Thankfully, Rose was uninterested in the counterculture – she was more inclined to enthusiasm about Tereshkova, the woman the Russians were sending into space, and she followed the progress of Jacques-Yves Cousteau as his diving saucer explored the bottom of the Red Sea.

"Rose will make something of herself," he admitted, and when the offer from Canada came for her to study with Dr. Annabel Winters, he and his wife were excited and supportive. Neither of them realized at the time that he was putting her directly into the hands of Winters, an enthusiastic atheist and scientific advocate for his daughter that was enriched by a whirlwind romance with her eventual husband, the secular Simon Strongin. It seemed unlikely there would be bar mitzvahs for his grandsons.

~~~

Now, as Rose stood on the ferryboat that bright August morning, she caught the eye of another young traveller. Simon had noticed her the moment he stepped outside the main cabin and onto the deck. She was standing at the railing, blithely looking out and smoking a cigarette.

"You shouldn't smoke cigarettes you know. It's bad for your health," he shouted towards her in a cocky way. The pretty blonde turned her gaze from the starboard side of the *Princess of Arcadia* and stared at him.

"Excuse me?" she responded, bemused.

"Smoking. Well at least inhaling. You're not supposed to inhale," Simon offered. "At least that's what's coming out of Ottawa. Health ministry and all that."

"I'm an American. It doesn't apply to me." Rose smiled openly and then snuffed out the cigarette with her foot.

"You could have just thrown it overboard, you know."

"Oh no," she responded. "This ocean is too beautiful to mar with even one, tiny cigarette butt."

Simon moved closer to her. It was an ideal day for the ferry. A gentle wind was blowing in the bright August sun. "I've been reading about the magnificent tides. The funnel." She turned back to look at the water again.

"Yes, we're pretty unique around here," he flirted. "By the way, I'm Simon. Simon Strongin and my family has a small salmon processing plant over there in Nova Scotia," he pointed out confidently. "I'm actually on my way back there now from a business trip to St. John. My new car is below deck."

"And am I supposed to ask you what kind of a cool car you're driving," she laughed a little. "I'm afraid I'm on foot, Simon. And my name is Rose. I'm actually just a day rider. Plan to get off and then get back on."

"That's a long day on the water."

"Yes, but that's why I'm here. To study the Bay. I'm enrolled at the University of New Brunswick. I'm from Brooklyn. And I've never seen a harbour seal or a grey seal. Let alone a dolphin or a porpoise. At least in the wild. I'm afraid the Brooklyn Aquarium is the closest I have come."

"They're all pesky you know. They get caught in the salmon nets and cause a ruckus."

"That's because you're interfering with their habitats," she threw back, wrinkling her nose defensively.

Simon smiled, running his hand through the inky black hair he had combed back and applied a slick pomade to. He liked the response – it was feisty, a bit sexy, and he studied her briefly. She was dressed in a floral shirt-waist dress under a dark brown wind breaker jacket and was wearing flat shoes. He could tell, as he got a little closer, that she was slightly taller than he was. It was 1963, and she definitely did not have the heavy eye makeup look that he had seen on so many local Canadian girls who wanted to mimic Brigitte Bardot or Elizabeth Taylor, though he could see a trace of a light colored lipstick that accentuated her lips. He put his hands on his hips and said in a smart-alecky way, "Well, you'll have to figure out some way to tell them it doesn't do them any good to get trapped."

"Dr. Winters is working on that," she answered smugly. "Marine mammals are highly adapted to produce and perceive ocean noise."

"Really?"

"Don't you know that porpoises and seals and dolphins and lots of fishes can hear? They rely on sound to navigate, find food, and establish dominance. "

"And avoid predators. No?" He made his eyes bigger and smiled alluringly.

She felt a warm rush overtake her and looked at him closely, studying his features. "Ever since the sonar acoustic transducer was developed," she explained. But he wasn't listening. He took her ungloved hand in his, put his arm around her waist. "Passive sonars listen without transmitting," she continued softly. "The universe provides so many possibilities."

He studied her closely for a moment before asking, "Do you believe God has a plan for you and these animals?" She was taken aback, puzzled. "No. I want to be a scientist. I don't believe in God."

"Oh, good," Simon said. "Neither do I. Now let's go inside and get some coffee."

CHAPTER FOUR

Galilee, Israel - September, 2014

Simon's memory collapsed suddenly, like a splash of cold water thrown onto an unsuspecting face. The images and sounds, the warm powerful sensation of the past rushed by him, filtered by the sharp, contrasted noise of the present. He shook a bit, like a dog that has just come out of a bath. Nathan looked back at him and called out, "Are you all right, Simon? Are we on the right course?"

"Yes," the old man answered quietly.

Nathan wondered why Simon was being so cryptic about everything. "We'll just head north, northwest. It's not far," his father had told him at dinner last night, "and I know I'll recognize where I want us to stop."

"Can you give me some idea of how long it will take?" he asked now.

"I'm uncertain," his father answered and Nathan made a face. "Please. It's what your mother wanted. Not me. Just proceed slowly." And then, "Barbara, will you please come back and sit here with me now."

Nathan noticed Sharon turn her head towards him and roll her eyes as he returned to the boat's wheel, sitting on the padded white leather seat by the control panel. It's funny, he thought, how he could feel his mother's presence everywhere. Her remains may have been gathered into a vessel and placed in a wooden box at Simon's side, but her presence loomed far and wide. He heard her voice; he pictured her face. A quick flash of light, like a Polaroid in his mind, and he could recall vividly the day he told her that he had met Ricky.

"I hope he's Jewish," Rose had laughed, throwing her head back when she thought she had said something funny or endearing. But he knew his mother really never had a sense of humor.

"Really, Mama. Since when was that a requirement for any of your children?"

And then she told him how lucky he was to have been born when he was born. To be alive in the second half of the twentieth century, how different life might have been for both of them, fifty years earlier, or a thousand, or even two thousand.

Brooklyn, New York - 1962 & 1963

David and Lydia Fonseca expected their only daughter to be upright and morally sound, to be an obedient Jew, to associate with Jewish girls and boys, to join the local synagogue bowling team and participate in fellowship with the affirming community that gathered at their *shul* each week. This was the cultural standard for Jews raising their post-war families in the Borough of Brooklyn.

But Rose knew she could not be true to her own convictions and honor her parents simultaneously. Her only route was to be agreeable until she could separate from them and leave home. Unlike her current boyfriend Maury's feelings for his parents, it did not mean she didn't love her own. It only meant she needed to follow her particular path to fulfillment, and that was one of the intellect and not the soul.

Scrappy, but cute, Maury Waxman, who Rose had dated for a few months during her senior year at Brooklyn College, found every reason to despise his own father whom he once described to her as the "enemy." They disagreed on everything, had antithetical politics and, according to Maury, had "nothing in common." He wasn't particularly fond of his mother either.

"How bad could they be?" Rose wondered. But then again she had met so many students at college who rejected their own parents, criticized and condemned them. She had never felt that way about her own mother and father. She didn't seem to have the same conflicts with them that other girls were having with their parents over drinking alcohol, or rock and roll or beach blanket movies.

There were so many things happening all around her during those days in the early 1960's, changes that were coming fast. It seemed like a giant pendulum had been swinging in one direction, and it now was reversing direction. If she could just hold on a bit longer.

Of course, there would always be idiocy around her like the silly "duck and cover" air raid drills. The special bell would go off and the youngest grades would climb underneath their desks using their arms to protect their heads. The older children would be told with authority to "*Form two lines*" and then march off to the gymnasium where they would await the Soviets' inevitable dropping of the A-bomb, the burnt offerings of a society of the godless, bent on promoting the scientific and the atheistic. After all, didn't they believe that the struggle against religion was a struggle in favor of science?

Talking about the Soviets was a frequent topic at the Fonseca supper table.

"But Dad," Rose would often say in between mouthfuls, "it is a pointless exercise. We will all be disintegrated, burned to a crisp."

"It might not happen that way," her mother would answer. "The government knows what they're doing. Who won the war anyway, David?"

"Well, the Russians did, too. After all, they were our Allies. For a while at least," he responded.

"Don't let anyone hear you saying the Russians are your friends. That's not wise."

Rose interjected, "This is ridiculous," which she said often. "Don't you guys understand that we make the same bombs? Besides, *if* the bomb gets dropped anywhere within twenty square miles of Grand Army Plaza, we will all cook like a piece of toast. We'd get third degree burns in a flash. Instead of hiding under a desk they should give us fire-resistant suits to cover our skin."

"Rose, you will make a really good doctor someday. I know you will," her father would say and her mother would nod in agreement. "Now let's just eat."

Rose had the feeling that Maury's dinner table talk was more combative. He lived in Canarsie, a working class neighborhood in Brooklyn on the Jamaica Bay. His background and upbringing wasn't that terribly different than Rose. He, too, was a Brooklyn-born Jew, grandson of Russian and Polish immigrants, though he got to attend Hebrew School and she didn't.

"My bar mitzvah was a joke," he told her. "All that crap, memorizing things I couldn't wait to forget. Sadistic rabbi who should have taken a bath more often."

On their first real date he picked her up in his father's car, a beat-up 1954 rust-colored Plymouth. It was early spring, and he called for her at her house near the intersection of Sterling Place and Eighth Avenue. Wearing a pair of Levis, he dressed it up with a pullover sweater covering a casual shirt. He wore his hair fairly short but with a bit of the popular wet look. He got out of the car and pulled out a package of Pall Mall cigarettes, packed it down, and pulled one out, cupping his lighter in his left hand to shield it from the wind.

"You want one," he asked her as she walked down the long stoop of the family's chocolate brownstone.

"Maybe later," she said as he lit up. She was wearing her favorite outfit, a pair of cropped pants and a tight-fitting black knit sweater with a wide, collared boat neck. It set off her long, straight blonde hair nicely.

She expected him to compliment her or at least open the car door for her, but he just went around to his side, "Wow," he said looking around and realizing exactly where he was, "this is right near where that plane went down."

"Yes," Rose told him, a bit disappointed, "it crashed into our neighborhood. Went down like a jackknife into a church and killed all those people who were on the ground."

"Happened right here. Shit!"

"Forget about all the others who were on the planes. Look over there," she pointed straight ahead through the windshield as she seated herself in the car, "you can still see the burn marks on those buildings across the way, and they're still rebuilding the stores and bar that disintegrated."

"Yeah. Killed that guy just out walking his dog. Shit, imagine looking up and seeing a piece of a plane spiraling down over you," Maury said. "Talk about bad luck."

"We weren't home at the time. None of us. I was still at school, Dad was at work and my mother was somewhere."

"I heard people thought the Russians had dropped the A-bomb. It was that loud. One plane whacked the other into three pieces and then just sailed on, burning in the skies, until it fell down near here."

"Well, what would you expect? It was a mid-air collision. Right over New York. Makes sense, no?" Rose said logically.

It *was* a terrible disaster. Two planes flying over New York City had crashed into each other: a United Airlines propeller on the way from Chicago to Idlewild Airport and a TWA jet bound for LaGuardia from Columbus, Ohio. It had been a miserably foggy and rainy December day with snow on the ground, some fifteen months earlier. The bodies of over 120 people were strewn all over an airfield in Staten Island and in Park Slope, Brooklyn. There were limbs hanging from trees in people's backyards. Burned corpses. Unimaginable horror. Body parts tossed around like broken appliances. They found some fuselage in New York harbor. Rescue workers, searchers and first-responders combed through the Brooklyn neighborhood succumbing to smoke inhalation and burns. The tail section with the letters U-N-I-T-E-D was sticking out of a pile of rubbish with flames shooting out like a roman candle that had been stuck in a sculpture of Lego-like bricks.

"That one boy who survived, though. That was tough going for him," Maury said. "Imagine surviving a plane crash like that, your body burned like an atomic bomb had exploded. You make it out alive and then, POW. You're dead."

"Yeah," Rose agreed, "he was only eleven."

"That really sucks."

"People said it was a miracle he even survived. But after all, he *wasn't* strapped in. So when the door flew open, he flew out with it," she explained, although the gritty details of the so-called boy survivor were well known by then. "Not sure that qualifies as a miracle."

"Yeah," Maury agreed, "well, all the prayers didn't do the kid any good anyway."

"The only miracle might have been if he had actually missed the flight," Rose added.

The boy had died during the night. Not from his burns, or damage to any of his internal organs. The thing is, he had inhaled the burning jet fuel. So his lungs had been compromised, and infection set in. He had expired from pneumonia less than twenty-four hours after the crash.

Rose and Maury's first date turned out to be rather uncomplicated. They were headed down to Shore Road Park trying to get as close as possible to the Narrows to watch the progress of the construction of the Verrazano Narrows Bridge which had started a few years earlier. Fort Lafayette, the old fort that had been plopped down in the Lower Bay between Brooklyn and Staten Island, had made way for the eastern tower of the new bridge. It was touted as the world's longest suspension bridge, a marvel of engineering and one of Robert Moses's pet projects.

The authoritarian New York City parks commissioner had already altered the landscape of the city's infrastructure, and this was another project that he had pushed forward for his grand vision of the city.

They were standing on the concrete walkway, watching the ferries go back and forth, overlooking the flickering lights of Staten Island just beyond the bay.

"It's a bit romantic for a first real date," Rose thought, but she *had* been drawn to Maury after all. They met in a class they were enrolled in together, a literature and discussion class called *The Quest for Enlightenment*. The Professor was a wiry, snooty man with bad acne and a large mustache who was quite content to promote his own opinions, but reluctant to hear others. Rose had played it safe in that class but Maury, who was majoring in philosophy, was well on his way to arguing persuasively.

"Except, of course, in the classroom of someone who has a stick up his ass," thought Rose.

They had gone through the *Bhagavad Gita*, Hesse's *Siddhartha*, *The Acts of the Apostles*, among others. The argument at hand was about moral uncertainty. Rose had been impressed with Maury's handling of the discussion which arose around the persecution of Jesus's followers by Saul of Tarsus and the stoning of Stephen, a disciple of the prophet.

Maury argued that Saul was blameless, saying, "What's the difference if he participated in the violence as the prevailing culture demanded the stoning of heretics," while the instructor proposed that "Faith, and obedience to an omniscient divinity, gave purpose and meaning to existence," and therefore, Saul's blindness and epiphany were justified.

It was a lofty argument and though Rose couldn't remember the ins and outs of it, she did recall that every time the class agreed with one of Maury's points, the Professor shut him down and insulted him, calling him reckless and arrogant. For his part Maury handled it well and this only increased his appeal to her as far as she was concerned.

"Using the Bible as a barometer of behavior is useless," Rose had later told Maury.

"And Professor Dickbrain is one of those guys who thinks his job is to shove his ideas down the throats of anyone who opens his mouth to disagree." Maury had complained to her. "At heart I'm a political nihilist and he just doesn't like that."

Though she had exchanged a quick hello with him once or twice, the first time they had actually talked outside of class was after a long night of studying for midterms in the college library. She noticed that when he spoke he had a way of twisting the side of his mouth a bit and making his eyes open wider. Rose thought he had nice eyes, and a nice mouth with thick lips. It turned out that he was a good kisser, though she had not done much of that with any boy.

She had gone to the library with her friend Rhoda, a stunning young woman with naturally red hair whose one ambition was to "be a nurse, get a job *inna* hospital and find a *doctah* to marry *huh*." Rose had an idea of what direction her own life might take, but at this point she couldn't say settling down to routine domesticity was part of it.

Rhoda had left the library earlier and Rose, who was carrying a heavy curriculum of science, decided to spend a little more time hitting the books. It was an Earth, Atmospheric and Planetary Science course, and it sought to explain the fundamental processes defining the origin, evolution, and current state of the earth and use this understanding to predict the future. Heady, but necessary stuff for a budding scientist.

Around eight o'clock she walked out into the rain and was heading for the IRT subway station on Flatbush Avenue to take her home when Maury came up beside her and asked her if she needed a ride. He had noticed her sitting in a carrel but didn't want to disturb her. He told her he had a car and he would be happy to give her a lift. At first she hesitated, but there was something appealing about his offer. Instead, they went for coffee and bagels at a 24-hour coffee shop just outside the campus perimeter. Afterwards, she decided she didn't want him to drive her home after all. She said she had a few more hours of studying and wanted to go back to library. He was puzzled but agreed to return her to where he found her.

It continued to drizzle on and off and as he pulled away she went up to the pay phone, deposited a dime and dialed. "Dad, do you think you can come and pick me up in front of the Library? It's raining out."

The next time she saw Maury, he asked her to meet him for a movie. After that she started to see him more regularly, in and out of the '52 Plymouth, but she hesitated to call him her boyfriend right away. After a few dates Maury had tried to get to what he termed "first base" but Rose insisted that he "watch where he put his hands," and she would take things slowly. He didn't seem to put up much of a struggle with that.

"He's just a boy, a college boy, I'm dating," she told Rhoda.

"Well, ya not datin' any othah guys. So heez gotta be yore boyfriend," she retorted in the thick Brooklyn dialect that came naturally to her.

Rose often wondered why she, who had been brought up a short distance away from Rhoda, said "her" instead of "*huh*" and "coffee" instead of "*coughy*". Rhoda also spoke in a vernacular that Rose thought betrayed her true interest, one which didn't seem to be nursing. Expressions like "*Did he coppa feel?*" and "*Did ya get a love bite?*" were gradually introduced into each conversation. She also used the word "*retard*" a lot. Rather than be annoyed though, Rose was amused by this.

The reality was that Rhoda, whose figure was a classic 36-24-36 and who projected a sexual insouciance, would never have gone "all the way" until she was lock, stock and married. Rose, on the other hand, disciplined and controlled, had already decided to cede her virginity to Maury. She wanted to be the one to initiate a sexual experience, and she did not want to go off to graduate school, the next summer, as a virgin.

Although her mother had never talked about it, she was certain that her father was not her mother's first lover. She had no factual basis for this except once, when the two of them were talking, Lydia Fonseca had said wistfully, "Sometimes you settle for a man who will be your friend. Not necessarily the one who made you feel like a woman."

Rose introduced Maury, her potential lover, to David and Lydia who, seeing that he was both pleasant and Jewish, were polite, if not enthusiastic. David Fonseca trusted his daughter's judgment even if she was inexperienced in certain matters. He knew that his plan for a successful medical career for his daughter, as well as her own ambition, superseded any relationship between two young people of the opposite sex.

As an only daughter one would have expected that Rose's mother and father would be scrutinizing every aspect of a casual relationship she was having with a young man, but they agreed that he was well-groomed and intelligent even if he was studying a subject that was useless. And Fanny Siegel, her mother's mother, who moved in with them after the death of her husband in 1953, had been a wannabe feminist in her day, an early proponent of birth control and an advocate for gender equality. She was often vocal about "leaving Rose to be as independent as she likes" and, since she still wielded some authority in the Fonseca household, her daughter and son-in-law were duly obedient. After all, Maury had been bar-mitzvahed and had two older brothers who both worked in the garment district in Manhattan. His father was a member of the Knights of Pythias and his mother was active in Hadassah. These were important economic, social and cultural accomplishments to the Fonsecas.

Rose decided she did not want to have sexual intercourse in the back of an automobile so she waited for the right opportunity to invite Maury to their house on Sterling Place. They had been dating since March and now, at the beginning of the summer, Rose had taken a part time job babysitting for two families who lived within striking distance of the Fonseca home. Maury, for his part, had been working in the Waldbaum's supermarket near Canarsie, first as a stock boy and then later on at the Delicatessen counter.

They were sitting in the front seat of Maury's father's car when Rose announced, "My parents and grandma are going to a family function out on the eastern end of Long Island on Saturday. I can't go because I have to babysit the Cohen boys so they're going without me." Then Rose began to organize the enterprise, "They won't be back until very, very late." The last three words were said with deliberation.

"So, this means..." Maury was excited.

"This means you've got to make sure you can be done with your shift and get over to me by nine o'clock," she plotted. "The Cohens said they'd be back a bit before then, and it's just a short walk for me back home."

He reached out and pulled her towards him folding his arms against her tightly. She teased him a little pushing him away. "No, let me explain," she went on, but he was positively ebullient and wouldn't let her go.

"My God, Rose you smell sooo good." He started playing with her long blonde hair, taking the strands in the fingers of his right hand while keeping his left hand tucked into the small of her back. He could feel himself getting an erection.

"All right, Maury. Now stop it. I want to work this all out in advance." She, too, was beginning to feel aroused.

"I don't know how long we will have to be alone in the house so get yourself to me on time. Their affair doesn't start until seven o'clock, so I think we're safe until eleven."

"And *our* affair will start as soon as I get through the front door," he snickered and she squinted her eyes and grinned a little bit. "Oh Rose," he couldn't contain himself, "I don't know how I am going to wait until Saturday. I really like you, a lot."

"And I like you, too, Maury. A lot. You know you'll be my first. Well, remember what we talked about. You must bring a condom. There's no way I'm going to…"

He cut her off, "I'll take care of it. In fact, I've already taken care of it." He reached into the back pocket of his black work pants, pulled out his wallet and took out a Durex Condom in a sealed wrapper. "I took it out of the drawer of my father's nightstand. It's lubricated," he smiled widely.

They both started to laugh together, and then Rose drew him back to her taking his right hand and placing it on her breast. He made a bit of a circling motion and squeezed a little, very gently. She tilted her head at a forty-five degree angle, exposing her long, graceful neck and he put his mouth down on it, kissing it attentively and then, after he heard her moan softly, a bit more aggressively. Rose felt his warm mouth, the bristle from his unshaven face, especially the stubble on his chin which pressed against her and created a sensation that she could only anticipate would be more potent in a few days and a few nights.

Six months later Rose was ready to break it off.

She was circling her senior year in college, getting ready to land, and she decided she needed some space in order to prepare herself for her future. She had made the decision not to go to medical school. It was a huge decision that put her in potential conflict with her father. But, true to his character, David Fonseca listened carefully to what she had told him.

"Dad, I want to understand the world around me, and be a part of making things better, but I don't feel called to medicine," she explained. "I know I'm smart enough to make something of myself, but I can't see myself treating the human species."

"Well, we want our daughter to be a doctor," he said.

"I *will* be a doctor. Just not the kind of doctor like you and mom know."

She had taken coursework and studied Molecular Biology and Comparative Animal Physiology as well as Evolutionary Ecology, and after a series of visits to the New York Aquarium which had opened at Coney Island a few years earlier, she felt herself drawn to marine mammals and the oceans. She reasoned that it was already embedded in her DNA – her ancestors, both from her father and mother's sides, had made great journeys across oceans to come to America. She had begun to research areas of scientific interest and became intrigued by the burgeoning field of bioacoustics. She spread out wide and researched programs in the United States as well as abroad but her introduction to the University of New Brunswick at St. John, and subsequent fellowship, came accidentally.

In her senior year, Rose had been working on a pseudo-science group project for a seminar that required her to research a crypto-zoology study. Her group had chosen the Yeti. Throughout the first half of the twentieth century there had been reported sightings in the Himalayan mountains of Tibet and Nepal of the Yeti, an ape perhaps, but certainly a large bipedal animal, a species that was unknown and undocumented to science. After 1953, when Sir Edmund Hillary had successfully reached the summit of Mount Everest, there were widely circulated reports of the expedition and others to follow of large, unaccountable footprints and sightings of hairy, humanoid creatures.

"This material is a hoax," Rose told her fellow students. "There's definitely going to be some reasonable, sensible explanation one day."

Explorers and adventurers had been smuggling alleged pieces of the Yeti out of the region for some time. Sir Hillary was visiting the Khumjung Monastery on an expedition to Nepal in 1960, and he came upon a "scalp" of the mysterious creature. He had then sent it on to a number of laboratories in the west for further testing.

One of these was the University of New Brunswick at Saint John. There were photographs of New Brunswick, Nova Scotia and the Bay of Fundy in the magazine article Rose had examined, and she became intrigued. After accumulating as much information as she could about the school, she consulted an advisor about applications for International students and made contact, in person, with the Graduate Program's biology research scientist and teacher, Dr. Annabelle Winters. Coincidentally, Winters was coming to New York City in the late Fall of 1962 to attend an academic conference and staying at the Hotel Piccadilly on West 46th Street in Manhattan.

"I'm so excited you're going to meet her," Rose's mother told her, "and at *that* Hotel. It has air conditioning, you know, it's near shopping and the theatres. They call it the meeting place of celebrities."

"I know, Mom, I've seen their advertisements, but I don't care about those things. You do."

Lydia Fonseca did not have a formal education, but she wasn't stupid. She had finished high school and went to work as a switchboard operator at a chair manufacturer in the late 1930's at a big factory in Williamsburg before she met her husband David, a blind date in Coney Island that had been organized by her brother's wife.

"Well, Dr. Winters obviously is interested in interviewing you for the school. What are you going to wear? Do you know who the competition is?" she asked.

"It's not a beauty pageant. She's seen my transcript and my test scores. The thing is, I need to convince her that my primary research interests correspond to hers," her daughter responded.

"Oh, all that fancy college talk, really." But her mother was right on the money about the upcoming interview. Rose had indeed agonized over what to wear to meet the woman who had the potential to be her mentor.

"What did a budding scientist look like?" she wondered. She opted to treat the meeting like a job interview and selected a cotton floral dress in blue and black and a long-line bra and girdle so everything would stay in place nicely. She wore flat shoes so she would not accentuate her height and made the decision not to wear a hat.

Her appointment was for nine o'clock and she got on the IRT at Grand Army Plaza and rode the subway up to Times Square with the crowd of daily commuters going to their offices in Wall Street and in midtown Manhattan, walked three blocks to the hotel and met Dr. Winters who had told her she would be waiting for her in the hotel lobby.

When she arrived, Rose looked around the hotel lobby to try to pick Winters out of the crowd. They hadn't agreed exactly where to meet in the busy lobby, but Rose had seen a photograph of her in the University brochure that was sent to her home. The photo showed her wearing a lab coat, and she'd had on thick black-rimmed eyeglasses. Inside the lobby there were a few possibilities, but she eliminated them quickly, then considered the agreeable-looking woman who was sitting alone on a small, richly upholstered camelback sofa.

"Dr. Winters? Are you Dr. Winters? It's Rose, Rose Fonseca," she announced as she reached out her right hand for a handshake.

Winters looked up and responded with a smile as she rose to greet the young woman. She wore a grey boucle suit with three-quarter sleeves, a white linen blouse and had long black gloves. She had on a felt pillbox hat that was pinned to her head that sported a bouffant hairdo, perfectly shaped.

Her appearance and dress was totally unexpected to Rose, to whom she immediately said, "You certainly are prompt. I appreciate that very much. It has been quite fortuitous for both of us that I had a trip planned to New York City this month. It's difficult, of course, to evaluate students for assistantships who live abroad or are unable to come to New Brunswick without personal contact."

"Yes, I am much obliged for giving me this time to meet with you," Rose answered respectfully.

She hadn't realized she was staring at the older woman, a little shocked by the professor's surprising appearance. Winters was entirely too glamorous, she thought, to be a biologist.

"I'm sorry," Winters inquired, "was I not what you were expecting?"

Rose began to blush.

"Oh, no. Please forgive me. It's just that the photograph I saw of you was from the laboratory, and ..."

"Oh that's certainly understandable. My hair was pulled back into a tidy bun and I had on those thick black-rimmed eyeglasses which I need to read the charts. Unlike the idea that many men have about women in science, we do clean up quite nicely," she said.

"I'm so sorry if that came out awkwardly," Rose felt foolish now.

"Miss Fonseca, I am the only woman on the faculty of the Department of Biological Sciences. The sole female out of fifteen. My colleagues would much prefer a man, I think, or at least a woman who would fit their idea of what I should look like. Plain, perhaps. A spinster sporting a small mustache?" she continued directly. "Well, if we're keeping score, you don't look anything like what I was expecting either. I was impressed by your academic record, your writing samples and, of course, the recommendations that came from your professors."

"She certainly got right to the point," thought Rose who loosened up a bit.

"So let's go inside the restaurant, order some breakfast and see if we like each other," she said, smiling. Rose followed her, a little timidly but thinking to herself that Winters was a formidable woman.

Once they were seated and had ordered beverages, Dr. Winters unfastened the pin from her hat and removed it, placing it next to her on the table.

"Of course, it would be perfectly acceptable for me to keep my hat on in the restaurant, but the rules of hat wearing, like so many other rules, are extraordinary to me. Don't you agree, Rose?"

Rose, a little suspicious, wasn't exactly sure what Winters was setting her up for.

"Take this hat, for example," she lifted it up, "if I were to doff my hat to a stranger it would be considered inappropriate, no? But not if a man tipped his hat."

Rose shook her head in assent. "Now let's say that if I went into St. Patrick's Cathedral," the older woman continued, "I would be required to keep my hat fastened to my head. But if a man were *not* to remove his hat it would be seen as disrespectful.

Yet if that same man enters a synagogue it would be considered disrespectful if he did *not* wear a hat. How do you account for this variety in houses of worship?"

Rose thought quite carefully before she answered the question, "I avoid them entirely."

After that Rose felt that they had connected extremely well, and she could tell that the interview had nothing whatsoever to do with her potential to engage in scholarly research or discern a vocation in the natural sciences. The scientist and teacher had already determined that.

Through a series of questions that were uncommonly ordered and systematic, Annabel Winters attempted to get to know who Rose truly was. If she was to take on a promising student, she would assess her potential through a pseudo-scientific analysis. She apparently had already developed her own hypothesis about Rose, designed an experimental method to confirm or refute the hypothesis and drew conclusions. Whether or not this experiment was repeatable was another story entirely.

~~~

That evening David Fonseca called out excitedly when he came through the inside frosted glass door of the vestibule at the top of the brownstone's stoop, "How did it go? Was she impressed with you Rose?"

Rose was sitting in the small parlor to the left of the narrow front hall, reading through an assignment for tomorrow's class in Advanced Cell and Molecular Biology. She had a few large envelopes scattered around on the floor with applications and brochures from Cornell University, the doctoral program at the City University of New York and the California Institute of Technology.

"I'm in here, Dad," she called. He put his coat on a peg behind the door, placed his black fedora over it and pushed his narrow leather briefcase into the corner. He could smell and hear the sounds of supper preparation coming from beyond the hallway in the back of the house where his wife and mother-in-law were fussing.

"I'll take a kiss, please. Thank you." He looked around, "What's all this?"

"More stuff from schools. But I think I really want to go to Canada. I can't explain why, but I have a feeling that Dr. Winters is going to change my life."

"I thought so. But St. John is so far."

"Not as far as California."

"Maury will be devastated," he said with a slight twinkle in his eye.

Meanwhile she and Maury had settled into a rather prosaic routine. Over that summer he had become increasingly argumentative. Not so much with her, but with everyone and everything around them. He still had another year of school in front of him and then his I-S deferment status would expire. Military manpower policies were being debated and enacted by the Kennedy administration in case a call-up of troops might be necessary in Southeast Asia or other Cold War conflicts.

Rose was sympathetic and told him not to be alarmed, but selfishly she was more focused on where she would be in a few months and that did not include being with Maury.

Their dates had become mainly movies (they had seen *Lawrence of Arabia* which she thought intolerably long, but loved the psychotic elements in *Whatever Happened to Baby Jane*), and they went dancing a few times with Rhoda and her date, had sex a few more times in Maury's father's car and once at his house when his parents went up to the Hotel Nevele in the Catskill Mountains for a weekend. They regularly watched the progress of the construction of the Verrazano Narrows Bridge and took the Staten Island Ferry back and forth between St. George and Bay Ridge, Brooklyn. Eventually, it was the boat she chose to be the venue for the breakup.

On a crystal clear evening in October, Maury picked her up in front of the brownstone. She sat on one of the steps near the bottom of the stoop smoking a cigarette pensively. When Maury pulled in she snuffed the cigarette out on one of the steps and got into the car. He had started to wear his hair a little longer and grow his sideburns out.

"I reject everything that Moe and Ada have given me," he announced.

"But why?" Rose asked, lighting another cigarette. She had recently started smoking mentholated cigarettes and was experimenting with different brands, "Did you just argue with them?"

"Because they are happy with the status quo, because they believe money will solve all the world's problems, because they voted for Nixon, because they call Negros *schwarzes.*"

"They're still your parents, Maury. They brought you into this world."

"Yeah, and they're pushing me out of theirs. As soon as I have my degree you know I'm heading out to California."

"What's out there?" she asked.

"People who don't want to sell out! New York is bullshit. The square root of bullshit. The entire east coast is bullshit."

"Oh, come on. California is where movies are made. Talk about selling out."

"Utilitarianism, baby!! The real pursuit of happiness. That's what it's all about. And California here I come," he shouted out the car window. "You'll come with me, no? California can change your life," he said confidently.

"Oh, stop showing off, Maury. You're just a crazy mixed up Jewish kid from Brooklyn."

"Yeah, but that's what you like about me, right?" he shot back at her. Rose thought he was probably on target there.

"Are you hungry?" he asked her.

"Honestly, I'd rather just talk. Let's go for a ride on the ferry."

Maury knew that Rose adored the transient but panoramic ride on the Staten Island Ferry which would transport people and cars from the 69th Street pier near Owl's Head Park in Bay Ridge to the St. George Ferry Terminal on Staten Island. *The Hamilton*, a small, compact ferryboat, was waiting for cars to board.

When they made the turn onto the corrugated entryway, the harsh lights on the pier and inside the boat illuminated its grey-green façade and cast bleak shadows through the two dozen or so oval-shaped windows that lined the perimeter of the car deck. They walked upstairs to secure a private spot at a railing. Rose felt comforted by the night air and the smell of the Bay. She pulled out a cigarette, and Maury reached over to light it for her then took one of his L&M's out and lit his own.

The rough clanking of the ratchet wheel started, the ferry whistle blew three times and then *The Hamilton* departed, pushing its bulk away from the pier, forcing the chilly water up against the moorings and splashing intermittently onto the deck. Ahead were the flickering lights of the north shore of Staten Island, its perimeter lights fluttering in counterpoint against the on again, off again, lapping of waves against the battered hull.

Rose looked at him and said, "Are you serious about going to California? I mean, after school."

"Well, yeah, Rose, I guess. I don't know. I get mixed up. Sometimes I'm certain about everything and then, in a flash, everything seems questionable."

"Because sometimes things seem a lot better than they actually are. You know I'm going to be applying to graduate schools, right?"

"Right, but I thought you wanted to stick around here," he said with concern. "I mean, my plans are still uncertain at this point."

"No. The truth is it's time for me to move on."

It was a succinct way of putting it. Maury looked at her with a furrowed brow and ran his hand through his hair.

The boy had been hurt at first, but not angry. When the ferry arrived in St. George they both got into the car, and Maury drove off wordlessly, making the wide U-turn at the end of the ramp to get back on. But for that portion of the trip he decided to stay inside the car while Rose got out to go upstairs for the return ride. When the ferry docked back in Brooklyn, it was mostly a silent ride back to Rose's house with the two of them smoking furiously.

"We're bound to run into each other on campus," Rose told him as she opened the passenger car door and got out.

But oddly, it only happened one time, later in the semester.

She was walking to the subway and she noticed a small group of students on Flatbush Avenue who were gathered near the basement steps of a store that had a "For Rent" sign posted on it. A waft of smoke went by and she was sure she knew what it was. She had smelled it before when she and Rhoda had tried to smoke pot a few years back, but she didn't really like the way it made her feel. She turned her head and saw Maury, his back leaning against the black wrought iron railing, holding a small joint pressed between the thumb and middle finger of his right hand. Their eyes met fleetingly, but Rose pretended she hadn't seen him and proceeded to walk straight ahead.

CHAPTER FIVE

Galilee, Israel - September, 2014

Simon looked out at the crystalline water as the Sundancer pressed on, hugging the western shore of the lake. It was getting close to noon, and there was a warm sun in the sky. Off in the distance he could just begin to make out where the shore curved, the broad and then wider coastline which yielded the pebbled beaches at Ilanot and Arbel, and the low roofs of the farmhouses at Migdal, a bit beyond. It was all coming back to him. Yes, this was where he and Rose and the girls had been before. They were getting close.

"Daddy. What are you thinking?" Barbara asked, approaching Simon, placing her hand on top of her hat to secure it in the wind."

"I'm thinking that this is the last time we will all be together," he continued.

"Oh, Daddy, I'm sorry," she told him, and then he took her hand in his and the two of them sat looking out at the water, peaceful and blue.

After a few seconds he looked at her and said, "You know, the first time I met your mother I had never met a nice Jewish girl from Brooklyn before." He laughed. "We were so young, excited to have found each other. We had no time for anything except ourselves. And then you and Sharon came along."

"I know how lonely you are without her. This is so hard for you. I know it is," she tried to console him.

"When your mother was out in the Bay," he told her, "or on the Ontario, she would say 'Simon. I'm a scientist and I believe in science'. And I loved to tease her, you know, in that silly way that non-believers have always been challenged. 'What about goodness or evil?' and she rattled off that our moral sense comes from Darwin. For our own profit. Not to obey a creator. 'The Old Testament was absurd' she said, "and the 'love one another' commandments in the New Testament were really 'love another Jew' not just anybody else."

Both Nathan and Sharon looked back a few times at their father but stayed in their seats in the front of the boat. Barbara sat there listening intently.

"So what happened to her? Why did she wait until the end to tell me what happened. To make her change her mind?" Tears began to well up in his eyes.

"But that's very common. When people face their own mortality," Barbara said.

"Why did she keep secrets from all of us?" he continued. "Why at the end of her life did she tell me that Nathan is not my son. *Not my son.*" And then he began to weep, his face shaking lightly, his hands trembling.

Barbara shook her head. "Oh, Daddy, of course he is your son. Just look at him! Of course he came from you! At the end Mama was delirious." He could see that his daughter had tears in her own eyes, too.

"She had no idea what she was saying," Barbara continued. "She had morphine coursing through her veins. She said a lot of things that weren't true."

"If only I could believe it."

"You can," she reassured him, putting her hands on top of his. "Daddy, do you remember when I organized the CHPC to set up in the house?" Hospice at home. She had already known that Rose's grasp on reality was dying along with the rest of her.

"How can I forget?" he answered.

"Well, that morning she reached for my hand and said, 'Barbara, take care of your father. But don't neglect your husband.' But Mama I'm not married, I told her. And she looked at me with a puzzled expression and said, 'Your husband, David I mean. Where has he been?'"

"What?" Simon was puzzled.

"I said, Mama, David and I were never married. It didn't work out. And she looked at me with the saddest face and said, 'I'm sorry, dear. Sometimes I get all mixed up.'"

The wind had shifted slightly and Nathan turned the wheel to accommodate the position. Simon gathered his composure and stood up as Barbara exchanged a circumspect glance with her siblings. She didn't really want to tell them about her conversation with him — she wasn't sure she ever would repeat what her father had said. How could what he said be true?

She looked out over the railing and could see how tranquil the scenery was. "Are we getting close, Daddy?"

"Yes, sweetheart," he answered her, "now would you go up there and tell Nathan to cut the engine and let us float." He watched her walk towards the bow of the Sundancer; his devoted child Barbara, always compliant, always dependable. And then seeing Rose in his mind's eye and hearing her voice. The two of them sitting quietly on the back porch of the Lake Ontario townhouse they moved into for their retirement.

His wife was pouring tea from an earthenware teapot in the shape of a cube, a reproduction of a silver pot designed for pouring tea on a moving ship. Nathan had sent it to them from London.

"Do you think any of our children will find a life partner?" he had asked her.

"That's an odd turn of phrase, Simon. Is that how you think of me? As your life partner?"

"No, Rose. But I'm not sure any of our children will find a marriage quite the way we have. Barbara has certainly had a hard time," he explained.

"No time for men? Is that what you mean?" Rose commented.

"I think she's hard on them. There's a lot of her mother in her." It just came out.

"What's that supposed to mean?"

"The two of you share a certain quality. A drive, an ambition. I don't know. Something that propels you to put up walls, to isolate yourself from those around you."

"Is that what I've done Simon?" she asked a bit spitefully, reaching for the teapot to refill her china cup, "Well, she's a litigation attorney. A good one. She has a deep sense of obligation to her vocation, and she might not be able to make room for anything else. Sometimes there just isn't any more room. Do you want some more tea?"

Simon held his cup out to her in quiet agreement while she filled it adding, "and Sharon has already been down the aisle once, and I don't see her making that trip again. So I guess it's up to Nathan. Do you have a future scenario for him, Simon? Does he settle down into a comfortable marriage, like us?"

"I'm the most hopeful about Nathan," Simon admitted. "He *is* more like me. Loyal, authentic. Though he wears heavy armor, he wounds easily. And he doesn't have the ordered, disciplined mind of his mother. Planning things out, having all the pieces in place. Knowing what comes next."

"Oh, Simon, whatever are you talking about? That's what made me a good scientist."

"I'm talking about the future, Rose," his voice raised slightly. "I never knew what would come next for me. You were always able to picture yours."

Atlantic Maritimes, Canada - October, 1963

By now Rose had already decided she would make love to Simon in his house, an elegant Victorian home on Young Avenue in Halifax. It was the second time she had boarded the ferry from St. John to Digby and now, two months after that first ride, the weather had turned sharply colder and wetter.

This time, though, she was better prepared for the four-hour journey. She packed a sandwich and beverage along with her books for some uninterrupted study. She knew once Simon picked her up at the terminal there would be no time for anything else. The drive from Digby on the northern shore of Nova Scotia to Halifax in the south would take another two additional hours. But it was a Friday morning and she didn't have to be back on campus until late on Sunday; she would take the last ferry back then and spend Sunday night in her own bed. In Halifax she was going to meet Simon's father, Karl, a widower whom Simon frequently talked about with great admiration.

Though Simon was just slightly older than she was, to Rose he seemed much more mature and worldly. They had talked non-stop when they had first met, almost two months earlier. He was very funny, she thought, and he told her amusing stories about the people who worked for him and his father, in what she affectionately began to call "the fish factory." Local people whose Scottish and Irish ancestors had settled this part of the Atlantic Maritime provinces generations ago and spoke English with their distinctive regional speech, a flat accent with a very nasal "r."

"Simon, you've distracted me totally from my purpose," she scolded him that first day they had met. "I was here to take in the beauty of the Bay of Fundy," she tried to explain as they sat together for a while with coffee and the Breton crepes that Rose thought were quite delicious.

"You can take in my beauty instead," he joked. "Besides, there'll be plenty of time for that on your return trip. That is if I let you get back on this ship and turn around."

"That's highly unlikely. I have a big day planned for tomorrow with my mentor, then an orientation, and I still have to get my living arrangements together," she answered.

But when the *Princess of Arcadia* finally docked in Digby and she walked with Simon towards his car to say goodbye, he turned to her and said, "I'm taking the return trip back with you."

In a way he was similar to one of the famous tidal whirlpools that could be found in the Bay. Churning like a vortex, unpredictable and inexplicable. After that ride back across the Bay there was no stopping him. He put Rose in the passenger seat of his 1962 red Chevy Impala convertible, drove the car off of the ferry and turned around, stopping to purchase a ticket for the both of them back to St. John and talking non-stop. Rose had never met anyone who had done something so spontaneous as that. And though a part of her thought his assertiveness a bit bossy, another part was intrigued.

You couldn't really say they were inseparable those first two months. That was entirely impractical as Rose began to be immersed in her studies and life at the university and Simon was compelled to return to his responsibilities at L&J Strongin Fisheries. But the suitor had returned to St. John every weekend since they had first met, a rapid courtship that started to occupy almost all of Rose's leisure time, little that there was those first few months under the keen but nurturing eye of Dr. Winters.

Rose was trying to adjust to a new environment, a vigorous graduate assistantship and a burgeoning relationship with a man who was intent on pursuing her. But she was reluctant for Simon to spend the night with her in the small one-room flat she had just moved into at the perimeter of the campus in St. John. She had a single bed, a small desk and a chair and the kitchen consisted of a two-burner gas stove, a GE Toaster Oven and an ice-box the size of a dictionary. Simon had visited her room but never had spent the night. He had taken her all around St. John on the weekends in between her reading and writing assignments. They had gone to the City Market, walked in Lowell St. Park and went out to see the Reversing Falls on the St. John River.

Though barely twenty-one years old, Rose felt that she had achieved to some degree a little independence. She had a phone conversation with her father and mother on the two extensions of the phone in the Brooklyn house a week after she had arrived in Canada.

"Oh dear, we were so worried about your traveling, especially when we hadn't heard from you," her mother said.

"But Mom, it all worked out fine. If something had happened the police would have notified you."

"Don't be funny, Rose," David Fonseca jumped in.

"Some of my friends from school became Peace Corps volunteers, Dad. They're on the way out to Africa or somewhere, and I doubt they're calling home."

"Canada isn't Africa, and Ma Bell lives there as well," he went on.

"Well, I'm doing fine. They've fixed me up with a room just off the campus. It's small, but adequate, and it's not far for me to walk anywhere. I meet with Dr. Winters all the time. She's invited me to her house for dinner. Isn't that nice? Do you know she's married and has a grown-up son and daughter?"

"What are you eating?" her mother asked.

"Oh, mostly earthworms," she teased.

"What!!"

"They do have normal food here in Canada, Mother."

"Have you made any friends?" her father jumped in.

"I met a very nice young man who is from this area."

"Oh? What's he studying?" her mother asked, secretly hoping it wasn't something useless like Philosophy.

"Well, he's not actually at the college. He's a businessman. I met him on the Bay of Fundy ferry. Remember the pictures I showed you? His family has a business. They're in the fishing business. And he's very nice." There was a long silence from both extensions.

"Do you think that's wise?" her father asked quietly.

"He's *just* a friend. But he's been awfully nice to me. Same age as me and his name his Simon," she filled in. "Look, I'll write to you and grandma regularly, and I'll try to telephone whenever I can. But please, please do not worry about me. I am an adult and I feel safe and excited to be here."

"Love you," both her parents said overlapping each other.

"By the way," she giggled a little before she put the phone on the receiver, "in case you were wondering ... Simon is Jewish."

~~~

So here she was on a brisk October morning, riding again on the St. John to Digby Ferry and thinking that by spending the weekend with Simon at his house, she would be making love to him. A part of her could sense that Simon's attraction to her was "love at first sight." Rose wasn't sure if she felt exactly the same. At least not at this point in the relationship.

But she had opened herself up to the possibility that she could fall in love with him.

"Like any good scientist this needs further analysis," she thought, "and repetition." She gathered all the data available to her, no matter how small.

For his part, Simon was exceedingly compliant. He always complimented her on her appearance, paid for everything, from the smallest cup of coffee to a meal in a fine restaurant, bought her sweet little gifts: a pair of wooden candlesticks with dolphins glued onto them, a book or two she thumbed through in a used book store and said was interesting.

"Oh, Simon, this is too much," she said when he presented her with a gift a few days after they had met on the boat. It was a polished clamshell of Nova Scotia agate, collected from a beach on the Bay of Fundy and then handset into a silver filled wire. "It's really beautiful, but let's take it slowly."

"I saw this and thought of you, Rose. It makes me feel good to do things for you. You're all by yourself here," he reminded her.

She unfastened the tiny metal clasp, and he helped her put it around her neck. They had kissed gently after that, the second time their lips had touched each other. There was nothing more than that, but Rose liked the way he smelled and the sensation of his breath on her mouth.

After that, whenever they saw each other, Simon would hold her hand and often kiss it, stroke her slender neck and play with her hair. And he would kiss her straight on her lips whenever he departed. But he never tried to touch her anywhere else on her body.

Sitting inside the passenger cabin on the ferry she couldn't help but wonder about that. The sole lover that she'd had was Maury Waxman and their relationship, a mere year ago, seemed like ancient history to her now. She had no idea what made a good lover and what made a bad one. But now she felt older, more experienced. She wondered how many women Simon had sex with. She thought he might compare her to them.

But she was also nervous and a little excited to meet Simon's father and stay in his house for two nights. Father and son lived in what was described to her as a majestic house in Halifax, and Rose was quite impressed as she walked into the large vestibule hallway and was introduced to Karl Strongin.

Simon's father Karl was the kind of man who adored the company of women and was uncommonly charming and solicitous to Rose from the moment they were introduced. His wife, Simon's mother, had been killed in an automobile accident ten years earlier and Karl, a prosperous businessman, was an easy and desirable target for many middle-aged women. Curiously though, he remained uninterested in another marriage.

"I see my son has an eye for a beautiful woman," Karl had said in heavily accented English, "and he tells me you're a scholar and a scientist."

"Yes, well, a graduate student really."

"And what are you studying?" he asked.

Rose was unsure exactly how to answer but decided she would show off a bit, "I'm working on navigational warning systems, for fish and marine mammals. To keep them from fishery nets," she plunged right on.

Karl smiled broadly, his eyes widening, "I know, I know, and I am happy for someone to help me. We compete, you know. These animals and my business. They die because they are chasing the bait fish which are small enough to escape the nets."

"We are researching navigational warning systems. Attuned to species," she answered. "Each breed must have some form of acoustical compatibility."

"Ah, of course," he smiled with big chalky teeth, "we are compatible, you and me. And my son? Well, he will not let *you* escape."

Simon blushed a little. Rose thought the elder Strongin was charming. She could see what Simon had inherited from his father: the wide, prominent nose and forehead, strong jaw and full lips, short but muscular build and the bright blue eyes.

And she loved his story. The insightful, courageous young German-Jewish boy who risked everything to get to North America. It was an entirely different narrative from her paternal and maternal grandparents who had at least boarded their ships with their families intact.

The Strongins had been in Nova Scotia for a generation. Karl was self-sufficient and determined. He had applied to emigrate from Hamburg and found himself in Halifax in the spring of 1934. Eventually, he charmed himself into a job working on a fishing boat that collected Atlantic salmon, mackerel, herring and swordfish, where he exploited his talent for chutzpah and the language arts. He had a working knowledge of English and, to a lesser degree, French, which he spoke well though he retained a slight distinguishable accent in both. He quickly moved off the boat, into the fishing factory's back office, then to the front office and eventually, took an entrepreneurial position in a start-up company that caught, processed and distributed salmon – a classic immigrant success story.

By the late 1930's he had encouraged his sisters and brothers to apply for refugee status, but only his brother Max gathered his belongings and went to America. The remaining family hesitated. They did not want to pay an emigration tax, and eventually when the Nazi government restricted the amount of money that could be transferred abroad from German banks, the opportunity to leave diminished.

After that Karl Strongin lost touch both by telephone and post, and the ultimate disposition of his remaining family was an all too familiar story at the end of 1945. By then his son Simon had been born, Anglicized from Shimon, and named in honor of a long-dead relative.

~~~

Karl and Simon enjoyed an amicable and respectful relationship, a marked contrast from what she understood about the Waxmans back in Brooklyn. Firstly, Simon had a cushy upbringing, living in an ample home in an affluent part of town and he benefited, like Rose, from being an only child. A series of miscarriages a few years after Simon's birth had set the stage for Laila Strongin's difficulty in getting pregnant again, and Simon became resigned to not having any siblings.

The weekend turned out to be highly illuminating. It was almost like reading through an academic textbook about Simon and his family. Rose learned that Simon had attended a highly-respected private school, chartered by the Anglican Church. There were other Jewish boys who were enrolled, but Simon never seemed to connect with them, and though he didn't remember anything blatantly anti-semitic from students or teachers, he always recalled feeling a bit out of place.

He had tried learning the violin, with encouragement from his mother who had studied the piano when she was a girl, but he had no aptitude for it and was annoyed by the amount of practice it might require. He played sports, to the best of his ability: curling, hockey, cricket, soccer, even ice skating, but he never felt confident. He attended the Hebrew school at the Shaar Shalom Synagogue, which had been founded in 1953 and had ties to the progressive Masorti movement.

Growing up, Simon had made a few close friends, a boy from the synagogue, a sister and brother who lived in a house on a neighboring street, but he deemed these relationships ones of convenience, rather than necessity. He had started to notice girls when he was thirteen but was more excited by another event that helped to shape his adolescence. He began to work for his father during the summer before he entered the high school.

Simon's father was a hands-on man, and though he and his partners owned their business outright, he had been more fulfilled by being involved in the day-to-day activity of a seafood processing company. And so Simon was put out on a fishing boat when he was thirteen and then brought him into the factory the next year. Moving fresh and frozen seafood around as well as negotiating with local buyers and supply partners was a complicated business. By age seventeen Simon had been thoroughly inculcated into the daily operation of a successful, seasonal fishery. His father had no doubt his son would be a strong partner in the family business.

For his part Simon never really challenged that idea. It felt natural for him to follow in his father's footsteps. He was a well-read and curious student but not a particularly good one and his social skills were more highly developed than his academic ones. He flirted with the idea of perhaps becoming a lawyer. But the more he thought about the commitment to an academic life – undergraduate college and then law school the notion became less appealing.

Perhaps because he knew the history of his father's own pilgrimage, a risky and uncertain expedition, he was content to let his journey occur uninfluenced by either world events or great expectations.

Karl often talked to his son about his voyage from Hamburg to Canada in the early 1930's. "I was younger than you are now, Simon," he would tell him, "when I decided to leave my mother and my brothers and sisters. I didn't like what I was seeing around me. Hitler and his cronies had just been elected. Everyone thought they were just a bunch of disorganized hooligans, well, at least the Jews in our community. 'Oh, it's temporary,' Mrs. Katz our upstairs neighbor would tell my mother, 'Hitler is too crazy, too extreme and you'll see, he will be pushed out before you know it.'"

"Why didn't all your brothers and sisters leave with you?" Simon had asked his father.

"They were ostriches. If you were a Jew in Germany you always *knew* you were a Jew. It didn't matter if you converted, or married a Christian. It's something you carried in you always. Because you were made to! So, they reasoned, what's the difference between *this* man in the government and anyone else? There will always be anti-semites among us. There will always be two Germanys."

"But something inside you told you to leave, right?"

"Yes, son. I was different from the rest of them. I did not believe that having faith in the God we prayed to would keep me alive. I knew deep down inside me that if I was to survive, I would have to make the choice to find my way out. It was a struggle for me. To leave my mother. But she understood. She did not want to leave the place where your grandfather, was buried."

"But Onkel Max. You got him out. Right? You sent for him."

"I wrote every week to my family. Every single week begging them to leave. To come to Canada. Or to try to get to England. Or America. They all had so many excuses. But Max had been involved with a young woman whom he loved very much. He wanted to make a life with her. She told him one day that she was pregnant, and he was prepared to marry her. But shortly afterwards, he discovered that she had lied to him. She was going to have a baby except the father was another man. Someone she had secretly been seeing. He was crushed, and this is what gave him the push to survive," Karl explained to his son.

Max had been able to get himself to Liverpool and then to New York City where he became Americanized as quickly as possible. By 1941 he had joined the U.S. Army and been deployed to Fort Dix, just across the way in New Jersey. After the war he went to school on the GI Bill, met a woman from the Bronx and married her in 1951.

"The rest of the sad story you already know my son," he continued. "I never saw my mother again. Or my other brothers or sisters. Except for Onkel Max and your mother, Simon, you are my only family."

Simon remembered one time when he was much younger asking his father, "Are you ashamed to be Jewish?" and Karl answered back, "No son. I've just never found it beneficial."

~~~

The night Rose arrived at Karl Strongin's house, after they had dined on a dinner of roasted salmon, potatoes and Brussels sprouts followed by a strawberry charlotte sponge cake prepared by Karl's cook, Karl excused himself and retired to his bedroom on the second floor of the house. Rose instinctively got up to help clear the dining room table.

"Please sit down, Rose," Simon told her, "you don't have to do that. Someone will be back soon to take care of that."

"You're serious, Simon?" she asked as he got up to pour a little more wine into her glass. Rose did not have much experience with wine. She drank it on Jewish Holidays and a few times at a dinner or social function. But this did not taste like the wine she'd had before. Simon seemed to know what he was doing.

"Yes, my father has a couple who take care of things for us. Even before my mother lost her life. Who do you think prepared this meal? They live close by and come and go as they are needed. They will appear early in the morning before we wake up, and all of this will be accounted for."

"My mother and grandmother did everything in our house. My father wouldn't even bring his plate into the kitchen," Rose told him. "It's traditional for men to be waited on. But our kitchen was kosher. You know what that is, right?"

"Yes, of course," he snickered, "I did have a bar mitzvah you know. Although I think that was the last time I was in a synagogue."

"I ate a lot of Jewish food growing up. Mostly fatty cuts of beef, potato pancakes, cabbages, chicken soup with matzoh balls. Once in a while my father's mother would come and cook something exotic from Morocco. You don't get a lot of that sort of food up here now, do you?" she asked him.

"My Uncle Max is a New York Jew," he blurted out.

"Huh?" Rose started laughing and a bit of wine spilled out through her nose. "I'm sorry, but that was so funny the way you said New York Jew."

"Well, he didn't start out that way. He was converted by his wife, my Aunt Pearl. Well, I guess she's my Aunt. I only met her once when she and Uncle Max came to visit us. They have no children so they put all their resources into buying things to make Pearl happy. My mother was very polite to her, but afterwards she told my father that Pearl was *vulgar*."

Rose rolled her eyes, "She sounds positively dreadful."

"Well, she looked a little like Shelley Winters and wore a lot of makeup and used perfume in abundance," he went on. "And she had a fur coat and hat which she kept on a few times in the house saying she wasn't used to a house being "that cold". She wanted to know where the Jewish food was."

Rose began to laugh again, and then she looked up into Simon's eyes. He was sitting adjacent to her at the table, and the clock stopped for her. She'd heard that it was possible to glimpse a person's soul through the eyes. Something about that moment, the deep blue of his irises with minute flecks of aqua, the curve of his chin, the clear unlined forehead, the dark, even growth of his beard shaved much earlier that day, the fresh smell of the soap he used to wash his hands and face, the black hair on his forearms beneath the rolled-up sleeves of his white dress shirt, the warmth of his breath, all collided into a sensation that told her this man would complete her. She was not looking for a husband, but she knew instinctively that she and Simon would be bound together for life.

They would make love that evening, something she did not want to postpone. Simon took her hand and quietly led her up to the third floor of the house where his bedroom was. There was a small lamp on a nightstand next to the bed that was turned onto the lowest setting. He sat her on his bed, which was covered with a cotton Irish quilt, soft patches of greens and blues, while he went over to an RCA Victor portable record player, turned it on and placed the needle down on an album of The Drifters.

If left alone, not a soul in sight.

Then he unbuttoned her long-sleeved ivory blouse and slipped it off tenderly. She could feel her breasts begin to swell inside her bra, aroused by his warm hands. He seemed to know exactly what he was doing. Rose sat at the bed's edge, staying silent and letting Simon be in control, taking in his movements, watching him closely.

To tell me what was wrong or right.
I'd try to make a start.

He removed her shoes confidently and then gently lay her down on the quilted coverlet. Standing over her he reached down and began to unfasten the kick-pleated, black pencil skirt she had worn on their second date. Wrapping his arms around her buttocks he pulled the skirt down unhurriedly over her thighs, down her smooth legs, then removing the sheer stockings nimbly from each leg. He took her left foot in one hand, and massaged it with the top palm of his other hand. Then he gave equal time to the right foot.

She lay there on her back stretched out in her long-line white cotton bra and white rayon panties, her long blonde hair splayed against the spring green and dark navy of the bedding that had surrounded Simon as he grew from a young boy into a man.

And listen to my heart,
And say something good is going on.

Then he methodically removed his own shoes and socks, one at a time, looking into her face, not once looking down. To Rose's surprise, he lay down next to her, turning her on her side spoon-fashion and pressed himself against her curved body. He spread her hair to the left of her head and began to kiss her neck. She felt the hot air of his breath exhaling and tried to picture what he looked like lying next to her, seeing how their bodies fit together.

"Do you want me to undress you, Simon?" she found herself murmuring.

"Do you want to?" he asked.

She hesitated and then whispered, "Yes."

She turned over and placed her hands on his shoulders. His body was narrow but firm, with a muscular upper torso. She unbuttoned his shirt from the bottom to the top and he helped her remove it. Underneath he was wearing a white tank tee-shirt which accentuated the outline of his upper body. His chest was covered in a light coating of hair, but nothing like the dark, unruly chest hair that Maury had sprouting everywhere, pushing through the collar of his shirts. She lifted Simon's cotton vest and began to kiss his chest, massaging it smoothly with her fingers and palms. He tried to help her lift the shirt over his head, but she stopped him.

"Please," she said gently, "let me."

She unfastened the buckle of the brown leather belt that had been looped into his trousers, unfastened the single button that kept the pants closed, and slowly drew down the zipper. With the soft palm of her hand she could feel him grow underneath her touch. She slid both of her hands inside the trousers' band pulling them down from underneath his buttocks until they reached below his knees. And then she rolled the pant legs, one at a time, until she fully removed them. She could see the faintest hint of wetness in his eyes. They both lay there, still and silent. When he finally climbed on top she drifted in and out of a blissful dreaminess, feeling the weight of his body on top of her.

As it turned out, they would dress and undress each other that entire first weekend. Rose grew to know every inch of Simon's body and he would know the same with hers.

CHAPTER SIX

Galilee, Israel - September, 2014

She was everywhere, Simon thought. Inside his eardrums, hiding in the small hairs of his nostrils, cloaking the irises of his weary eyes. The brown box next to him was nothing but dust.

His son had stopped the engine, as his father had asked him to, and the boat rocked back and forth. Simon put his hand over his forehead, like he was saluting, trying to pick out a point on the shore. And then he spied the landmark he was searching for, a small dock and pier that jutted out into the lake. Beyond that he could make out the verdant grass lawns, an abundance of small cottages, buildings and gardens along the grass's perimeter that led the way to open, manicured fields and story-book orchards. It was Ginosar. He recognized it all.

There were swimmers in the lake at the pier, and on one side, a large tourist boat had docked. It had been built to look "old" but was essentially an overly large dug-out wooden canoe with clunky wooden railings and a canvas tent posted on the interior that could accommodate a couple dozen tourists.

Isolated at one end of the landscape was an odd-shaped ultra-modern building of glass and stone that looked like a concrete layer cake cut in half and flanked by elegant stone pavilions, stately palm trees and Aleppo pines. The museum was built to honor Yigal Allon, an important Israeli political and military figure and a founder of the kibbutz. It was also the permanent home of that archaeological wonder, the "Jesus Boat". Of course, the excavated boat had not been there forty years ago.

Simon's mood seemed to turnaround, and he started walking towards the front of the Sundancer where his three children were collected. "We've arrived," he announced pointing towards the shore. "That's where we're going in a little while, Nof Ginosar. This is where it began. The start of the story your mother wanted you to hear. Girls, do you recognize any of this?" But they both shook their heads, "no." Indeed, neither had any recollection.

From the corner of his eye Simon could make out the beach at Ilanot, slightly to the south where the Chazon expedition had been set up in 1974, and instantaneously, it brought him back there. He was younger then. Things were clearer then.

Suddenly, without warning, a motorboat passed by, furiously spraying water onto the Sundancer and pushing Simon down onto one of the built in bench seats on the side of the boat. "Fucking Christian pilgrims," Simon shouted. Barbara and Sharon ran over to him as Nathan grabbed the wheel.

"No. Fucking inconsiderate Israelis, Simon," Nathan responded immediately. "You know how arrogant they are. Like

Mama's colleague, the *esteemed* archaeologist, Dr. Noah Chazon."

The mention of that name raised Simon's temperature a few degrees. But how could the scientist's name go unmentioned this entire day? Chazon had invited them to Israel in the first place, and from the moment Simon had met him he was mistrustful. Especially twelve years later, in the mid-1980's when Chazon and Rose had participated in an academic conference in California. That's when the ancient boat had been discovered here in Israel and, after the news of it hit the press, Rose had returned from Los Angeles, changed and uneasy.

Something had started out there in California, right after a conference of the International Bioacoustics Council and, following that, Rose's second more urgent trip to Israel to see Noah who been given a peripheral role in the boat's excavation by the Israeli Department of Antiquities.

Yes, that's when it happened. Simon was certain. That's when the changes that haunted their marriage began to take place. Whether Noah Chazon was the cause of those changes or a result of them was something Simon wrestled with for many years after.

Galilee, Israel - July, 1974

The first time Rose saw Dr. Noah Chazon she thought he was a god, or at least the model for one of the beautiful creatures depicted on an Italian ceiling by a Michelangelo or a Raphael. Annabelle, her mentor, had described him as *exquisite*.

Rose had viewed a film clip of an archaeological expedition he captained for the Israelis, the revelation of a Babylonian siege tower which had been uncovered in Jerusalem's Jewish Quarter at the beginning of the 1970's. A series of arrowheads had also been excavated, artifacts giving testimony to the violent clashes between the Israelis and the Babylonians in 586 B.C.E., and Noah was explaining the significance of the ashes, soot and charred wood that helped to date and classify the discovery. A tracking shot of him reaching down to pick up a handful of dirt jumped to a closeup of his thirty-ish long face, bushy black hair and apple green eyes. Speaking in Hebrew with a confident voice, his skin was suntanned and radiant, and he sported a modest beard. Rose hadn't a clue what he was saying until a series of English subtitles started crawling across the bottom of the film as he delivered his narration in a dark, rich baritone.

When she finally met him in person, in the summer of 1974, the four Strongins had just arrived in the residential building at Ginosar and were standing at the bottom of a staircase. They looked like happy vacationers with their suitcases, sun hats and sunglasses and a bag containing toys, books and games to keep the youngsters, Sharon and Barbara, occupied for a few weeks. Simon and Rose were chatting informally with Leor, an Israeli archaeology graduate student who was one of Dr. Chazon's many research assistants and the designee charged with organizing the hospitality needs of the expedition members.

Chazon came walking quickly down the wooden staircase of the two story building. He spotted the top of Rose's large sunhat first and, as he descended a little further, Rose heard his heavy footsteps and turned her head up and to the right. That's when they saw each other for the first time.

She recognized him immediately from the film she had watched a number of times, but he also seemed, momentarily, to recognize *her*. Perhaps he had seen her photo somewhere before as well? There was the smallest moment of awkwardness, almost imperceptible, before Chazon leaned over the railing, pausing for a brief moment and said, "Dr. Strongin, I presume?"

They both laughed at the joke, "Leor told me you had arrived, and I'm very happy to meet you." She extended her hand out to him, and when he finished descending the stairs he took it into his. It was twice the size of her hand, and it felt wrapped like a warm towel. He placed his other hand on top of hers. She noticed the prominent blue veins on the top. They were strong hands like those of a longshoreman or laborer. Here was an intellectual who also knew how to use a shovel.

"Let's get you situated, and then we can talk," he said in excellent English. In that same fleeting moment Rose took him in, noticing his clean and bright white teeth with a small space between the front two, the full lips and eyebrows, the broad shoulders which carried a well-developed torso that wore a cotton tee-shirt with a patch pocket on the left side, and strong muscular arms which were revealed freely.

Simon missed none of it. "Is that Mama's boss?" Sharon asked.

Her father furrowed his eyebrows and said, "Yes, he's apparently the man in charge."

"Let's go to our room," Barbara, all of six years old, announced.

"I'm so sorry," Noah apologized, "These are your children, of course. And you are the husband?"

"I'm the nanny," Simon said.

"Pardon?"

"The part-time nanny. The rest of the time I'm the husband."

Rose blushed slightly and introduced him, "This is my husband, Simon. I couldn't be here without his support." She turned towards him and made a silly face which Noah could not see. "And these are my little jewels, Sharon and Barbara who are also very excited to be here."

Sharon gave a tentative smile and Barbara stuck out her hand as if offering a handshake.

"Well, we will all get to know each other then. I'm afraid there are no other children except those who live here at the kibbutz. But we all take our lunch together in the common room, with everyone who is collaborating," Chazon said.

"That's nice. But I may be out with the kids swimming or on a boat ride," Simon responded quite quickly.

"Oh, we have built in plenty of time for leisure," Chazon answered. "Really. We don't work every hour of the day and night."

"Simon, we can figure out our own schedule once I meet the whole team," said Rose.

"It's quite simple," Noah explained, "we have a light breakfast at six-thirty and meet at the site by seven. We already have a few canvas tents set up and our equipment is in place. By noon it will be too hot to do anything useful, even under a canopy, so we return to the common room for a midday meal, do our notation and documentation, read, discuss and then return about four o'clock for another few hours until it's too dark to do anything profitable. After that the team is usually on their own, though if we find something worth arguing about we can have an evening session on the porch with a glass of the fine wine they produce in the hills. Not all of the team is with us here in Ginosar. Some are staying in Migdal and others are staying outside of Tiberias."

"It sounds like paradise Dr. Chazon," Rose began say until he interrupted her.

"Noah, please. Just call me Noah."

Just then Leor, came into the hallway. "Let me help you with your things, Mr. Strongin, and I'll show you to the rooms upstairs for your family," the young man said kindly.

"Simon, please. Just call me Simon," he said with a puckish grin and the same inflected voice just used by Chazon. "Noah, nice to meet you. Girls, after you." After which he ushered his two daughters in front of him, up the stairs, as Rose lagged a beat behind.

"I'm very excited to begin," she said as she ascended the stairs. Though she might not have meant it that way, one could have thought it sounded flirtatious. At least Simon did.

"Yes, looking forward to our work together," he answered politely. "I'm honored to have you as my colleague." He looked at her again curiously, making note of something.

"Is there anything you want to…?" Rose heard herself saying, lingering a beat longer. But the Israeli had already taken a step backward, turned around and began to walk away. Quite by accident they both swung their heads to look at each other at the same moment. In that split second Rose thought Noah had seen something in her face, a sense of recognition. But she didn't fully understand. At least not then.

Simon had been observing this. From the top of the stairs he looked down. Chazon was standing at the bottom. Rose was on the staircase, midway between the two of them. For Simon it would be that way for many years.

CHAPTER SEVEN

Galilee, Israel - September, 2014

The intrusive motorboat that passed closely by the Sundancer had caused a slight quake, splashing some water on the deck and shaking the boat slightly, but the old man had already overreacted. With so many memories drifting around him, he had a hard time holding onto the present. He had to put Chazon out of his mind, at least for now.

"I cannot have this!" he bellowed at his three children. "This should be a solemn occasion. Please."

"What did I say?" Nathan muttered inaudibly under his breath. "Why does he think he's the only one who hurts?" There was quiet except for the lapping wake.

When Rose had first brought up the subject about what to do when she was gone, he couldn't bear to even approach the matter. But she had pressed him in an orderly, methodical fashion, the way she approached much of her vocational career. Eventually, he consented to letting her present her wishes to him. Though he was uncomfortable at first with what she had asked him to do, his gradual acceptance of both the procedure and specificity of the tasks afforded him a contentment that was mollifying. Now he looked around the boat at his three children standing together not knowing what to do or how to proceed. He walked up to Sharon and took her hand.

"Daddy, what do we do now?" she asked.

Simon sighed, thought for a moment and then, rather matter-of-factly said, "It's time we say a prayer." He took the wooden box from the seat next to him and handed it to Barbara to hold. Then he took a long piece of paper that had been folded in three and removed it from his jacket pocket.

"Come children and stand with me," he asked, "it's time to gather around your mother while I try my best."

"*Yit'gadal v'yit'kadash sh'mei raba. Amein. B'al'ma di v'ra khir'utei v'yam'likh mal'khutei b'chayeikhon uv'yomeikhon uv'chayei d'khol beit yis'ra'eil.*"

It became very silent on the boat. The wind had died down, and there was no visible traffic now on the water except for the far away sounds of some swimmers to the west. But they seemed muffled and indistinct. Simon read the prayer with exquisite authority, mustering up the scant Hebrew he learned as a boy, most of it all forgotten. It was the *Kaddish*. The prayer for the dead. An exaltation of God.

"Did you know this was the one piece of the Hebrew liturgy your mother could recite from memory?" he told his children.

"No. I never knew that," Barbara said in a surprised voice.

"She told me she learned it as a young girl. Of course, she could not say it out loud. Women were not permitted to recite it. At least not in the house where she grew up. But when your grandfather passed away, she conjured it up from her memory, and I was astonished."

Barbara chuckled a bit, "So much we never know." Sharon smiled in agreement but Nathan stood stiffly looking out at the water, avoiding eye contact with his father.

"Let's all sit down now and listen to your brother," he indicated to Nathan. "Would you play for us now, son?" Nathan reached under the seat obediently and took out his clarinet. He had predicted that his mother would request this, and his father had gently reviewed it with him at dinner last night.

It took a few minutes for him to assemble the instrument, moisten and insert the reed, and tune to the pitches. Sharon and Barbara sat on opposite sides of their father while their brother, standing a few feet away from them, began to play the achingly beautiful melody from the Fauré *Pavane*, opus 50, Rose's favorite piece of music. It had been Nathan's first concert solo in an arrangement for piano and clarinet when he was only fifteen and performed as a guest with the Canadian National Youth Symphony. It brought him to tears the first time he heard it.

Now he didn't need to generate tears. They had already been notated in the compliant melody, supple and heartbreaking, proceeding *dolce legato*, pulsing a course of sound, repeated, flourishing profusely then resolving. Five notes that could produce a phrase so affecting. And then the final section, *sempre dolce*, trill, retreat to *pianissimo*, a series of triplets he smoothly attended and then, finally, *crescendo*, whole notes to half notes to quarter notes, *piano* to *pianissimo*. Quarter note. Rest.

His mind flooded with memories. The piece had been so practiced it emerged effortlessly, the salutary effect of conjoining fingers and breath over many years. He lost himself in flickering flashes of his mother. He pictured her face, her hair, the paisley shawl she had worn for years, and the bland, cotton nightgown he had last seen her in when Barbara had called him that morning. He passed through remembered fragments of conversations with his mother, pushing and reassuring him, urging him beyond diffidence, encouraging him in his study, affectionately but without excessive sentiment. The gentle words of reprimand when his precociousness overstepped boundaries. The shock of surprise, but then quiet recognition, when she realized a man he had introduced her to was his lover.

When he finally stopped playing and put the clarinet down, the music lingered for a while like a bloom of jasmine. The four of them sat quietly until Simon turned to Barbara, "I'd like you to read something your mother requested."

He handed her the unfolded paper. She looked down at it for a moment, a little puzzled, then back to her father who smiled gently, "Please."

"This is from The Gospel of John, Chapter 21," she began. Nathan and Sharon had bewildered looks on their faces.

"*The Gospel of John*? You're kidding. Right?" Nathan interrupted. Sharon shot him a look.

"It's just a Bible reading. She must have picked it out."

"I wouldn't have thought she'd pick it out of the New Testament," he responded.

"She did," Simon responded bluntly. "She had plenty of time to think about this. Your mother spent a lifetime figuring out how to warn cetaceans of the presence of fishing nets. Why should this be any different? She may have been secretive about some things but she was clear about this. Go on, Barbara, please."

"*Jesus showed himself again to the disciples by the Sea of Tiberias; Gathered there together were Simon Peter, Thomas called the Twin, Nathanael of Cana in Galilee, the sons of Zebedee, and two others of his disciples. Simon Peter said to them, "I am going fishing,"* she read in a clear, calm voice. Simon had put his head down with his hand on his forehead.

"*They said to him, 'We will go with you,"* she continued. "*They went out and got into the boat, but that night they caught nothing. Just after daybreak, Jesus stood on the beach; but the disciples did not know that it was Jesus. He said to them, "Children, you have no fish, have you?" They answered him, "No." He said to them, "Cast the net to the right side of the boat, and you will find some." So they cast it, and now they were not able to haul it in because there were so many fish. That disciple* whom Jesus loved said to Simon Peter, 'It is the Lord!' When Simon Peter heard that it was the Lord, he put on some clothes, for he was naked, and jumped into the sea."

Nathan asked Simon directly, "How did she come upon that fairy tale?"

"Apparently from Noah Chazon."

"Huh?"

"Nathan, you of all people must know she'd still been in serious contact with him. After all, you brought him up! Did she never talk to you about him? She must have said something." His tone was a little sinister. It confused all of them.

"Yes, of course, I knew about him. We all did," Nathan answered defensively. "He was her colleague here in Israel. And elsewhere. I know they had worked together and the girls met him way before I came along. Right Barbara?" She shook her head. "But I never did meet him," he went on. "Just the wife though, you know. The psychiatrist. That one time. And very briefly at that. She told Mama she wanted to meet me. It was sometime after her husband had died. I don't remember exactly when. She was traveling through Toronto. Ages ago I think."

Atlantic Maritimes - May, 1974

Ages ago. Simon closed his eyes. He could recall in vivid detail exactly when the Chazons entered their lives. They came by way of an academic opportunity, unanticipated but auspicious. Rose had explained to Simon that her career and her job security depended on her ability to investigate, produce and publish.

Karl Strongin was still alive then, and the family business was humming along nicely, growing and expanding in both Nova Scotia and New Brunswick. Simon never pressured his wife to earn a separate living, but Rose was her own person. So both Simon and Rose were building separate, but mutually beneficial careers for themselves.

Then one day Dr. Winters, her former mentor and now her colleague, stopped by her office to pass on an invitation.

"There's an interesting opportunity for you, Rose. In Israel, of all places," she had explained. "The Israeli Department of Antiquities is in the middle of a project to map underwater archaeological sites in the Sea of Galilee, to amalgamate a national database."

"Wow. I've never been to the Mideast before."

"Your people are from there, no?" Winters had inquired.

"Not exactly. Well, maybe generations and generations ago. But more recently they were European refugees who had made their way from Northern Africa at some point. Though that line is, at this point, untraceable."

"One of the leaders, Dr. Noah Chazon, from the University of Haifa who I met at a conference a few years ago, has asked me to recommend someone with experience in bioacoustics and an interest in fisheries," she explained, and Rose perked up now with keen interest. This was indeed her area of specialty and it could be an enormous opportunity for scholarship and recognition in scientific and academic circles.

"The project is to analyze and clarify a series of undressed stones from the Roman period that may have been used to create an artificial harbor to improve the grip of anchors attaching to the bottom of the lake. There is evidence that the concentrations of these stones may have formed artificial fish nurseries."

The Sea of Galilee was subject to the natural phenomena of precipitate storms that blew winds westerly or, in the case of the *sharkia*, a powerful wind that whistled its way down from the Syrian desert to the Galilee regularly. It can on occasion cause giant waves in a spiral vortex, tossing boats around without mercy. With few natural harbors in and around the lake, it seemed natural for ancient mariners to try to create artificial shelters to harbor and anchor their fishing vessels.

Winters continued with a wry smile, "Are you interested?"

And three months later Rose had signed onto the team. She would be collecting and analyzing underwater acoustics in and around the site near the Tamar, Ilanot and Arbel beaches on the shoreline of the Galilee, a short distance outside of the northern Israeli town of Migdal. Their base of operations would be at the kibbutz at Ginosar, less than one kilometer away.

The expedition would be comprised of Dr. Chazon, a group of his students from the University at Haifa, three marine biologists from the Hebrew University in Jerusalem and their assistants, a marine structural engineer from Cornell University in New York, and an observer from the British Museum in London. The University of New Brunswick had funded travel expenses for Rose and a small stipend from a research grant that Winters pushed through effortlessly.

Simon remembered vividly how excited Rose had been when she told him the news. They were sitting in the dining room of the small but efficient house they had bought in St. John shortly after they had married, though Simon still kept his "room" in the house on Young Street in Halifax. They had finished clearing the supper dishes together, and Simon had taken the girls to their bedroom to get them ready for bed while Rose finished up.

He had just come down from putting the two young girls to bed. Sharon was in the middle of the second grade and Barbara was in kindergarten, bored and unchallenged. Sharon pretended she wasn't interested in hearing her father read out loud and would usually lay in bed with her own book, but she couldn't fool him. He knew she was listening.

Barbara, though, was still keen to hear the continuing story of *Charlotte Sometimes*, a young girl attending an English boarding school who awakens to find herself transported back in time to 1918 and living in the body of another girl. Simon would read until he saw their eyes flutter and close intermittently, then stay shut for more than a few seconds. His words would trail off and he would slip out quietly. When he parked himself down in the dining room Rose sprung the news.

"This is a big opportunity for me, Simon," she explained as she was putting the kitchen in order. "I've never been associated with an international project before, and Annabel seems to have manipulated the whole thing in my favor."

"Yes, it sounds exciting. I'm just wondering if the girls and I can be away that long though."

"It's the summertime. They are out of school, and you know I won't leave them. I'll be busy during a good deal of the day and they need their father."

"And my father?" he asked her. "What about him?"

"Simon, come on. He'll be okay without you for six weeks. You know that," she moved up closer to him putting her arms around his waist. "You smell good," she told him.

"It's not me. It's the Baron," he laughed, acknowledging the spicy scent he had used for many years. He put his mouth on hers sideways and kissed her, "Do I have garlic breath?" he asked. He could feel them both getting aroused.

"Yes. But so do I. Blame it on supper. The girls are sleeping, no?"

She unfastened the small rubber band that folded her long blonde hair into a ponytail and shook her head to let it fall into place then started to work the buttons on his dress shirt, one at a time, with her fingers, "Remember how we used to undress each other?"

"Are you starting something with me?" he teased.

"No. What makes you think that?" But by then she had already pulled his shirt off, and he was pulling his white undershirt over his head as she was beginning to work on the buckle of the brown lizard-skin belt.

After that there was no turning back. Rose would sign onto the expedition at Ginosar with Simon and her daughters joining the entire time. It would boost her confidence and advance her career, but it would also, most importantly, bring her into the world of Noah Chazon. Once she had been there she could not turn back.

Galilee, Israel - September, 1974

A few short months later, on the final day of the visit to Israel, the strange, extraordinary circumstances occurred that could not be explained. Rose and Simon had been over and over the same ground. As many times as she had revisited that scene outside of Ginosar, when Simon and the rest of the group "found her," she could not remember where she had been for almost three hours. Time had stood still for her and all she could recall was walking down the long slate path, from the common area in the kibbutz, to the small beach where the research team had been set up.

After that her mind had gone blank. She appeared agitated, but otherwise she had no physical injuries, bruises, contusions, not even a scratch to indicate that perhaps she had fallen and blacked out. Her eyes were clear and lucid, her breathing normal. Her pulse and heart rate were slightly elevated, but that was easily explained by the stress she felt when she realized she'd had no recollection of those hours that stretched from early morning to just before noon.

Her clothing was all in place, a white sleeveless blouse under a sky blue smock and coffee-colored huarache sandals she had bought a few years ago in a market outside of Cozumel. Her hair was in place, tied back exactly the way she had prepared it when she stepped out of the shower earlier that day. She just had a veiled, foggy feeling and felt as if she had walked into a cloud and come out the other side, three hours later.

The only real manifestation of anything unusual that had happened to her was a slight twitch in her right eye. *Blepharospasm*, the involuntary movement of the eyelid.

When she walked into the common room and saw her daughters, both of the girls had run up to her and grabbed her legs, wrapping their tiny arms around them. "Mama, Mama!" they cried out. Sharon and Barbara were small children then and though Simon had tried to hide his concern and spare them any outright fear, he couldn't disguise his nervousness when they kept asking, "Where's Mama? Don't we go home today?"

"Rose, my God what happened to you? Where were you? We couldn't find you for hours and hours." Simon had rushed up to her when she walked into the small lobby being used by members of the expedition that had been set up by the Marine Archaeology Unit of the Israeli Department of Antiquities.

"We looked everywhere throughout the kibbutz, down by the beach, up and along the shore. Nobody has seen you since breakfast," Simon pushed out, practically hyperventilating.

"I must have sat down somewhere and fallen asleep. It's the only explanation."

"We searched everywhere. On the beach, throughout the parameters of the dig, all over the kibbutz, we even sent some of the students down on the Tiberias road in case you had started walking and got lost. Nobody could find a trace of you," Simon told her in a frightened voice. Noah had walked into the room a bit earlier and was perplexed by the activity.

"What's going on here?" Chazon asked. But when it was explained that they couldn't find Dr. Strongin, his reaction was strange.

"This doesn't make any sense," he said, without emotion. "I had to do a few errands this morning in Migdal. If she was on the road I would have seen her."

Simon asked him, "Didn't you notice us all scattered about when you returned?"

"No. I went to my room to tidy up some notes. We are finishing up over the next few days, you know," Chazon responded directly to him in a tone Simon thought was haughty. "I'm sure she will turn up."

But when Rose walked wide-eyed into the room a few minutes later, Simon was sure Noah and Rose had locked their eyes, even it was just a fleeting, imperceptible moment. And in that transitory moment he thought he saw relief in the Israeli man's face. Had they been together?

It's true that Noah was extraordinarily beautiful, Simon had to admit, looking at him from across the room. He was tall and lanky, with a head of curly black hair – the kind you'd enjoy walking barefoot through, and Simon could see that Rose had been drawn to him immediately. But so were most of the other women (and no doubt a few of the men) who collaborated with him on the project. Regardless, Simon could not believe that Rose would betray him.

"Rose, do you remember anything at all?" Noah asked her directly in front of all the onlookers. "Anything? Where you were walking, specifically?"

She looked shellshocked. "No. Just the beach."

After a period of sighs of relief, brief questions and no answers, Simon and the girls took Rose by the hand, and they walked back together to the kibbutz guest house quarters where they had been staying.

"I'll have to phone the airline and see what we can do. There's no way we will be able to get back to Tel Aviv and make our scheduled flight out of there," Simon told Rose.

Both Sharon and Barbara attached themselves to their mother's thighs and held on. "I'm so very sorry to have given you all such a scare. But I'm perfectly alright. Really." But there was no plausible explanation readily available, and they needed to pack their things and get back to home to Canada. Rose's semester had started, and she was already a week behind.

That's when Simon noticed the fluttering at the bottom of Rose's right eye. Imperceptible at first and then more noticeable. He was sure she wasn't even aware of it.

They gathered their belongings and said their goodbyes, boarding the dusty bus that would take them to Tel Aviv, a few hours drive away.

When they arrived at the airport their departing flight, TWA 841, had already left. Simon thought it was a bit of a mixed blessing anyway. The travel agent had put them on a circuitous route that was delivering them to Athens, departing about one hour later for Rome, and then, after a brief stop there heading back to Toronto and a short flight to Halifax.

"I was able to get this sorted out, Rose," he explained to her as she waited with the girls and their luggage inside the departures terminal, "though I had to turn on the charm." Rose seemed fine to him at this point. Perhaps a bit aloof, but Sharon and Barbara had been visibly shaken earlier in the day, and Rose was glued to the two of them on the bus ride from Ginosar to Haifa and then to the Ben Gurion airport.

"We're on a flight to London tomorrow where we will switch planes for Toronto and then catch a flight to Halifax. At the end of the day it will be a lot easier on all of us, though we will be arriving one day later." But none of it was easier on Rose or Simon. They had to spend the night in a hotel room outside of the International Airport.

Simon had waited until the girls were fast asleep before he began to test Rose's memory again. The room was L-shaped, and there was a sleep sofa in the long side of the L which had been made up for the two children to share. A larger bed was fixed on the shorter side of the L, close to the bathroom, and afforded Simon and Rose a bit of privacy.

"Simon, I just *don't* remember anything. I'm so sorry and I'm frightened as well. But I can't tell you anything I don't know," she had repeated to him. "After breakfast I just needed to walk down to the lake and take a look around. I'm not even sure I know why. I think I grabbed a cup of coffee and took off."

"Were you going to take some photos?" he asked.

"No. I didn't need anything. We were all done."

"But you must have had a reason. We were leaving in a few hours and you had finished up your part of the project. We had to pack and get ready," he stated eagerly looking for some answer.

"Yes, I know. I know. But there was something I had an urge to do. Something that was driving me, moving me forward. I can't explain it. I just can't."

"Well, we are taking you to see a doctor when we get back. You need a neurological examination. You need to figure out what happened to your memory."

Simon had noticed the facial tic come again. He was unsure whether he should mention it or not. Instead he pulled her over to him.

"Rose, I love you. I want all to be well. When we couldn't find you I didn't know what to do. We would be lost without you," he began to stroke the side of her face, massaging her temples, working in his index and middle fingers under her left eye, gently rubbing underneath. He brought his lips onto hers and felt her respond easily. He turned off the lamp that was next to the bed.

"I need you," he told her.

"The girls," she responded softly.

"They're out like a light. They won't hear anything," Simon assured her as he gently stroked her inner thigh, lifted the edge of her nightgown and they quietly made love.

Rose had drifted off quickly after that. Simon stayed awake for a little while, listening to her light snoring. "Where were you, Rose? Where did you go?" his mind repeated until his eyelids were heavy and he slipped willingly into sleep.

Hours later, the morning light had filtered in through the flimsy hotel room drapery when Simon awakened to find Rose already in the bathroom. That's when he turned on the small television, which was hidden in a console that did duty as a dresser as well, tuned into the BBC World News and saw the news of the disappearance of TWA 841. The plane had vanished over the Ionian Sea, on its second leg from Athens to Rome. Another plane had been in the area and witnessed what appeared to be the separation of an engine from one of the wings. All of the crew and passengers were lost.

"I don't want the girls knowing any of this," Simon told Rose within seconds of hearing the news. "This is horrific. Those poor people. I'm not sure I can handle this."

"Please, Simon. Get a hold of yourself. It's God-awful. But we were lucky."

"Sssh. Rose. Please. I don't want to talk about it. I just want to get us all home."

But Rose's mind had already gone into overtime. She replayed over and over and over again the events of the previous day. But still she had no answers.

Details were sketchy at this point. TWA had already disavowed any report that even suggested its aircraft was a victim of sabotage. There was an investigation underway. But that didn't matter because the activity at the airport had increased beyond belief. Israeli security, which had already been beefed up over the years since the Arab-Palestinian-Israeli conflict had grown out of control, had gone into overdrive because a terrorist organization in Southern Lebanon had claimed they had put a suicide bomber on the flight. But at this point it was conjecture and speculation.

Most passengers subjected to airport security scrutiny went about their business, boarded their flights, and arrived at their final destinations with minimal discomfort. The Strongins negotiated their flights home with ease though Simon played the news broadcast over and over in his mind. And newspaper headlines everywhere contained large banners describing the incident.

~~~

Once the family had planted their feet back in Canada, the necessity of getting back to the normal, quotidian chores at home and work imposed its own priority. Though the story of the sabotaged American plane continued to dominate the news headlines in Canada, it faded into the background of Rose and Simon's lives as they both returned to their routine.

Simon embarked on a rigorous travel schedule in the Maritimes, and Rose began a new semester at the College in New Brunswick. The Galilee Marine Harbor Project was an essential piece of her tenure dossier, and she needed to get to work on assembling her part of the project and coordinating with Dr. Chazon and the other principal scientists involved with the expedition. But it was hard to get far away from the near-miss.

When her parents, friends and colleagues discovered that she and the family had avoided the fatal flight she was flooded with comments and observations about the nature of chance and randomness.

"It's hard to get back to normal Simon, with everybody all over me about getting checked out," she complained to him.

"That won't happen until we find out if you are okay."

By now, Rose had accepted that the eye-tic was not just going to go away. She had made an appointment with a neurologist in St. John the week after she returned. The doctor gave her a thorough exam along with a complete neurological evaluation including electromyography and a nerve conduction velocity test. The results were unremarkable. Nothing out of the ordinary. Blood samples similarly demonstrated a healthy thirty-three year-old woman. No additional quantitative testing or further study was required or called for.

A colleague of hers had talked to her about the rapid eye movement. She was a Hawaiian by birth. "Most people see this as a nervous tic but in our culture," she related to Rose, "it can signal the arrival of someone new, someone unexpected. Of course, we all know that this is a bunch of nonsense. After all we are scientists. Not witches."

But Rose, never one to submit to superstition, read a number of accounts from African, Indian and Chinese folklore. Each of the cultures associated something with the rapid eye movement of the left eye, although it varied from culture to culture. At the end of the day though, it was the Hawaiian colleague who was onto something that had the most validity. The culture that produced the superstition proposed that it was associated with an impending birth.

Eventually the eye fluttering began to subside. It appeared less frequently and, within a few months it had all but disappeared. This had, however, coincided with Rose's announcement that she was pregnant.

She hadn't been feeling great and this, coupled with the fact that her menstrual cycles always had an irregular nature to them, led her to think that pregnancy was a distinct possibility.

"Simon," she said one night after he had put Sharon and Barbara to bed, "there's a good chance that we're going to be adding to the family."

"What?" he had responded, startled, "How do you know?"

"How do I know?" she laughed, "Well, I've already given birth twice so I have some fair idea about what my body feels like before, during and after."

"No, I'm sorry. It's just that we haven't, you know, we haven't been at it that much these past few months."

She threw her head back, her long blonde hair gathering to one side while she twisted it together and fastened a red rubber band around it. "Simon, don't you know the facts of life?" she laughed. "You only have do it once. There are some girls who just *look* at their boyfriend and are knocked up."

"I don't know that this is a good time for another child," Simon said in a voice that was filled with worry. Then he turned sharply lugubrious.

"Stop it, Simon. What is the problem? It can't be money. We have enough of that."

"No. It isn't that. I'm sorry. I can't explain it. Please, let's just find out for sure."

"Look. We're going to have a boy. I know it," she blurted out. It was almost an announcement, asserted confidently.

Then Simon looked at his wife with great intention, taking in the curve of her mouth, the shape of her lips, the velvety ponytail she had just created that flopped up and down on the nape of her neck, absorbing the blonde, almost-Nordic looks that had drawn him over to her on the Digby ferry.

Only now he caught a glimpse of something he hadn't seen before. A detachment, perhaps, an aloofness that frightened him. It was the first time he considered that Rose might have had secrets. It was a glittering realization, a moment that, in his heart of hearts, he knew was guided by those three missing hours.

CHAPTER EIGHT

Galilee, Israel - September, 2014

"Just look at him. He's somewhere else," Nathan thought to himself. Simon was sitting on the foldout bench with his eyes shut tightly. "What's going on Simon? On the inside."

Nathan and his older sisters were huddled together at the front of the boat waiting for something to happen, some instruction or at least a directive from their father. The old man just seemed to withdraw the moment Chazon's name had materialized.

Of course, Nathan knew who the Israeli scientist was. How could he not? During that summer his mother and father had separated, if Rose even mentioned Chazon's name, Simon would turn red with indignation. But that was almost thirty years ago. He thought they had put all of that behind them.

He didn't really like lying to his father, but he promised his mother he would never tell him that Noah had come to the house at the end of that summer, back in the mid-1980's, before Simon and Rose had reconciled. They talked alone together in Rose's study for about thirty minutes, and then Chazon had left as quickly as he had arrived.

"Please, Nathan," she asked him nervously, "this is something you won't understand now." And he had complied dutifully. It was a secret that sealed mother and son.

All Nathan could recall was that when the Israeli took his hand to shake it, he felt his whole body shake. He started to perspire and his mouth went dry. It scared and confused him at first, but later on, as he got a little older and thought back to their meeting, he understood what it had meant.

"So Chazon was still a looming presence in my mother's life," he thought. Even after he believed she had pulled away from him, both professionally and personally. For Simon's sake. For the sake of their entire family.

Sharon broke the silence, "I don't get all this. Prayers, readings, Jesus. I don't understand." She was perplexed, "I thought Mama had just left instructions for her ashes to be spread out over the water. I don't get it all," she repeated emphatically.

"She obviously felt some strong attachment here. Even though it had been many, many years," Barbara jumped in. "Look it's almost over. Let's just go on, do whatever needs to be done, have some lunch and then we can head out of here and back to the hotel. The sooner the better." She walked over to her father and touched him on the shoulder, "Daddy. Let's continue. Please tell us what to do next."

The old man opened his eyes and scratched the nape of his neck, "I guess it's time to dispose of your mother's remains."

A slight breeze that had begun to come up from the faraway shore began to be more pronounced now. But it was too early in the day for a *sharkia,* the wind that comes down from the Golan Heights and can cause huge waves. The Levantine *sharkia* is supposed to blow the bells in front of houses as a signal that it's time for the family to gather around for the evening meal. But the sun was still straight up in the sky, hours to go before it began to settle in the west. Nonetheless, the stillness was broken, the boat started rocking, and the passengers all had to steady themselves. Then suddenly a whiff, a spray of a scent penetrated the boat. It came up unexpectedly. Nathan sniffed at it first.

"Do you smell that?" he asked, "Is it lemons? Oranges? Something very distinctive."

"I smell spices. Coriander, maybe," Sharon offered.

"Don't you recognize the smell?" Simon said observing his three children. "It's the fish tagine your mother used to make with the charmoula. Her grandmother had taught it to her. From Morocco. That's what you're smelling."

"Daddy, I love you but that is way too weird," said Barbara.

"Maybe. But if you think of it, why not? The wind has always been a messenger. Look at where we are now."

An eerie silence and then the wind left as quickly as it had arrived.

"Let's walk to the back of the boat," Simon requested and the Strongins found themselves standing in a circle underneath the bimini-topped canvas that shielded them from direct sunlight.

It was time. Simon handed the decorated box to Barbara who held her hands out as if she was waiting to transport firewood. He opened the lid gently, removing a ceramic urn that contained the contents of Rose's remains.

"There's a formula to consider," the cadaver-like funeral director told him, "based on the deceased's weight. To calculate the size of the container." By the time she was dead Rose was down to a little more than one hundred pounds, and Simon and the mortician had agreed on one that was small and portable.

There was something else in the box as well, wrapped tightly in a thick velvet cloth and tied rather formally with a gold brocaded tassel. That would have to wait for now.

"I think we can all participate in this," he instructed his children. "Why don't we start, eldest to youngest and scatter a little, hand off and then I'll finish up. Does that seem like a good plan?" His voice cracked, "I've never done this before."

"Here Sharon," he said, "we need to start with you."

Sharon took the container from her father and studied it. "This is all that remains of my mother," she thought. "And when I die, my daughter will reach down and scatter me around. And her daughter, perhaps, and so on and so forth and on and on and on."

She could make herself dizzy thinking about this endless spiral and, if she didn't get a grip, she could have just collapsed there on the boat. Crumbled into a thousand somber pieces. She used to do that as a child when she lay awake, thinking about spirals and coils and the spinning of the universe.

When she was put to bed as a young girl, before she fell asleep, she would drive herself crazy thinking about nothingness. "What if there is *nothing*. Then I wouldn't exist and there would be no Mama and Daddy, or Barb, or people, or the earth, or the world, or anything. Just a big blank of nonexistence. But how could that be?" She would work herself up into a frenzy that exhausted her. Only the physical demands of girlhood, one that necessitated sleep, were able to overtake her, causing her mind to shut down and allow her to finally drift off.

Holding what remained of her mother, she heard the conversation she'd had with her once she started to go to school and met children who were being raised in so-called religious families. A young schoolmate told her that she must choose something to believe in, otherwise she was going to die right away.

Sharon ran home to her mother and asked, "Mama, am I going to die?"

Rose took her daughter's two little hands and said tenderly, "Yes, Sharon, you are – but not for a very, very long time."

Now, here she was scattering her mother's ashes into water, some six thousand miles from her home, and thinking about her own mortality. She retracted her hand, took a deep breath and handed the box over to her sister.

Barbara, for her part, stepped up to the railing. She quickly poured some the ashes out, immediately placing the cover back onto the urn, as if the rest of the contents would escape and not allow her brother and father to participate in the ritual.

"Nathan. Here," she said, holding the urn towards him as if it were an oblation.

He removed his dark sunglasses, placing them on his head, took the vessel from her and pushed the lid up to look inside. His deep brown eyes were liquid. He looked at his father and then at his two sisters, finally turning to the western sky. In one quivering motion he emptied some of the contents out into the water.

"Goodbye, Mama," he said quietly.

Ontario, Canada - July, 2013

It was just a little over one year ago. A humid, sticky Sunday afternoon, about ten months after Rose had her diagnosis. Nathan came to call on his mother and father, bringing his boyfriend Ricky with him. He had just come off a three-month Canadian tour with the orchestra and would be resident in Toronto for the next few months, rehearsing and performing. It would be good for him to be somewhat settled in one place. Good for him to spend more time with his mother, and healthy to have a regular routine with Ricky, even if he wasn't hearing wedding bells yet chiming in their future.

"Hello, Simon," he said to his father when the door opened, "we're here. We brought groceries to make lunch. And I picked up some other things."

"That wasn't necessary. I'm not housebound, you know," Simon responded defensively.

"Well, we wanted to. I hope it doesn't throw anything out of balance."

Ricky shot him a look "*be nice, Nathan*" and interrupted, "Hi, Simon. And a nice Oregon Pinot Noir for you." He extended his hand out for a handshake. Simon took it, clasped it into his and brought him in for a hug instead. They had met a few times before, and Simon was growing fond of him. Somewhat younger than Nathan, he reminded Simon of his own son, without the edge. Ricky was charming and effusive, and even more importantly, Rose admired him. He worked for an advertising agency, on the creative side, and the two of them talked about books, and films. Ricky was quite solicitous Simon thought, "He knows how to play the old lady card," and this, in his mind, was admirable.

"Come in, gentlemen," he said. "Rose is inside, sitting on the sofa. She's not feeling too terrible today, coughing a little, a bit raspy."

Nathan handed his coat to Ricky, kicked off his loafers at the front door and walked through the hallway that divided the downstairs into a study and living room to the left and kitchen and dining room to the right. He placed the grocery sacks on the kitchen counter as Ricky and Simon trailed behind.

"Where's my old girl?" Nathan said loudly with animation, and then, more softly, "God, Simon, it's warm in here. Why don't you have the air conditioning on?"

"Your mother gets cold," he answered without emotion as Nathan started to open the buttons of the cotton shirt he was wearing.

Ricky cut in, "Nate, why don't you go and say hi to your mother and I'll stay back with your dad, unpack these things and come in shortly."

Nathan walked into the long living room. It contained many of the same pieces of furniture that outfitted their house when they lived in Mississauga throughout most of the 1980's. He recognized a few interesting articles that had been in his grandfather's house in Halifax. An oak sectional bookcase from the turn of the 20th century, a Biedermeier mahogany bust stand, a French baker's clock. It was fascinating to him that these pieces, some more than a hundred-fifty years older than the remainder of the furniture, looked more alive and vital than the ordinary but new, beige fabric recliners and matching sofa his mother had settled on.

She was seated upright, her head drooped and her eyes were closed. A yellow wool blanket was spread across her lap. Nathan could see she had lost more weight, accentuated by the length of her hair, still long and flowing. She had on a floral printed housedress that was covered with a short, white cardigan. Her reading glasses were hanging around her neck, supported by a braided eyeglass chain. Next to her, on the cushions of the couch, was today's *Toronto Sun* and the *Globe & Mail*, some issues of *Scientific American*, a current *National Geographic* and a few books with thin slips of paper marking page locations. On a small adjacent hassock was a suspense novel, a book of poems and a copy of C.S. Lewis' *Surprised By Joy*.

A small nesting table sat in close proximity holding a box of tissues, a glass of water, a mug containing some cold tea, an empty packet of Splenda, and a portable device known as a Transcutaneous Electrical Nerve Stimulator (TENS). It was battery powered, about the size of a small transistor radio, and contained two electrodes which generated a series of electric impulses that could neutralize pain in a specific area of the body. It was one of the only forms of pain management that Rose had agreed to simply because she knew that the idea of electrical stimulation to relieve pain was as natural as standing on a fish capable of generating electricity.

Of course, Rose knew all about electrogenetic and electroreceptive fish, uncommon in North America, but rampant in the fresh and sea waters of South America, Africa and the Middle East.

When the pain was too unbearable, Simon would insert the two electrodes in parallel positions near the point of discomfort and turn on the TENS. The relief was always temporary, but at least it brought her a small reprieve.

Nathan leaned in to study his mother's face and, at the same moment, her eyes opened, large watery pools of pale sky. The recognition was instantaneous, and the eyes brightened immediately, a smile forming at the corners of her mouth.

"Mama, I'm here for a visit," he said.

She straightened herself up a bit, backing up on the couch, "Did you bring your clarinet?"

"Of course. But I brought Ricky, too. He wanted to see you."

"Oh, good. Where's your father?" she asked.

"In the kitchen. We brought some things to make lunch."

"I'm not eating much these days."

"You'll enjoy this," he sat down next to her, looking around at the books and magazines, and took her hand in his. "So many things to read! It's a regular library here."

"I find it hard to concentrate on one thing. So I distract myself as much as I can," she cleared her throat and coughed for a moment. "Hand me some water there please."

"Mama, you've always been surrounded by books," he laughed.

He kissed her hand gently, "I'm so glad I could be here today. We're in town for a while. It's the 90th season and the orchestra is going to be spectacular. We're working on a Brahms concerto for Emmanuel Ax and we've got a Beethoven and a Rachmaninoff and there's a wildly special benefit performance with Mr. Christopher Plummer reading *Henry V* for the Walton film score. My God, remember how *gorgeous* I thought he was as Captain Von Trapp? Well, you thought so, too, Mama," he baited. "Maybe we can get you out to one of these?"

She tried to pull herself up a little, but it was a struggle. "Did you ever think you would see me like this, Nathan?" she asked.

"Like what?" he answered nervously.

"Don't be ridiculous. I'm a sick old woman. Well, not that old, but still sick."

"Well, we are here to cheer you up!" he said brightly. "And where's my co-star anyway? Ricky! Get your cute Puerto Rican butt in here and say hi to my mother," he called out loudly to him.

"It's not Puerto Rican, you racist," Ricky shouted back from the kitchen, "it's Cuban!"

Ricky came into the living room with Simon trailing, each holding a glass of red wine.

"A little early in the day for the grape?" Nathan said.

Ricky whispered mildly, "Bitch. Hold this while I give Mama Rose a kiss." He handed the glass to Nathan who stole a sip, and leaned in to give the woman a peck on the cheek. "Actually, it's not even Cuban. We've been in Canada for a few hundred years. I think we intermarried with the Algonquins and the Hurons. You know, my folks named me Ricardo because my father worked in television. For the CBC. And my mother read somewhere that when an episode of *I Love Lucy* aired in the 1950's, the one that featured the birth of little Ricky, the water pressure in New York City dropped after the first commercial because so many people were watching, that they had all had to pee during the first commercial. It was a flush marathon."

Nathan rolled his eyes, "What a bunch of baloney." But Rose grinned widely, her eyes sparkling, and Simon's face was bright.

Then Simon announced dramatically, "Rose, we're going to have a good day today. Nathan and Ricky are fixing us lunch. One of your favorites! And then there will be some music."

"Oh, Simon. You sound like a barker at a circus tent," she answered him. "Honestly, I may be dying, but I'm not senile."

"Your mother doesn't have quite the same appetite," Simon warned.

"It's not a problem," she said and then shivered for just a moment, shifting in her seat.

"Do you need me to get to you something?" Nathan rushed to ask her, but Simon had swooped in and began to spread the blanket that covered her lap. When he had opened it more fully it made his wife look even smaller and frailer.

There was an awkward pause, and then Ricky said, "I hope you two will be able to see Nathan's new house soon. A dear friend of ours, who is a first-rate interior designer, has made extensive contributions. Apparently animal prints are "in-fashion" and you can't go left or right without seeing a leopard pillow on a chair or a zebra rug on a floor," he chortled.

Rose started to cough again, just a little, but it was continuous. "Well, it's hard for your mother to get around now," Simon started to say.

"Is there nothing I can do to break up her day? Nothing to distract?" It came out a bit more spiteful than he wanted, but patience was never one of Nathan's advantages.

His father looked at him, taking off his eyeglasses, "What I meant was, transportation is a bit of a challenge now. For a variety of reasons which we will not go into now in front your mother."

"That's ridiculous. We can just come here and pick her up and help her into the car. There are hardly any stairs …"

"It's not the stairs," Simon started to say, "it's the breathing. And the bladder. And the pain. In case you didn't notice."

Rose's eyes started to get bigger. "That is unnecessary, Simon."

Nathan bounced up from the couch like a rubber band, "Oh, for Christ's sake. I forgot something. In the kitchen. I'll be right back." He was sweating and a bead of perspiration started to drip down the side of his face onto his neck. Simon followed him right out, his face turning red.

"I'm glad you are here Nathan, but I don't appreciate your telling *me* how to take care of your mother."

"I'm not doing any of that. I was just saying,"

"Saying what?" he interrupted. "Do you think it's easy watching her deteriorate more and more every week when there's nothing I can do about it? Nothing anyone can do."

Nathan reached for the sack of groceries that he brought in and tore open the package of asparagus, grabbing a paring knife and a wooden cutting board that leaned against the side of one of the cabinets. He began to peel and then cut the asparagus. His father stood there quietly watching him for a moment and then sat down at the small dinette set that was pushed into an alcove in a corner of the kitchen.

"Nathan, all we ever do now is argue with each other. It's been like this for years. Why, I ask myself? Why can't we ever agree on anything? Was it always like this? When you were a boy you were much more forgiving."

"When I was a boy I thought I had a chance," his son responded.

"A chance at what?" the older man asked. Nathan put down the knife and turned to his father.

"A chance that I could get you to love me," he blurted out. Simon was stunned.

"But I haven't ever *not* loved you. I don't understand why you would say something like that. What have I ever done but help you? Support you. Protect you. I did what a father should do for his son."

"Because you took me to music lessons? Bought my education? What choice did you have?"

"I had plenty of choices. I never, ever made any demands on you, son. Never once did I try to entice you into coming into the business with me. It would have been a business of three generations. I never showed you scorn, or discouragement or interfered with your relationship with your mother. I supported you, stood by you when you were sixteen and announced to us that you had a boyfriend."

"You told me you were not surprised, but disappointed," he countered immediately.

"But only because of the obstacles you would have to face, Nathan. Not because I didn't love you."

Nathan turned back to the kitchen counter and grabbed an onion. "I'm making an asparagus frittata. I hope you will like it."

"Tell me, son. What have I done?"

Nathan could feel the tears welling up inside of him. Maybe the onion was the catalyst, but the sobs erupted quickly. A forty-year old man in tears is a painful sight to observe.

"I can't stand to see her like this. I just can't," Nathan cried softly.

The rest of the afternoon went along quite nicely. Rose was able to sit up at the dining room table and eat lunch with her son, his boyfriend and her husband. Along with the asparagus frittata, Nathan had made a hearts of palm salad and a garlic bruschetta, making sure that everyone knew it was pronounced *brus-ketta* and not *bru-shet-ta*. He pampered his mother, setting her napkin on her lap, telling jokes and reminiscences and cut into quarters the Red Velvet Cupcake he had bought for her at The Cupcake Shoppe, a *chichi* bakery off of Yonge Street. That afternoon he even paid Simon a compliment.

Ricky, for his part, was just as delightful, regaling Rose and Simon with stories about his crazy Latino-Canadian family. He was a convenient buffer for Nathan at the lunch table. After the meal Nathan helped his mother back into the living room while the dishes had been cleared by Ricky and Simon. She was quite tired, and he propped the pillow against the back of her head and covered her with the soft blanket she had been using.

"Nathan, I'm not going to live much longer," she started to say.

"Stop, Mama, stop," he began, shaking his head, "I don't know how I can …"

"You will go on without me," she tried to speak with strength, but the words were hoarse and powerless. "Listen to me my sweet son. You will not drown. *I will not let you drown.*"

"Mama, what are you talking about?" but he could already see that she'd drifted off.

Later on, after she awakened, he assembled his clarinet and played for a little while. The *molto perpetuo* by Paganini, followed by a series of klezmer tunes that livened up the afternoon. During the last of the klezmer songs, a slow dance called a *khosidl*, he saw Simon take Rose's hand and rub his thumb into her palm. It was the last time Nathan played music for his mother when she was alive.

Galilee, Israel - September, 2014

"Goodbye, Mama." Nathan looked up, holding the urn, unsure of what to do next so he held it out for his father to retrieve. By this point most of the contents had already been emptied. Simon took it from Nathan, upended the urn, and shook it lightly. The remaining ashes trickled out. Then, almost as an afterthought, he tossed the vessel into the lake where it bobbed around briefly and then faded from their view, lost in the foamy ripples of aqua and white; a golden artifact for some marine archaeologist to find millennia from now. He turned to his children, "Let's go downstairs and eat lunch. It's time to eat now."

~~~

It was another hour before they had finished the lunch that was prepared for them by Arkin. There was also a wine bucket containing two bottles of a Yarden sauvignon-blanc, cultivated out of the nearby Golan Heights Winery. They ate quietly with minimal conversation just listening to the regular if uneven sound of the lake water hitting the side of the boat. Inside the walnut-wooded interior the cabin felt claustrophobic, and Sharon who saw that Simon had closed his eyes decided to go up the ladder and onto the deck. Nathan followed her up shortly afterwards while Barbara stayed to clear the plates.

It was a familiar repetition of the family dynamics. The eldest would rush off to accomplish some task while Nathan, the prince, never cleared a dish nor involved himself in the disposal of trash. Barbara, the buffer sibling, had eventually assumed responsibility for the routine of the daily domestic chores of a household that had both a working father and mother.

"He's exhausted. You can see it all over him," Sharon told her brother, her eyes darting down towards the deck below. "All of this elaborate preparation."

"How much of this do you really think was Mama and how much is Simon?" her brother asked.

"I don't think he made any of this up. Our mother was very organized in everything, from our evening meals to her experiments. Even in her crazy periods she was orderly and logical." She gave him a look of resignation and then slipped her hand into the bag she had left on the deck and lit a cigarette. "They're Israeli-made. And now apparently they're kosher for Passover," she chirped liked a banal TV ad.

"Kosher poison, you mean," Nate said. "What kind of a Jew are you, anyway?"

"All of that is still so silly to me," Sharon said.

Though they were still close to the shoreline it seemed placid at the moment with only slight rumblings now and then of other craft out on the lake.

"You played beautifully," Sharon told her brother. "It was very moving. You always make me weepy when you play," she complimented him.

"Thanks, honey. It felt good and appropriate. A *pavane*, a formal dance. Symbolic, no?"

"What do you mean?" she asked.

"You know, solemn and proper. Avoiding confrontation, pretending things didn't happen. We talked around things or just took notes and went about our business. And today Chazon reappears. Really? Dead for years but involved in her memorial service."

"She changed, Nathan," Sharon continued, "it's hard to pin down when, but you know she did. I think of so many things I thought she did wrong when we were growing up, but then I see myself doing the same things, saying the same things to Michelle."

"Not our mother," Nathan laughed.

"I used to think that she just didn't care," she said. "It wasn't until I was much older and juggling Michelle and my patients that I realized how focused she was on her own work. She used to keep us attached to her when we were young. Like a bird. But then, after her children fledged, they were on their own."

"It made Simon agitated when you or Barbara were away or staying at a friend's house. Remember he was a basket case when you first went off to school," Nathan reminded her.

"After you came along Daddy was never comfortable unless we were all together. He didn't like being separated from her, from you, from anyone of us. It was something deeply seeded in him. It was Mama who changed. Not him."

Nathan nodded in assent, "Yeah, I remember. It started in California. It was Los Angeles that did her in. That sad paradise."

CHAPTER NINE

Los Angeles, California - February, 1986

Rose opened the door of her hotel room and picked up the newspaper that had been placed on the carpeted threshold outside, an amenity for guests at the lavish Los Angeles Biltmore. It was the last week of February, and she was attending a conference of the prestigious International Bioacoustics Council, participating in a panel discussion on *"Evolution, Ontogeny and the Development of Acoustic Behavior"*.

At forty-three she had achieved a level of success in her field, and though tied to an academic calendar at the University of Toronto at Mississauga, she had climbed her way profitably through years of academic discourse, research and publication into a position of security and flexibility.

A few years earlier, in 1982, Rose was offered an opportunity to work in Toronto, and she and Simon had begun the fatiguing negotiation about relocating west to Ontario and away from the Atlantic maritime provinces where Simon had lived all his life.

"We'll still be near the water, of course," Rose had argued, "and the children will adapt. The girls are starting high school soon, and Nathan hasn't had time to get used to any school here in St. John. Nothing ventured, nothing gained."

"I'll be leaving my father. And the Company is located here."

"Yes, I know that. But haven't the two of you been seriously talking about entertaining one of the buyout offers? I know it's hard for you, but your father is not that active anymore. You're here with us in St. John and not in Halifax all the time anyway."

"Yes, but ..."

"Let me finish, Simon," Rose maintained, "your father can come live with us – if he wants to. It will be good for the kids to spend more time with their grandpa."

But Simon knew that could never be arranged. Karl wouldn't make the move to Ontario. He stayed in his house in Halifax, living as independently as he could, cared for by the middle-aged local couple who were caretakers, cooks and companions. The Strongin investment in fishing and food processing ultimately was redeemed, and the growing Canadian national company, which paid to take over Simon's and Karl's share in L&J Strongin Fisheries, kept the name intact for twenty-five years when they were eventually bought out by an even bigger company. It was a continuous story of larger fish devouring smaller fish.

Simon had not competed with his wife. That had never been a factor in their relationship. He had always admired her for her scholarship, supported her accomplishments and bolstered her confidence. Even if he didn't quite understand the nuts and bolts of what she was doing, he was her champion. The family had all followed Rose's research projects in and around the Bay of Fundy, northwest in the Georgian Bay and Nottawasaga Bays.

But he couldn't help notice that the spouses of his employees and friends were housewives, women contented with raising children, supervising the help, restoring and decorating historic houses, joining social societies. This was a world that Rose had no interest in and Simon, to his credit, was not resentful or annoyed. He simply wanted her to be happy doing what made her happy. But he became increasingly brooding when she would find it necessary to leave the children and their home, and now this new trip to California was worrisome.

"We need a break from each other, Simon. It's only Los Angeles, and I'll be back in less than a week," she explained, sitting across from him at the dining room table before she flew out. "Only a week."

This had been coming for a while and he knew it. He had never been particularly comfortable with Rose's traveling. Something always gnawed at him when she left the children and their home. He often thought this insecurity was planted in him after she disappeared in Israel, that deep down she'd had an undiagnosed condition, a fugue amnesia that would rear itself unexpectedly. But over the years he had gradually become accustomed to her attending a conference here and there and nothing unforeseen had occurred.

Since their arrival in Toronto a few years back her research expeditions were mostly local, centered around Lake Ontario. Any locations that were further away were coordinated with him around school holidays and summer breaks so they could all travel together or, at least, spend part of the time as a family.

"What about Nathan?" he asked his wife when she brought up the trip.

"What about him?"

"He hates spending time alone with me. The girls aren't around." Both Sharon and Barbara had started in college by then, both at schools in Quebec.

"He has to practice his clarinet anyway. Please Simon, embolden him. He is gifted. You know that. I can't always be the only one to encourage him for God's sake," she said. "He's just a boy, not like you Simon. He's not like you."

"It's not a question of whether he's like me or not. He just doesn't *like* me."

"That's ridiculous. He's a boy. And besides I know what this is all about anyway."

"I don't know what you're talking about."

"Come on. You think the main reason I'm going to L.A. is to spend time with Noah."

There. She had said it outright.

"No. I wasn't even certain he would be there," Simon responded insincerely.

"Yes. *Of course,* you did. And yes, Chazon is going to be there. But as my colleague, Simon. Not my lover."

"How can you even say such a thing? Why do want to provoke me?"

"Because that's what I know you're thinking," she shot right back.

He knew she was right. He had talked with Chazon on the telephone a number of times when the scientist telephoned the house and he had spent that disagreeable time with him in the Galilee. But Simon, who considered himself an astute judge of character, was put off.

"I don't like him," he told Rose.

"You don't even *know* him. And I haven't really seen much of him in over twelve years. We are on the same panel. He invited me to participate. That's all there is to it. He's a happily married man."

"And is that what we are?" he asked bitingly. "A happily married couple?"

"Yes. Exactly. Look, nothing's going to happen. You know what I'm talking about. We've been over this ..."

"And we keep coming back to it."

"When, for God's sake, will you just let this thing go?"

"You were *both* missing, Rose. At the same time. Only he knew where he was and what he was doing. You're still foggy on it." Insinuations. Wounding words.

"You know what the doctor said," she was cutting him off.

"The great disappearance mystery and I cannot relinquish it to a closed case file. It's our unfinished business," he shouted.

"No, Simon. It's yours," she said now with anger in her voice, "and I'm done discussing it. I've never been unfaithful to you."

"Do you think I ever cheated on you?" he asked.

The response came immediately, "No. Never. You're not even capable of that kind of breach. You wouldn't sacrifice the things you love for something as meaningless as screwing someone else."

"It's him I don't trust. He's a player, Rose. A fucking Jew Don Juan. Your ears would bleed if I told you all the things people said behind his back when we were at Ginosar. It made me uncomfortable then, and it makes me uncomfortable now."

"We are not having an affair. I don't want to have an affair with him."

"But admit that you find him attractive. Admit it." He was badgering her.

"This is just ridiculous, Simon. He can't help the way he looks. And I have two eyes, for Christ-sake. What am I supposed to do? Not look at him?" She paused to catch her breath, "This is more about you than me. So while I'm in California working on my career, why don't you take your son and drive him up to Montreal to see his sisters. They'd like that."

Rose had never been to Los Angeles before. The city had calmed down a bit since the Olympics back in 1984, but there was always something to get hysterical about in California. The West Coast always seemed a world away to Rose who, having grown up in New York and lived in Eastern Canada most of her adult life, thought of L.A. as a tawdry city filled with celebrity fads and devil-worshipping serial killers. At least that's how it was portrayed in the media. One could certainly be anonymous in the spread-out, highway-driven template. She remembered some pop song calling it "lonely."

Nonetheless, Rose knew there were colleagues of hers who would use the opportunity to be away from their wives and husbands to pursue extramarital affairs, or at least what was described to her as a zipless fuck. But for Simon to think she would be sexually intimate with Noah made her indignant.

She started to flip through the newspaper she had picked up when the loud, strident ringing of the telephone startled her.

"Oh, I'm surprised you're actually there in your room," Simon said.

"And a good morning to you Simon. A bit early for sarcasm, no?"

"No, no. I thought you needed to be up at the crack of dawn for these things, having breakfast and schmoozing with the top minds of the day." It was nine o'clock Los Angeles time.

"Ha, ha. You're a real joker. I've got the big panel presentation in a little while, and I've been preparing here in my room. I had some breakfast sent up. I don't know why I feel nervous. Ridiculous isn't it. How's Nathan?"

"He's fine. He wants to say hi." He put his son on the phone.

"Hi, Mama. When are you back home?"

"In three days. I have a very early flight on Sunday and will be back late afternoon."

"Oh, good. No school today!"

"I know, that's why your father stayed home with you. Are you practicing?"

"Yes, and you don't have to ask me that same question every time you talk to me. I'm twelve years old, not ten. Besides, he has been checking up on me to be sure I do what I've been told."

"Well, I'm glad you're both being so obedient. Give me your father again. Kiss."

Simon got back on the phone. "Everything is fine here, Rose. Really. Just concentrate on what you need to do. We miss you."

"And I miss you guys, too. But it was worth it. I've been recognized by so many people here, and if I needed an ego-feed, well, this is the place for me to get it. Oh," she remembered, "you know who else is here?"

"Surprise me," he answered sarcastically.

"Stop it."

"Okay, okay. I'm sorry, go on. Who else is there?"

"Joanna Manion, the young woman from Vancouver who was my graduate research assistant when I first got to U.T. The young woman with the "D" cup. You must remember her Simon. Your eyes came out of your head the first time you met her."

He started to chuckle, "Touché. I hope she's doing well."

"Yes, she's at Cal Tech now. And, of course, Annabel is here. I haven't seen her for a few years. She looks terrific. She's ageless."

There was a pause in the conversation that went on a little too long for it to be a technical phone difficulty.

"Simon, are you there?" Rose asked.

"Yes," he paused, "and Noah. How has that all been going?"

"Honestly, I haven't seen much of him. You know what a celebrity he is," she snickered wickedly, "but yes, we've been meeting in spurts to get prepared for today."

"Okay. I just wanted to say, well, to say, I'm sorry we had that disagreement before you left."

"We've moved beyond that now. I'll see you in a few days. Wish me luck."

"Bye." And the phone call was over.

She was glad he apologized though it didn't really make any difference. Everyone needs to have their own secrets.

She opened the door to a corridor of elegantly trimmed doors and listened to the bells and whistles of the bank of elevators down at the end of the wide hallway. Ambient music played through circular speakers inserted into the ceiling. She picked up the *LA Times* that had been tossed against the door, unfolded, and took note of the headline, "Marcos Flees Philippines After 20-Year Rule." Nothing she cared about reading. Making a trifold of the paper, she tucked it under her arm, grabbed the smart Coach briefcase Simon and the children had given to her for a recent birthday, and headed down towards the elevators. Surprisingly, when it arrived it was empty, and she pressed the button for the lobby riding all the way down in silence.

The sumptuous foyer of the Los Angeles Biltmore Hotel was noisy and bright as the gated elevator opened onto the grandiose lobby revealing a wide staircase leading to the series of ballrooms that had been reserved for the conference. The lobby stretched out in front of her, and her eyes adjusted quickly to the brightness after coming out of the dark, subdued carriage. But oddly, it seemed to her that the light had focused her eyes in a specific direction, almost manipulatively, like a flashlight, leading to one corner of the lobby where a brown-skinned woman sat alone. Without realizing it, Rose had walked over to her.

"Do I know you?" Rose asked the striking woman sitting serenely in a gold-brocaded club chair. The lobby was quite active with guests checking in and out, luggage strewn about, waiters carrying silver trays with cocktails amidst the frescoes and fountains, columns and chandeliers that characterized the Hotel's Spanish-Renaissance design.

There was a constant buzz of noise and activity all around but, to Rose it appeared that the woman was centered in a state of serenity. She was dressed in a traditional sari, blue silk richly decorated with a peacock design. Her features were Indian, large wide expressive eyes, dark coffee colored eyebrows and long, wavy black hair. Rose couldn't guess her age but thought somewhat younger than she.

"I'm sorry," Rose repeated. "Have we met before?"

"I don't think so. Perhaps?" the exotic woman answered in the accent of Indian English.

"Sorry to disturb you. It's just that when I came into the lobby something compelled me to look in this direction and I thought I recognized you. From somewhere."

The woman laughed, "Perchance in another life?"

The two of them locked eyes. Rose felt slightly awkward. She could have sworn they had met somewhere before: a conference, project, lecture. Somewhere.

"Well, I don't mean to make you uncomfortable," the woman continued, "but we are all in recognition of each other somehow. Our consciousness filters our experiences, but they remain indelibly etched into our souls."

Rose smiled and thought, "Oh, she's a kook". She might have then excused herself and moved on, but for some unexplainable reason she wanted to stay. The woman could sense this.

"You're a scientist," she went on.

"Yes. How did you know?"

"There's a large conference happening here. Signs in the lobby and many, many intelligent-looking men and women with plastic tags around their necks carrying important looking papers and portfolios," she rattled on in that inflected-Indian English so recognizable to the American ear. "I'm not a detective, by the way."

Rose had today's *L.A. Times* rolled under her right arm. She removed it, placing it down on a small lobby table and extended her hand out, but kept the small briefcase close by her side.

"I'm Rose Strongin and yes, I'm here to be a plenary speaker on one of the IBC conference panels."

"I'm pleased to meet you, Rose. I am Shatapattra. It is a mouthful, I know."

"Not really. May I sit just for a minute?" Rose found herself asking.

"Of course. I am in no hurry," the stranger admitted. She lifted her right arm to adjust the long, draped cloth that extended from her shoulder and Rose caught a glimpse of a small tattoo on the inside of her forearm, two overlapping triangles, inked in blue. "In fact, I come here often to sit and meditate."

"In this lobby? But it's ridiculously loud."

"Meditation is a mental discipline. In order to meditate you must change the way you think about noise. All sound is vibration. Therefore incorporate it into your devotions."

Rose was astonished. She had built a career around listening to vibrations in an arena of silences — beneath the surfaces of water. She had never connected it with meditation.

And then the woman said, "It will bring you closer to God, my dear."

"Excuse me?"

"In proximity to God. This is the foundation of all that we are and all we can be."

Normally Rose would have felt uncomfortable having such a personal conversation with a stranger in a public lobby. But she thought the woman projected an audacious wisdom. It felt natural to continue the exchange.

"I'm afraid I have not developed my spiritual side at all, Shatapattra. My days are taken up with research and teaching and my nights are negotiating with my husband and children."

Her companion laughed, "You have the awareness of God already. That's all that is needed to begin. When you clear the veil of your mind, when there is present only the state of nothingness, you are free to walk the path to union."

Rose looked at the clock. She had to be on her way to the next event but something bound her to her chair. "This is ridiculous," she thought. She had wanted to give herself some preparation time before the panel assembled, and now she was devoting her free time to a stranger in a hotel lobby engaged in a discussion of a topic she was entirely uncomfortable with. And, on top of it all, she couldn't get rid of the nagging feeling that she had seen this woman before.

"I'm not sure I understand what all that means, but I will give you this," Rose attempted to explain. "I grew up in a strictly Jewish house doing things and thinking things because they seemed to be rooted in obedience to my mother and father, not because I actually believed them. But away from all the silly stories I was taught, after I had taken a course in religious philosophy, I came across a deeper and less compliant cogitation. In particular, I was intrigued by the idea of "nothingness." What the rabidly orthodox Jews called *bittul bim'tziut,* the entity of nothingness – viewing yourself as nothing at all."

Shatapattra smiled in a knowing, almost self-satisfied way.

"I would go to the beach and put my entire body underwater, close off all the senses and think there is nothing but timeless emptiness," Rose continued. She seemed to rattle on, almost trancelike.

"Do you know why I come here to meditate?" the Indian woman asked.

Rose stared at her blankly.

"This Hotel is a holy shrine. Yogananda died here. The glorious Paramahansa Yogananda. This is the place where his soul left his body," she announced as a matter of fact, "a little more than thirty three years ago."

Rose was astounded. Although she did not know much about the man, she knew he was a lion and the well-respected Indian guru who had shepherded the practice of meditation to the west.

"It was at a banquet to honor the Indian ambassador. The guru was reading one of his poems. '*Where Ganges woods, Himalayan caves, and men dream God -- I am hallowed, my body touched that sod*'. And then he brought his hands to his chest, looked up and died."

"Heart attack?" she asked.

"No. It was time for him to leave the world. He had attained enlightenment and left his body," said Shatapattra.

Rose pondered this last statement, considering the Indian woman's words carefully. The Los Angeles Biltmore Hotel as an actual destination for a pilgrimage? The inscrutable juxtaposition of the ancient and the modern. The extraordinary intersection between the state of nothingness and the opulent materialism of a western hotel in an American city.

"How fascinating this all is. I'm speechless," said Rose suddenly, "but I need to get to my conference."

"I'm so sorry to have intruded on your time," Shatapattra answered as she rose delicately from her chair smoothing the creases in the powder blue cloth that draped over her shoulder.

"Oh, no. Of course not. You've been a most fascinating diversion for me. Goodbye," Rose added reaching for her briefcase and clutching it to her chest insecurely.

"The pleasure has been mine, Dr. Rose," the woman answered. And then, almost as an afterthought, "perhaps we will all meet again one day when we find our Dalmanoutha."

Rose turned and started to walk away. "What a strange way to say goodbye," she thought. Perhaps this was some sort of Hindi or Indian expression of farewell.

But seconds later Shatapattra called out to her, "Don't forget your newspaper." Rose stopped and turned around, locking eyes with the woman. Shatapattra handed her the folded paper and said calmly, "There's a story on page six of the International Section. You may find it quite riveting."

Rose looked puzzled, but smiled and retrieved the newspaper. She started towards the staircase that would take her to the conference ballroom that had been set with tables and chairs and a long dais for the panel's speakers. But as she traveled through the long, swanky lobby filled with cigarette smoke and the bustle of travelers, in a split second, an instinctual flash and a powerful memory emerged.

She remembered where she *had* seen Shatapattra before. It was in the early 1970's when she traveled to the Galilee to meet

Noah and assist his work with the sonar traducers on the harbor project. That woman was part of the research team. She was sure of it. Rose remembered her quite clearly, though back then she was dressed as a Westerner in jeans and a smock. Though she was younger then, the face and features were the same.

But even more convincing was the small tattoo on the inside of the right forearm, just below the palm. Rose had remembered seeing it many years ago. The Hebrew Star of David, perhaps three inches in diameter, inked into the flesh.

She looked back across the room to see if Shatapattra was still there, but she had already vanished, an evanescence mysterious and unexplained. Rose stopped short of the conference venue, flipped open the *L.A. Times* to the International section, page six and began to read.

Israeli Archeologists Rush to Excavate 'Jesus Boat' From Sea of Galilee
February 26, 1986 from the Los Angeles Times

A few long minutes later she entered the hotel conference room and Chazon asked, "What's the matter, Rose? You look as if you've seen a ghost." He stood up from the folding chair he was seated on in the middle of a row of similar chairs set up behind a dais. Although Rose was above average in height, the Israeli scientist towered over her.

"Well maybe I have," she answered cryptically, "I'm just not sure. I had the strangest conversation in the lobby with a woman who called herself Shatapattra, but I'm one hundred percent certain she was one of your researchers."

"Shatapattra? One of my researchers? I have no idea who she is," he answered a bit perplexed. "How do you know her?"

"I don't *know* her," she responded emphatically. "I just met her. The meeting was accidental. I mean, it just evolved. It was an accidental meeting, yet it felt like I had been manipulated into it. Frankly, I don't understand."

"Rose, you're upset. We have to present in about fifteen minutes. Are you going to be okay?" The room began to fill with the conference participants, some milling about pouring coffee or juice, others claiming seats with their portfolios or briefcases.

"There was a young girl from India who worked with you on the harbor project. When we first met. Don't you remember her?" Rose asked aggressively.

"I'm sorry," Noah began to say.

"You *must* remember her, Noah. She had a tattoo on the inside of her forearm. Of a Star of David. She was a fucking Indian for Christ-sake. How many other Indians were on that dig?"

"Lower your voice please, Rose. I'm worried about you," he answered sternly.

"Noah, that is bullshit. You have to remember her. She worked with us at Ginosar," she blurted it out. "Did you see today's newspaper? They found an ancient boat," she announced, almost defiantly, "outside of Ginosar."

"What?" his eyes widened. "No, I didn't know. How curious nobody from Israel phoned me," he interrupted her.

"Here," she shoved the newspaper under his nose, "dredged out of that yucky mud we had to endure. Two kibbutzniks tripped over it during the drought. They think it could be over two thousand years old," Rose explained. "Your bosses in Jerusalem have kept it under wraps for a few weeks now. This woman showed me the newspaper article. Pointed right to it. Your Indian researcher." Rose was about to go on when Chazon cut her off. His eyes widened and his face took on an ominous demeanor.

"Oh, I think you're remembering Malik. I'm so sorry. She was British. Anglo-Indian. Her name was Anne Malik. She was born in England and worked briefly for me through the British Museum partnership. Now I do remember. She was involved with some sort of Jews-for-Jesus group. That's why she was so eager to work with us in the Galilee," he explained.

"So you *do* remember her. I'm not crazy," Rose was relieved.

"Well, yes, but Rose, I'm sorry. It could not have been her you met."

"Why not?"

"Anne Malik is dead. She died in a plane crash a few years after our work together. It was very sad, very tragic."

Rose stared at him. She could not believe what Noah was telling her. How could that be? Could she have imagined the entire conversation? No, it was impossible.

"Listen, we will have to deal with this later because now we have to make an important presentation. Can we please just put this whole thing in abeyance for now. I promise I will go over all of this with you when we are through," he assured her. Chazon wrapped his large, warm hand over hers and led her to a chair next to his on the dais.

~~~

When the panel discussion was completed and the ensuing round table discussion wrapped up, Rose was more than relieved. Noah had been the moderator; his confident presence was always appealing to conference and symposium organizers. Although she had put both the strange meeting in the hotel lobby, and the newspaper article on the discovery of the ancient boat, in the back of her mind, whenever her thoughts wandered they found their way back to those same events.

A luncheon had been organized in one of the larger meeting rooms for all attendees, but on their way down the plush hotel corridor, exchanging concise pleasantries with colleagues coming and going like ants in a colony, Noah grabbed Rose's wrist and took a left turn down a perpendicular hallway.

"A slight detour," he said. "I'm not hungry for any

'rubber chicken' today and I'm not going to watch you in distress anymore until we get to the bottom of this."

"Well, I'm glad it's over. My focus just wasn't there."

"You did fine, as usual. You make an outstanding appearance and speak with confidence. But it's not your science I worry about ... "

"Noah, I didn't make it up. It happened. She was real. I recognized that tattoo she had. I couldn't place it at first but then it came back."

"Yes, the Magen. I know. The Shield of David. How could you even be sure that's what it was, to tell the truth? "

"Of course it was, Noah. I grew up a Jew. I was surrounded by them growing up. She was assigned to the British Museum group but I passed by her many times on the way back and forth to the site."

"That's not what I meant. You think that sign is unique to the Hebrews? It isn't. It was incorporated by ancient Hindus into their worship of Brahma, Vishnu and Shiva, their holy trinity," he explained hoping it might open up more possibilities.

"That's beside the point," she answered.

"It's a coincidence. They happen all the time."

"I don't believe in coincidences. Especially Indian women who have the same tattoo of a Jewish star on their forearm. Come on. What are the chances of that?"

"What are the chances that Greatbatch would invent a

pacemaker for the heart while building an oscillator to record animal heartbeat sounds?"

She scrunched her face in doubt, "Look, why would *she*, this person, whoever she is, lead me to a newspaper story that is directly related to the area we were working in?"

"You told me she knew you were a scientist. Maybe she thought you'd be curious about a science article. It could be another coincidence."

"I'll repeat myself, Noah. I don't believe in coincidences," she said decisively.

"Coincidence is God's way of remaining anonymous," he snickered.

"So quoting Einstein is going to calm me down?"

Hotel guests and conference participants passed them by, some nodding in acknowledgement. One of them, a pretty girl named Joanna Manion, waved to Rose telling her she would see her at a session later that afternoon. Noah passed a long credenza which had piles of daily newspapers on it and grabbed the *L.A. Times, Wall Street Journal* and *U.S. News and World Report,* flipping through them and scanning the Science articles as they walked down the long corridor.

"This is fascinating. Amazing. It could be one of the most important finds in the western Galilee," he told her.

"The boat was found very close to where I was lost. Remember?" Rose said quietly.

"But you were found," Noah jumped right back, "and you were also found to be fine. Not suffering from any memory lapses, neurological problems, manifestations of physical abuse." He thought for a moment and then said, "And remember – it saved your life."

She shivered a bit whenever she was reminded of this. They headed towards the bank of elevators that led to the hotel's rooms and suites. It was much quieter here, just a porter or chambermaid passing through.

"There's not much else in these news accounts. I am going to make a call to Tel Aviv and get some more up-to-date information."

Noah pressed the elevator's button and then looked up at her, "You're a beautiful woman Rose. Even more so then when we first met." She met his eyes squarely.

"Where are you taking me?" she asked.

"Back to my room. I want to get something for you."

The elevator door opened, and they walked slowly together down the wide corridor, brightly lit with a classic gold-leaf wall covering.

"Oh, I don't know, Noah," she said, "I don't think this is a good idea." He saw the look on her face.

"Just be patient," he admonished. "I'll have you feeling better in a flash."

He turned the key into the door of his room and switched on the light. There was a thick piece of paper that had been folded and inserted under the space in the door. Chazon picked it up, disinterested, and tossed it on the desk that was just inside the vestibule.

"Just go sit down in that cozy armchair and take your shoes off," he directed her.

"It's the middle of the day," she answered.

"Maybe here in California," he shot back, "but somewhere else, let's say, in Tiberias, everyone is retiring for the night."

Then he went over to the closet, extended his arm to the top shelf, and pulled down a hard shell black suitcase. Unfastening the clasp he reached into a zippered pocket in the lid and pulled out a small plastic bag. As soon as he pulled the edges of the bag apart the incense permeated the room. Inside was the harvest of the plant cannabis, processed and pressed into a half dozen yellowed white cigarettes that had been rolled handily. He took one of them out, struck a match from a matchbook he kept in his pocket, and inhaled deeply.

"You got that through customs? Are you nuts?" Rose asked.

"Of course not. I made a contact five minutes after I got to LA," he said with charming immodesty. "You know how resourceful I can be." He handed her the joint. "Here. It will calm you down."

"I haven't been high in years. Besides, Simon would have a cow if he ..."

"But he's not here. So how will he know?" He puckered his thick lips and he grinned a bold smile. "And besides, in twenty years it will all be legal anyway. Probably prescribed the way your doctors here dispense the Xanax. This isn't exactly the only time we've gotten high."

It was an easy sell. Rose reached out and took a drag. It felt good going down her throat.

"They call it Californian Skunk. Can you believe it?" he said and started to laugh.

She leaned back and inhaled again, "You know this is one of the few things that really does calm me down."

Galilee, Israel - September, 1974

They two of them *had* done this before, on a moonlit night, at the end of the expedition that September. Simon had stayed back at the Ginosar kibbutz with the girls. Earlier that day Rose had finished mapping the underwater sound, had analyzed the fish and cetacean hearing, calculated the effects of sounds on the marine organisms using the Ishmael and automatic detection methods and reported back to the handsome archaeologist. He was quite pleased with her work. Her research indicated there was a high probability that a fishery had been constructed within the parameters of an artificial harbor in the Galilean Sea.

The expedition had now excavated enough stones to complete the picture that this was indeed a place for marine shelter and a commercial location to attract and catch fish. She could picture in her mind a bustling harbor of merchants and fishermen, hauling seine nets from their boats, salting and preserving the fish, and packing them for transportation along the old Roman roads to locations in and around the Galilee.

The night before Rose and her family were scheduled to return to Canada, Noah and a few of the researchers had decided to walk down from the common room to the beach at Ilanot. The group had passed around a few marijuana cigarettes as they walked the narrow, landscaped path out of the kibbutz's main entrance and down to the lake. The entire expedition staff had an evening session earlier. Rose felt a bit funny leaving Simon back with the kids, but it was late and they needed to be in bed. She, however, wasn't a bit tired. "I'll sleep on the plane. This is the most wonderful work I could be doing," she thought.

The golden moon created a stark beam of luminescence over the peaceful water, like a Hollywood spotlight shining on a movie star. Noah was clearly the luminary, and though he was already stoned by this time, he led the way confidently down to the rocky beach where reeds and other small debris had washed up. They all sat on the moist sand, feeling it run through their fingers, breathing in the exquisite, warm air. By the time Noah came up behind her the rest of the group was already dispersed. He sat down beside her, placing his arm around her shoulder.

She shuddered a bit not knowing if he was being sexual or if it was just the predictable effect of smoking weed. Nonetheless, she showed no resistance.

"In America and in Canada," he said to her in an imperious way, "you study things that are 200 years old. But here in the Holy Land, you study things that happened 2,000 years ago. Everything is ancient, even when it is new. Everyone is attached to their past."

He then released himself from her waist, and walked down into the lake. In the light of the moon she followed him as he walked into the shallow, dark water. Then she lost sight of him. She didn't know if it was five minutes or fifty, because she was staring up at the sky, studying the pattern the stars made, feeling the benign anesthetic effect of the pot when she heard a loud splashing sound and turned to see Noah emerge from the water. His clothes were drenched, his hair soaked, his eyes blazing like a dragon. It was an image she had not forgotten.

But now she watched the Israeli scientist, sitting across the hotel room from her, taking off his black Oxford shoes and plopping himself on the king-sized bed that had just been made by the hotel housekeeping staff. He threw over the bolsters and fancy pillows that dressed it and stretched out on his back, unbuttoning the top few buttons of his shirt. She recognized the small braided copper loop he wore religiously around his neck which he now caressed with his fingers.

They passed the joint back and forth in that dreamlike way when the effects of marijuana start to kick in, maneuvering everything in drowsy, slow motion. Yes. They had done this before.

"Noah, I have something to tell you," Rose said. "There was something about that day. When nobody could find me. I found something. Or I stumbled onto something, or maybe, it was something someone gave me. I don't know."

"What are you talking about?" he asked.

"A piece of wood. Driftwood, maybe, I don't know exactly. I found it in my pocket the day we left to return to Canada."

"And why are you telling me this?"

"It's very, very old. But it isn't preserved. And it isn't petrified."

"How do you know?"

"I had it carbon-dated in the laboratory at school."

"And what were the results?"

"They said it was probably 2,000 years old. Give or take. Trust me. It freaked me out," she explained. "It had been in the water a long, long time. Probably was submerged in a swamp or a bog. The scientist who dated it didn't think it came washing around a lake or river because the oxygen and physical abuse would rot it."

"So it's a good old-fashioned fossil. Why was this was important to you?"

"It needs the anoxic environment to stay preserved."

"Yes, of course. That's basic science."

"Well, guess what?" she continued. "I had it wrapped in a velour sack, un-conserved, exposed to dust and a multitude of airborne bacteria."

He shot up quickly. "That's peculiar. There must have been some mistake. What did you do with it?" he started to ask, but the telephone rang loudly and Noah climbed over the end of the bed to grab the receiver. "Yes. This is Dr. Chazon. What? Oh, yes. A fax? Let me see. Of course, it was under the door to my room. Thanks for sending it up."

"What's going on?"

"I have to read this fax." He took in the brief contents looked up at Rose and said, "I should have looked at this before. It's from the Israeli Department of Antiquities. They want me back in Israel. They're putting me on the ancient boat project. The one you've just read about."

"Doing what?"

"Helping with the salvage and the preservation. A miracle they're saying. A miracle that it was found so well preserved. But bringing it up is dangerous. It's a big, big deal for us Rose," he was getting excited.

"For us?" she asked. "What do you mean." She jumped off of the bed.

"No. Not for the two of us. For all of us." He looked at her with an intensity that almost frightened her. "*Don't you see*

Rose? Every time something points to the Bible's accuracy, it bolsters the legitimacy of Israel. Whether you are religious or a secularist, it tells the world, our story is the truth. When the modern and the ancient stories intersect, it means there is hope for all of us. It is the hope that the miracles are true."

But Rose always thought she didn't believe in miracles.

CHAPTER TEN

Ontario, Canada - February, 1986

A few days later, still reeling from the strange encounter with the Indian woman, the sudden departure of Noah for Israel, and the discovery of the 2,000 year old boat, Rose left the bright sunlight of an early Los Angeles morning and flew into the cold bleakness of an Ontario afternoon. It had snowed earlier that morning and though it had stopped hours ago the nasty wetness lingered on through midday. A rude wind had whipped around Lake Ontario and Simon was afraid Rose's plane would be delayed, but it was on schedule according to the screens in the arrivals lounge at Toronto Pearson International Airport.

Simon and Nathan were waiting in Air Canada's large international arrivals hall when they spotted her. She was walking quickly, her heels clicking loudly on the tile floor, as she pulled a small suitcase on wheels with her left hand. Over her right shoulder she carried her briefcase that she had secured with a leather shoulder strap. An elegant camelhair coat was draped over her forearm. She had cleared passport control and customs effortlessly.

The moment Simon spotted her he knew immediately something was wrong. He could tell by the way she kept her shoulders rigid, but more revealing was the slight twitch in the lower lid of her left eye. *Blepharospasm.* He thought Rose was over that.

"Mama, we're here," the twelve-year old Nathan waved both of his hands as if they were unfurled flags.

"Don't shout like that, Nathan. She will see us," Simon criticized.

The boy rolled his eyes "Sorry," but his apology overlapped with Rose's loud announcement, "There's my little man." Then, "and my big man." Simon grinned. She did look a bit worn out he admitted.

"Hello, Rose. We're glad you're home safely," Simon said at a distance. Nathan stepped out and she gave him a hug and then gave Simon a short peck on the lips. He could discern the faintest trace of cigarette smoke on her hair. She had given up smoking as a New Year's resolution just a few short weeks ago. It was the third attempt she had made, but he was confident this time she would be able to get through it. Of course, just waddling through a smoking section on an airplane was enough to have the sour smell of tobacco permeate one's clothing and hair.

"Me, too. Let's go home. I'll make supper for us," she answered.

"Oh, good. I'm hungry. He's not much of a cook," Nathan said pointing his index finger at his father who winced. But the boy caught his father's face and quickly added, "He did try. Besides, we went out a lot and one night he treated me and Thom and Cindi to sushi."

Thom and Cindi were two of Nathan's friends from the exclusive Hereford Academy, a twin brother and sister, both musicians from a family of musicians. Thom, like his mother, had taken to the piano when he was only four, and Cindi (short for Lucinda *not* Cynthia as she found herself having to recite with disgust all too frequently) was drawn to the cello. Though they weren't quite prodigy caliber, at least not yet, they were both exceedingly talented and confident players. Nathan rounded out the trio quite conveniently.

Rose glanced at her young son for a moment. At the prepubescent age of twelve, Nathan often projected a worldliness that made him seem older, and only the high pitch of his voice and paucity of body and facial hair, separated him from someone with more maturity. In disposition, he could be both funny and witty.

"I assume these qualities came from his father," Rose often told her husband. "I never really had a well-developed sense of humor. You always told me I took myself too seriously."

Over the years she had grown accustomed to Simon's smartly facetious, if often sarcastic, shots. Early in their relationship she found almost everything he said ridiculously captivating. But, like many things that happen over time in a marriage, what was sweet and charming early on evolved into something borderline annoying. Or even worse.

Not that Nathan was at that level of maturity. At least not yet. But he once admitted to his mother that a significant part of the appeal of his friendship with Thom and Cindy was opportunistic and grounded in the advantageous convenience to learn and play the Brahms *Trio for Clarinet, Cello and Piano in A minor*, opus 114. He had first heard the piece at a concert at St. Michael's Anglican Church in downtown Toronto shortly after he began his clarinet study. When he read that the trio was composed by the great German romantic as though the instruments were "in love with each other" he swooned. This, of course, entertained Rose to no end.

But her son's amusing quips and stings often belied his moods which could be filled with great sadness. Rose, an observer and analyst by nature, was more in tune with this than Simon who, though never blatantly insensitive, tended to dismiss many things as "growing pains."

Simon's relationship with his son was less easygoing than the one he had with his mother and so different from the rapport he had with his own father. It transcended any of the conventional ideas about father and son relationships. He didn't require Nathan to be interested or involved in his business life, or the mechanics of automobiles, power tools or outdoor sporting activities. These were thought to be traditional enterprises ascribed to fathers and their sons. They had been neither important to Simon nor his own father. And, besides, the only real interest Nathan had in the outdoors was boating, something

Rose herself had instigated when she wanted the family to accompany her on some early experiments in local waters.

No, it was something else. A distance between father and son that seemed to be built-in, unrelated to prevailing interests or the paternal-filial axis. It was something that neither of them had any control over. This past week was a perfect example.

"Do you need me to look over your exam booklets, son?" he had asked Nathan. He knew that there were essays to be submitted and Rose usually went over them diligently.

"No. I have it covered," the boy said.

"But your mother usually does this for you, no? I'm happy to throw an eye on it for you."

He answered, "It's really no big deal. It's just a silly essay about an even sillier book for my French class. And your French needs a bit of work."

"So should we watch some television together?" Simon asked his son.

"No. I don't think so. I've got to finish up some other reading for this week and I have to transpose a fragment from a clarinet concerto that my teacher wants me to practice."

"Okay, son."

He thought about this as he and Nathan scanned the terminal, waiting for Rose's plane to arrive. His son, just on the cusp of manhood, was wearing a dark blue pea coat and woolen ski cap. The same as his father, though Simon had a long, woolen scarf dangling around his collar. If they had been meeting passengers disembarking from a boat they could have been mistaken for crew, or fishermen, perhaps.

Simon reached out to pick up Rose's suitcase, but she intercepted him.

"I've got it," she said. "Just give me a hand with the coat." He felt her tense up when he helped her on with it. And then he saw the fluttering eye again, imperceptible at first and then, rapidly quivering.

"Are you cold?" He thought he would attempt to find out what was going on. "You seem a bit hyped-up." Her neck tightened and the eye fluttered even more. The coat also smelled of tobacco.

"Huh? No, I'm fine. Just tired. I know I'm behind you, still on California time. But it was a long week, a lot of hours, and I'm mentally exhausted."

"Did you sit by the window or on the aisle?" Nathan interrupted, as if he sensed there was something his mother could not be truthful about.

"A window seat," she answered quickly. "It was lovely looking down at all those fluffy clouds. I thought I might watch a film. I thought I might sleep, but I couldn't."

Simon continued to press, "Oh okay, yeah, I'm sure you're all wound up."

"I didn't say that," she responded coldly. "I just said I might sleep."

"Well yes, of course. Sorry. Okay, let's get out of here."

Nathan ran ahead to step onto the rectangular automated mat that would signal the large, double-glazed exit doors to open, playfully jumping on it with both feet simultaneously. His parents followed a beat behind as their son led the way out of the terminal, across the crowded lanes of ground transportation choking with shuttle busses and taxis, and towards the airport car park where his father had placed his '84 Volkswagen Quantum Station Wagon. It had just made the six-hour trek, each way between Toronto to Montreal last weekend, carting Simon and Nathan to McGill University to see Sharon and Barbara.

"How was the visit with your sisters?" Rose asked as they climbed into the car and began to circumnavigate the airport looking for the exit and highway to take them home.

"They treat me like a baby," Nathan complained.

"Oh, come on, no that's not true," Rose said."

"Oh, come on, yes, it *is* true," Nathan answered a bit whiny. "They hover over me like a bunch of roosters. Especially Sharon who thinks she's so hot because she's studying "Psychology." Big deal. She's always asking me questions saying, 'How do you feel about this or that?' Just ridiculous."

Simon smirked looking in the rearview mirror at his son.

"And Barbara is so bossy," Nathan went on.

"That's what big sisters do, son. I never had any. Neither did your mother. You're a lucky stiff," he said. "We can go again at the next school holiday, okay?"

"When pigs fly," the boy responded. It brought a smile to both of his parents. But then it got silent again and they continued to ride through the bleak landscape, each of them lost in their own thoughts. After a few minutes Simon looked at his wife.

"Do you have a big day tomorrow?" he asked.

But Rose, who had already floated up into the metaphoric ionosphere, didn't hear a word of Simon's question. She was looking out of the window at the ashen sky, her mind focused on Noah and their conversation in the hotel room in Los Angeles. When she drifted back into the Volvo she thought she heard in the distance Simon's voice overlapping with Noah's and then, "Earth to Rose. Earth to Rose. I asked you if you had a big day tomorrow," Simon repeated, "but you're obviously still out of it."

She turned back from the window and stared at him. "What? Oh, I'm sorry. I was just distracted. Just thinking about what I have to catch up on."

"So you *do* have a big day coming up?"

"Well I think so. Why?"

"I thought we would send Nathan over to have supper with the Beechers, and the two of us could go into downtown and have a quiet dinner and catch up. I know it's a school night but..."

The boy's head popped over the seat when he heard about the possible plan.

"Yes! I'd like that very much. I can just catch a ride home from school with Thom and Cindi, and then you guys can come pick me up later," he strategized.

"I don't think so," Rose answered, "I'm sorry Simon. I just can't make any plans yet."

He saw her eye start to twitch again slightly, flipped the directional signal on and turned onto Highway 427, the Queen Elizabeth Way. They would be back in their home shortly.

Later that evening Rose cooked a meal, and the three of them ate quietly with spurts of Rose asking Nathan about school, his sisters, his friends, his practicing the clarinet. The food turned out fine, but the strain on Rose was palpable. When Nathan finally retired to his room to watch television and the two adults were left cleaning up the kitchen, Simon made the first move.

"How'd it all go with Chazon? Were you two a big hit?" he pointedly asked, half serious, half joking.

"Not sure I'd describe it that way. But yes, the panel presentation seemed to get a lot of attention and the Q&A was pretty exciting."

Then silence.

"Where was his wife?" Simon asked. "He's a long way from home, no?"

"You know she's a physician with an Israeli government. She was there, I guess. At home," Rose answered flatly. "He had to leave the conference early and get back to Tel Aviv to join a project. It seems a boat was found outside of Migdal close to Ginosar." She added, "Not far from where we all were."

There. She had said it.

"That's interesting. Related to your work there?"

"Maybe. Don't know. But it's a well-preserved specimen. Could be two-thousand plus years old."

"Wow, that's a find. What's Chazon got to do with it?"

Rose looked at him like he had two heads.

"What kind of a question is that?" Her tone was unpleasant. "He's a prominent Israeli archaeologist and scientist. Particularly in underwater salvages. His area of expertise is in the Western Galilee. It's a huge find in the biblical archaeology community, and he's researched and developed methodologies for preservation."

"Yeah, he's a legend," Simon said, but by now Rose had started to get worked up.

"Goddamn it. Why are you always so sarcastic about him? Is it because you think he's interested in me?"

"Maybe. He's certainly maintained a prolonged interest in you. And he is particularly arrogant to me."

"That's just the way the Israelis are. They act superior. But let's face it, Simon. You always think I've been attracted to him. And what's the difference anyway? You're my husband. He's not."

"Or maybe Rose, maybe it's because the last time you said goodbye to him you were also strung out," he blurted out not sure now where this entire conversation was heading.

"Excuse me?" she asked indignantly. "Why for God's sake are you being provocative with me now?"

"Look at you. You're uptight and preoccupied. Your tone with me is raw. You haven't engaged me in any conversation. You ignored me throughout the meal, and now you're just answering questions because I'm doing the asking. I feel like the prosecuting attorney."

"Well, maybe that's because you imagine me the defendant." It was building. She was getting furious.

"Your left eye. Fluttering again. Can't you feel it? Can't you tell?" He blurted it out.

Then, abruptly, a wave of sadness overtook her. "Well, yes. I thought so. It just started."

"And I know you're smoking. You're not fooling anyone. Including your son." He said it almost triumphantly.

She sighed in an exaggerated way, "I'm not really smoking again. It's just that I was under a lot of pressure ..."

"Be stronger. Overcome it. Now I'm going to bed."

He left the kitchen and Rose, disconsolate, sat down in one of the kitchen chairs, placing her head into her hands, and began to weep. She had fought the tears all night, but now they came in a great swell, nothing held back, sweeping over her in a great rush. Something she needed to find was gnawing at her, but she hadn't the energy to confront it until morning.

~~~

The next day, in the bedroom she shared with Simon, Rose unpacked her small suitcase emptying the contents out onto the bed including the *L.A. Times* which was still folded neatly in three when she stuffed it into the bag. Simon had been up much earlier and had driven Nathan to school, a short distance away. She didn't have to be back on campus until early afternoon having anticipated canceling her office hours before she had flown out to California.

She sorted the items back onto the shelves in her closet or into the wicker hamper that had been already filled amply to the top by Simon and Nathan during the week. And then she went into her office, a small room a few doors down, which held a handsome teak desk she had bought from the IKEA store in North York.

A desktop computer and its peripherals were smartly assembled amidst a series of papers piled high, file folders with colored tags, assorted books and periodicals, and, in one corner, the Fred Fowler microscope she had transported from Brooklyn to New Brunswick twenty years prior. The desk contained a few photographs, framed inexpensively, including photos of David and Lydia Fonseca, Sharon and Barbara's high school graduation photos, and a sweet picture of Simon with Nathan on his shoulders from the coast of Mexico.

The office itself contained a spacious closet with shelves that held durable plastic containers, each neatly labeled with souvenirs, remnants, samples and contents of her work over the years. Another series of warren-like cubbies held a tangle of audio equipment, each also carefully labeled. The remainder of the closet was filled with odds and ends, apparatus and gear from her work on Lake Ontario and other nearby waters. This was only a modest sampling. Her office on the campus also stored assorted boxes and bags, cartons and paraphernalia of her experiments with students, colleagues and scientific pseudo-celebrities from Canada and the U.S.

On a wall behind the desk was an enlarged printer's proof of the cover of a book, "*Ethology of Marine Mammal Acoustic Communication*" by Rose M. Strongin, PhD. An expansion of her doctoral thesis, it had been solicited and published by the Science Direct Academic Press. The first inset page stated "This book is dedicated to my husband, Simon Strongin."

She secured a small step stool she had stored in the corner of the room, opened it up and stepped into the closet reaching for a plastic bin that was shoved way to the back. She had to move a number of other items around in order to reach it and finally, when she had grasped the grey handles that served as fasteners, she pulled it towards the front, reaching for it with both hands, and gently brought it down onto the desk. The identifying label was glued onto the container's cover and read,

ARTIFICIAL FISH NURSERY/ROMAN/1ST C.E./KINNERET, ISRAEL/AUG-SEPT, 1974.

"Being this organized does have some advantages," she thought to herself as she removed the cover and started to dig through the contents. It was mostly papers, journals and notes, a number of photographs labeled with names, dates and locations, a floppy disk looking as obsolete as a vinyl record. But underneath it all she dug out something from a black velvet sack that was closed shut by two loops of braided cord.

Inside the sack was a small fragment of wood, splintered from something larger. She didn't know what. It was about half a foot in length, mostly cylindrical, spotted with small, unappealing knots. She had no idea how she had obtained it; she only knew it was in the pocket of the jumper she was wearing the last day she and Simon and the girls were in Israel.

Now as she examined it she could see it looked exactly the same as the last time she had looked at it, just over twelve years ago. That was right after she had it analyzed, submitted to the comprehensive test that would be necessary to make a determination about the sample: an accelerator mass spectrometry radio-carbon analysis. The results had both surprised and confused her. But she knew there must be a good explanation, one plausible and logical.

She had come home that day twelve years ago, from her office at the University, removed the wood fragment from the airtight Ziploc bag and put it back into the velour sack. Her colleague in the Department of Physics and Geological Studies said it appeared to be a piece of timber from a ship. It was old. Very old. It did not show any signs of insect infiltration or signs of rot. It did not exhibit any checking or cracking, nor could her colleague find anything used to inhibit barnacle or woodworm. Without proper preservation, he told her, the sample would likely disintegrate. But it hadn't.

She remembered the night she had emptied her pockets, the night she and Simon and the girls had all stayed in the hotel by the Ben Gurion Airport. She was unsure then exactly what it was, but she had tossed it into a cheap, velour sack that contained the contents of some worthless souvenirs she had purchased at the Bukharian market in Tiberias. Trinkets to bring back and give her colleagues to say, "Look where I was this summer. A pilgrim in the Promised Land!"

And now looking over the small fragment of wood again she thought, "Where did I get this? Did Noah give it to me that night?" Then she began to feel her eye twitch slightly, and a warm sensation began to overtake her.

"*Rosi, Rosi. Are you alright? You could have lost your eye!*" A voice. A deep male voice. She jumped and looked around the room frightened. And then again, *"Rosi, Rosi. Are you alright?"*

"Is somebody there?" she shouted, spooked. "Simon, is that you?" But she knew it couldn't have been him.

Then that warm sensation again and she was unnerved. She looked out of the door to the office into the open hallway. There was nobody else in the house.

"You could have lost your eye."

Suddenly she turned, looking out of the office window that stood above the small snow-covered yard. It was empty, and that's when she realized the voice wasn't coming from outside or inside of the house. It was coming from *inside* her head.

She conjured a recent memory. It came up swiftly, overtaking her. She saw Shatapattra's tawny face and heard her repeat the words of the poem the great Yogananda was reciting just before his glorious death, *"Where Ganges woods, Himalayan caves, and men dream God — I am hallowed, my body touched that sod."*

CHAPTER ELEVEN

Ontario, Canada - February, 1986

A few hours later Rose was back on campus at the University of Toronto at Mississauga, rattled but determined to sort things out. "I trust you've all had a good weekend. I want to remind you that your passive acoustic monitoring projects are due at this time next week. Today, as your syllabus indicates, we will begin a new unit on methodologies for analyzing and studying the impact of marine sound created by both anthropogenic and natural environmental sources," Rose explained to her class.

"I'm so sorry to interrupt, Professor, but this is the unit we covered a few weeks ago," one of her students had interjected. Rose jumbled her notes a bit, seeing they were out of order on the table in front of her. The classroom was set up seminar style, like a horseshoe, with the professor seated at the center of one of the long sides. It was difficult to maintain any sort of distance from students in a venue as intimate as this. Her eye had quieted down, but she was anxious about it starting up again and having her students, especially those adjacent to where she was instructing the class, take notice.

She had taught a class like this many times before and, to some degree, she felt like she was just going through the motions, reciting from a script she had prepared, rewritten and refined over the years. But today, as she tried to focus on the sixteen students sitting around the table, she had a movie reel playing over and over in her mind, images and conversations intersecting with each other, rattled by the strange voice she thought she had heard in her office at home.

"Yes, of course. Sorry. I'm still a bit jet-lagged from a transcontinental flight," she apologized to the class. It was midway into the Spring semester, though the idea of spring was still out of reach, evidenced by the snow-covered ground, grey and slushy from plow gravel and the assortment of road treatment products. The latest being used by the provincial municipality was a byproduct of mineral ash. It had been pelletized and used for distribution to road surfaces, but also, apparently, due to its absorption rate, it made a great kitty litter. Still, it was a killer on the painted surfaces of automobiles and it transformed anything pretty and white into wet, ugly slush. Even inside the small seminar room one was constantly reminded it was winter on the outside. Wet coats and damp gloves, scarves and knitted woolen hats were hanging everywhere, some students even keeping their heads covered in the class, trying to keep as much warmth in as possible.

Despite the presumed youth and vitality of the twenty-something men and women, their complexions were pallid and charmless, a consequence of lack of sufficient sunlight. Rose had always called it "winter blues," and she suffered bouts of it all throughout her years in the Atlantic Maritimes. Not that she thought she was affected by it now, but as she looked around the room she found she was preoccupied and couldn't concentrate.

On top of the stranger's voice and the accompanying sensation she experienced, she also had a peculiar dream last night, one of those strange dreams where people and places metamorphose into each other. She dreamed she had gone back into her office at home, opened the closet door where she had hidden the odd scrap of wood and started to reach for it. Then she heard footsteps behind her approaching steadily. Her heart began racing and when she turned around quickly she saw it was Noah looking directly into her surprised face. He extended his arm to her, and she took it. He pulled her into his own arms lifting her up with one broad movement and placed her down on her desk, spreading her legs apart, inserting his unusually tall body in between them. Rose reached down for his trousers and began to unbuckle his belt and pull down the zipper. When she looked back up at Noah's face she saw it wasn't him, but another face instead. Another man with a full beard, grinning broadly. Large teeth with a small space between the front two.

Then, in the way that dreams often do, she was sitting up high, on the top of a boulder surrounded by beach and tide below. It could have been the shore near Ginosar or at Lake Ontario. An unidentified body of water. And then, unexpectedly, two hands reached out and pushed her, hard and purposefully. She tried to scream but found that she couldn't. She struggled harder and harder to make a sound but nothing would come out. Empty space magnified by a racing pulse and rapid heartbeat. Then nothing but an agonizing wail, devoid of sound.

It was a dream still so vivid and clear to her the moment she awakened. She felt her body shaking, her heart palpitating. After she shot up in the dark she still had the sensation of falling deep into a chasm, waiting to hit the bottom. She looked at the digital clock sitting on the nightstand next to the bed and could see it was 5:45 AM, still pitch black outside, but she knew she wouldn't sleep anymore that night. Besides Nathan had to be up shortly and coaxed through his school-morning ritual.

Sitting up at the edge of the bed, she put on her slippers and robe and went into the hallway. Simon, was already up and predictably in the kitchen brewing coffee. The evening had ended badly with him. She'd felt the urge to find a cigarette, but the thought of having to smoke it outside of the house in the bitter cold was enough to deflect the urge.

Instead, she searched for the *Sunday Toronto Star*, scouring it to see if there was a story about the "Jesus Boat." She looked around the living room and kitchen for the daily papers from the week, but Simon had already tossed them. She thought that on campus she would be able to find both the *International Herald Tribune* and the *New York Times* in the University library. She knew they received the daily editions as well as the weekend papers, sorted by work study students and subjected to clippings for archival files, copies made, deposited in buff colored files, inserted in a series of leviathan gunmetal cabinets while the original newsprint was catalogued and then microfiched. But that would have to wait for now.

Back in the classroom, once she cleared her head and found her place in the syllabus, she composed herself and then announced to the class, "Of course. How silly of me. It's time to move onto the topic everyone is excited about, the behavioral response of sea turtles."

A few students laughed, and then Rose turned around and picked up a large textbook. "We're going to be referring to a number of models and graphs in the Urick, *Principles of Underwater Sound*" so please turn to page 193, and let's make sure we all understand and agree on the variable parameters that were employed in the matrix."

After that the rest of the class seemed to proceed well, although Rose felt like she was on automatic pilot. She looked often at her wristwatch, counting down the minutes before the class had concluded. She was anxious to get over to the library as soon as she could before her office hours began. And she wanted to avoid a few of her colleagues who would be asking for a blow-by-blow about the Los Angeles conference.

When the class was finally over and students were packing up their textbooks, notebooks, and getting bundled to go back to their cars or walk to another one of the academic buildings, as expected a few students lagged behind with questions. She felt they were barking out their queries simultaneously and was slightly annoyed because the questions were ridiculously predictable and she had gone over the content of their responses a number of times before: "Will you review drafts of our papers?" "What is the format of the laboratory reports?" "What is the final length of the group presentation?" "*Have you ever been to Dalmanoutha?*"

"What?" Rose loudly interrupted the small group. "What did someone ask me?"

Small beads of sweat formed on her brow, and she stepped backwards, away from the encroaching students.

"Excuse me, Dr. Strongin, are you alright?" asked a perky young man wearing a blue parka with an Eskimo hood.

"What was that, Dalmanoutha? Why would someone ask me if I'd ever been there?" Rose barked.

The students looked around at each other perplexed. None of them had shouted out the question. They weren't sure what their instructor was asking. Rose looked into their faces, trying to find some recognition but she only saw puzzled, if slightly frightened, faces looking back at her. She wiped her brow. She must have heard wrong.

"Dr. Strongin, would you like me to get you a glass of water?" the perky one wanted to know.

"I'm fine. Really. Just a little beat from a long trip. Let's hold off the questions for now. I will have office hours later this afternoon, and you can see me or it can just wait until next class, okay? Nothing is that urgent."

The small group who lagged behind gathered up their belongings and began to file out slightly disappointed into the arctic cold. Rose, happily alone for a few moments, collected her discussion notes, gathering them into a bundle before placing them back into her briefcase. She felt a slight twinge in her temples, just the slightest trace of a headache coming on, and thought she would go back to her office for a Tylenol before heading out to the college library.

As she walked down the narrow corridor to the stairway that would take her to the natural sciences buildings she flashed on Shatapattra's odd farewell to her, *"Perhaps we will all meet again one day again when we find our Dalmanoutha."* What on God's earth was that strange woman talking about? Was it some exotic reference to the Yogi? Some arcane aspect of the Hindi? Or Buddhists? Or was it a reference to some alluring location, not on the physical plane, but one that was instead metaphysical?

She pushed open the green metal fire doors that closed off the internal staircase to the building and began the descent. The stairwell was completely empty on the third level where she entered. As she turned the corner to continue down the flight of stairs, which angled ninety degrees each six or seven steps, she saw a flash of light in front of her. A white light she thought might be the flickering of a fire alarm testing system. But then she heard a deep voice from somewhere behind.

"Rosi, Rosi. Did you bump your head?" The same voice she heard last night. *"Rosi, Rosi. You could have lost your eye!"*

Then the flicker of light, like the flashbulb of a camera, and she saw the outline of a small boy, maybe five or six years old, running and shouting "*It's my ha'av. It's his boat,*" the little boy shrieked. "*Ha'av!! Ha'av!!*" he screamed.

She turned her head to see if anyone was on the staircase above her, but she saw no one. Then more strange light, as if someone were shining a flashlight into her face. She dropped her briefcase and covered her eyes with her forearm until the light passed over her. Then she looked up and down the brick staircase, but there was nothing other than the muffled echoes of footsteps, perhaps a floor or two above her. Abruptly, she began to run down the remaining stairs, faster and faster, drawing her breaths more quickly and fully until she reached the bottom stair and kicked open the door that separated the building from the outside with her heavy snow boots. A blast of polar air hit her squarely in the face, adjusting her eyes to the grey light that filtered in.

There was still a lot of snow on the Inner Circle Road and its spoke-shaped paths, but she ran quickly, sloshing through the muck of wet snow and sand, splashing a white muddy mess onto the back of her boots and her coat. Now there were more people walking towards her, students and faculty, trying to get from one indoor sanctuary to another. Rose slowed down, waved to one or two of them, but continued on purposefully until she arrived at the Science & Technology Building where the biology faculty offices were located on the first floor. She slipped into the lobby entrance as steadily as she could, scurried down the corridor, and nudged open the door to her office. The pain in her temples had increased, and the bitter cold just exaggerated the impact. She dropped her briefcase on the floor and sat down on the small sofa that sat in the corner near her worktable and desk.

"What is happening to me?" she asked herself. "What is happening?" The telephone rang startling her as she jumped up to respond. She noticed her hands were shaking.

"This is Rose Strongin," she said nervously, her voice quivering ever so slightly.

"Rose? What's the matter? Are you alright?" Simon asked sympathetically. He could tell immediately something was wrong.

"Oh, Simon. I am so sorry. I don't know what's gotten into me. Yesterday and last night. And today I sort of had a mini-meltdown at the end of my class."

"I'm sorry, too. I know how stressful it can be traveling around on airplanes, and they are just petri dishes, your word my dear, for germs. Maybe you've got a virus?"

"No. I've just got a lot of questions about something that doesn't seem to have any answers," she responded.

"About what? One of your projects?"

"Maybe. In a way. I have to do a bit of digging. Some research. I'll be okay."

"Not that boat recovery thing in Israel? Has it jostled your memory somehow? Or is it Chazon?" He tried his best to hold back, but it still came out contemptuously. "Rose, cancel your classes. Come home please. You need to rest."

It put her right on the defensive. "No, I don't. I need answers," she said brusquely and put the phone down.

The McCallion Academic Learning Centre and Library was located near the Outer Circle Road of the campus, a short but chilly walk on foot for Rose from the building where her office was located. She had collected herself, prepared her notes for the next class, swallowed two Tylenol caplets and made an appointment for the late afternoon with one of the librarians, a vivacious black South African who had emigrated from Capetown to study in Canada.

Her name was Nkososana Bentley and she was, Rose thought, one of the most thorough colleagues she had ever worked with. She asked Nkososana to help her pull some recent collected newspaper articles about the "Jesus Boat" discovery from domestic and international dailies, weeklies and other news sources. Ms. Bentley was happy to comply.

But as Rose pored through the periodicals she began to realize they mostly covered the same information that was contained in the *L.A. Times* story. Less than a week had passed so she was uncertain whether there would be any follow-up articles quite yet. But she gathered from her reading that a number of prominent American, European and Israeli marine biologists, archaeologists and preservation specialists had been called in to consult with the local Antiquities Authority, including Shelley Wachsmann, the Israeli government archaeologist and J. Richard Steffy, the noted expert in their field of shipwreck analysis. It was said that Steffy read "wood" the way an ordinary reader would read a newspaper. The actual remains of the boat, like the piece of wood Rose had kept hidden for twelve years, had also been insulated from oxygen and parasites by the closely packed mud.

But she knew she had an "in" with Noah. If he was assigned to work alongside Wachsmann and Steffy, he might be able to find out something more. Something he would share with her that wouldn't be offered to journalists. Something that might unlock the questions that were floating in her mind, gnawing at her conscience, invading her dreams. She had always suspected her disappearance and subsequent memory lapse were somehow related to the mysteries surrounding the harbor project. The unknown surprises any archaeological expedition serves up might jog her memory, help her remember what had happened.

The sun begins to set by 4:30PM in the Ontario winter and Rose looked up around 5:30PM to see how dark it had become outside the large, smoked glass panels that were fitted to the library's exterior. She had been there most of the afternoon and had to go home soon. Nathan would be waiting for her. And Simon. She had a pang of guilt.

"I haven't seen my family in more than a week. What am I doing holed up in a library carrel when I should have just finished my classes and gone home?" she thought. Just like Simon suggested.

But too many things still nagged at her relentlessly. Noah's fervent, almost fanatical speech about biblical archaeology; her encounter in the hotel lobby with the Indian woman; the unconserved wood specimen lying on a shelf of her closet looking quite the same as it did when she found it in her coat pocket twelve years prior. And the word Dalmanoutha still ringing in her ears.

She tracked Nkososana down at one of the information desks in the library's wide entrance corridor.

"Ah, Rose, my buddy," the South African said in inflected English, with traces of the lilting Zulu dialect that her forebears spoke. She was a small, compact woman who had piled on top of her head a basket of dreadlocks, coiled and unruly, that she treated often with Jamaican black castor oil. "I see you've come back for more of me?"

"I'm afraid I am unsure of what I'm really looking for, Nkososana."

"That's what my job is all about. Do you think you're any different from the thousands of students who come to me cluelessly?" she laughed. "I've got all the answers lurking in the tips of my fingers."

"Point me towards an index search for the subject topic "Dalmanoutha." I believe it is a place. Perhaps not historical, but referred to. But it could also be a religious reference."

"How are we spelling that, Rosie baby?"

"D-a-l-m-a-n-o-u-t-h-a, I think?"

"Let me type it into the new indexing system we have just completed. We have an integrated library system and it gives me access to databases in libraries around Canada and in the U.S. There must be something I can pull up without having to wade, like a dirty duck, through the muck of the dreaded microfiche," she explained.

"Well, I can do the legwork."

"Just a few beats and I'll be back to you. I can use a few methodologies to search. By keyword and also Boolean."

Nkososana typed in some information on her keyboard that was attached to a large computer screen. It went to a hefty mainframe in the basement of the Library building and contained thousands of entries and cross-references to documentation in libraries across North America. Each month the College would receive a series of large reels of data that would be loaded into the mainframe computer and up-to-date information could be retrieved. A form appeared on her screen and she typed in some data, hitting an entry key and waited while the screen in front of her flashed. Then a few seconds later a string of characters appeared.

"Bingo, baby," the librarian announced, "Let me just point this towards the printer and you can get your report." She pressed a few buttons and seconds later the clucking sound of a line matrix printer started up, printing data across a large roll of flimsy green and white striped paper. The printer rolled around, huffed a bit like it was tired, and then spit out a sheet that contained typed information on it. The librarian tore it from the roller and handed it to Rose.

"Excellent. This is so helpful. Let me take this and get out of here. You too. It's time to go home," Rose suggested to her.

"My work is just beginning, honey. You think you're the only one needing my help today," she bantered. Rose thanked her and walked back to the carrel with the printed report. It said:

```
DALAMUNTHA or DALMANOUTHE (alt) or
DALMANOUTHA, referring to a location on the
western shore of the Sea of Galilee; attributed
to St. Mark in the New Testament. At present
there is no archaeological evidence for its
existence.
```

It was then followed by a long list of books, mostly Christian theological tomes, with BS call numbers and a series of translations of the New Testament including ancient versions in Syriac, Latin, Coptic and Greek as well as modern works dubbed The Revised Standard Version, *La Bible de Jerusalem,* The New American Bible and *Einheitsubersetzüng.*

Rose went down to the sub-basement stacks where works of Psychology, Philosophy and Religion were shelved, and pulled off a copy of the Revised Standard Version, fingering through the dusty pages until she found what she was looking for. In *The Gospel of Mark*, Chapter 8, verses eight through ten, there was a passage from the earliest known account of the story of Jesus and his ministry. Although she had never read much of the New Testament, she recognized this story almost at once. It was about the miracle of the loaves and fishes.

And they had a few small fish and having blessed them he commanded that these should also be set before them. And they ate and were satisfied. And they took up the broken pieces left over, seven baskets full. And there were about four thousand people. And he sent them away and immediately he got into the boat with his disciples and went to the district of Dalmanoutha.

Dalmanoutha had been mentioned only by the evangelist, Mark and was apparently a bustling, prosperous fishing town where pagans lived beside Jews on the Ginosar Valley shore.

"What does Chazon know about this?" Rose thought. "Was this what he was looking for all along? Was the harbor project just a smokescreen for another purpose, to find a first-century town?"

Her head was spinning. She folded the printed report up and placed it in her briefcase, put on her coat, hat and gloves and walked to her car, parked on the far side of the campus. The wind kicked up fiercely now, and it was a distressing journey.

It was close to seven o'clock when she arrived back at the house. Simon was sitting at the dining room table drinking a scotch.

"Have you eaten?" she asked him.

"No. I wasn't sure what to do. I didn't know when you were coming home. I'm not hungry, anyway."

"Where's Nathan?"

"I dropped him at Thom and Cindi. He's eating with them. I need to get him soon. It's a school day tomorrow."

She took off her coat and draped it over one of the dining room chairs. "I think I'll have one of those, too," she said and walked over to the sideboard, lifting the crystal decanter, a gift they had received from Karl Strongin on their tenth wedding anniversary, and poured herself a glass. She sat down at the table opposite Simon and began to sip slowly.

"Are you feeling any better," he asked her.

"Not really."

"I'm sorry." And then, "This boat. What gives? You're reading about it, collecting information. It's not even your area of specialty. I don't get it."

"It's important to me. To all of us. Don't you realize what it could mean?"

"No. Not really," he answered. "I read the newspaper article. Yes, I can understand how it's important to the world of archaeology to have such a specimen. But I'm not buying that Jesus hung out in it," he stated categorically.

"That's not the point. Noah thinks that ...."
"Ugh. Noah again."
"He's an important Israeli scientist and this is an important Israeli discovery," she answered defensively.

"I suppose he wants to bring you in on this?" Simon asked, hesitating slightly.

"No. It's not about that. Look I can't explain yet."

"You've never been interested in the Bible. You've always said it wasn't scientific. This is not your area of interest."

"Noah has asked me to be open to seeing things differently."

"What? How so? From a one-week academic conference in California? Really, Rose, I know that the west coast of America is a place for weirdo drop-outs and hippie-dippy New Age crap, but I never knew you took such an interest in western religions. Not even the one you grew up with."

"And your point is, what?" she tried to defend.

"Well, I'm no expert, but the Bible doesn't really prove anything. It's artificial. It merely asserts things," he reminded her. "At least that's what you've always told me."

"Are we really having this conversation? You're just wrong. The whole way that science began, the birth of science is based on believing in the faithfulness of God. Even for good little atheists."

"What? You're now believing in God because Chazon told you to?"

"That's stupid and puerile Simon, and you know it," she shot back quickly.

"This is a ridiculous argument. Let's stop right now." He stood up and walked to her side of the table placing his hands on her shoulders. "Let's go away next weekend," he had offered almost desperately. "A leisurely weekend in Halifax. We can catch up with so many people."

"You know I can't, so stop asking me. I've got work to do. I have to see this through." He pushed her away and then she was on her feet.

"See what through? You're not even on this project."

"I am. In my own way. I can't explain," she was walking away from him, heading towards the passage from the dining room into the front hall.

"I should have put my foot down and not let you go to that fucking conference in Los Angeles. All of this crazy shit started when you returned from meeting that man," he got louder.

"Let me go? Let me go? How dare you. You have no right, none at all to give me permission to do anything," she shouted at him.

"You're just a part-timer now to me, and you have been for some time now. Maybe the girls don't need you anymore, because they're at school and God knows how self-sufficient Nathan is without me. But I ..."

"You what?"

"I'm still above ground. Not buried in the mud someplace waiting for you to send down a wire to hear me," he said with an angry sadness.

Then he got up and walked past her towards the front door, pulling his woolen coat off of a hook that hung adjacent to the door. "I'm going to pick up our son now."

Rose sat at the table emotionless.

CHAPTER TWELVE

Ontario, Canada - March, 1986

A few days later, on the following Sunday after her return from Los Angeles, Rose decided to place the phone call to Noah. She had his home telephone number in Tel Aviv and, calculating the seven-hour time difference, she thought she might reach him around 9:00PM Israel-time. The week had been a tense one. Although she and Simon acted civilly towards each other, especially in front of Nathan, the boy could tell there was something odd going on.

"What's going on, Mama? Why has Daddy been sleeping in Sharon's room?" he asked his mother a few nights earlier.

"Honey, I've been irritable. Overworked. I'm a bit restless. It's better for your father to get a good night's sleep away from me," she tried to explain it away.

"You must think I'm an idiot. You expect me to believe that?" he countered. "Look I may only be twelve but I can tell that something's going on between the two of you."

"Don't be silly. Nothing is going on," she insisted. But the boy sensed that there was a lack of warmth, of authenticity when they were in each other's company.

"If it makes you feel any better Thom and Cindi's mother and father fight all the time," he told his mother, "and you should hear some of the things they call each other. Once Mr. Beecher called Mrs. Beecher a *cunt*. A silly cunt."

"Nathan! Where did you ever pick up that word?" she squirmed.

"I just told you," he answered precociously, "it's what their father called their mother. I *do* know what it means."

"Well, I don't like you repeating it," Rose shot back immediately, "and I don't like you eavesdropping on the arguments adults are having with each other. Besides we're not like them. We don't often argue. It's just that your father and I don't always agree about everything. Since you're already twelve going on twenty, you're bright enough to know that."

"Well, we weren't eavesdropping. We were all in the same room!"

"I wouldn't worry about your father calling me names, Nathan," Rose said.

"Oh, good," Nathan answered, "I don't want it to interfere with my plans for the weekend."

Rose had to chuckle, "I'm sure it won't."

Nkososana called two days after Rose found the reference to Dalmanoutha in the scriptural passage from Mark's Gospel. The librarian had left a message on her office phone. "I have something you might find interesting, Rose. Give me a call and I'll explain," it said. Rose assumed it was likely some additional newspaper accounts of the "Jesus Boat" discovery, but in actuality, Nkososana had found something much more intriguing.

"Oh, there you are, Rosie, looking as beautiful as ever," she called out liltingly to her, from her seat at the reference desk, when Rose walked into the main lobby of the library. "I've got something that might make your ears perk and your eyes brighten a bit."

She explained that the library had received a number of boxes of documents and letters from the late 19th century, donated by an enterprising couple who were caught up in the re-gentrification movement happening in downtown Toronto.

"The papers," the librarian told her, "seemed to have belonged to the descendants of the McBurney-Marshall family, a wealthy Toronto clan with roots in the community going back to the late 18th century. One of their descendants was a founder of the Northern Railway of Canada, and they had intermarried with, among others, the Eatons."

Apparently during a recent renovation at an old mansion near Queen Street, a series of trunks had been found in one of the attics containing photographs, diaries, correspondence, letters, contracts and other legal documents dating back before 1850. According to Professor Lewis Ingalls, of the Toronto Historical Society, they painted a "gloriously detailed picture of Ontario life and society in the late 19th century."

"Supposedly the trunks had been shoved in an unreachable corner of one of the two attics of the four-story

Queen Anne home," she went on. "The way they had been configured in the garret made them appear to be fixed because they blended into the eaves. But the restorers were fastening new insulation throughout and stumbled upon the chests. Many of the papers had suffered from exposure and deteriorated, but there were a number of items that were protected because they were folded into their original envelopes and placed in airtight containers."

The surviving documents had been photographed, indexed and archived by a group of graduate students whose area of interest was Ontario history. One of them, an ambitious historian, was intrigued by a series of letters, a correspondence between two sisters, Katherine Desmond McBurney, an American woman from Maryland who had married into the McBurneys, and her sister, Rose Frances Robertson, the wife of an Episcopal cleric. The two sisters had been separated by Katherine's marriage in 1880 but wrote to each other regularly as evidenced by the letters that Katherine had saved.

Apparently Rose Frances traveled with her husband on church-sponsored pilgrimages, and the graduate student who was analyzing cultural norms of British, American and Canadian women in the Gilded Age wanted to the use the correspondence between the two women as the foundation of her study.

"You see, this student works part time for me," Nkososana explained, "and when she came into work the other day she was reviewing the summary of data searches and saw the search that I had done for you."

"I don't understand," Rose said.

"She saw the reference to Dalmanoutha. Your search."

"And?" Rose asked.

"And … she said it had been referred to in a letter that had come from one of the sisters who had been traveling to the Holy Land. Sarah just mentioned it to me in passing and I thought I would ask her to dig up the letter and show it to you." She handed the letter to Rose who sat down in a chair in front of the librarian's desk. Her head was spinning, "Yes, of course. It might be useful."

July 13, 1890

My Dearest sister Katherine,

The descent upon Tiberias was as beautiful as everything must be that is connected with that lovely lake. Our camp is pitched on its shores some five miles or so north of Tiberias itself, close to a collection of houses on the lake near the village of Medjdel, the ancient Magdala. I can say little for I was never inside it but especially, as seen from the water, it appeared to be one of the most beautiful places we had yet come across.

Perhaps it was the illusion of the lake which made us think so, for some friendly travelers who visited the interior did not seem to be extraordinarily delighted. It is very dirty, I believe, and is inhabited chiefly by Jews; indeed it is like Safed, one of their holy cities. Other sects generally speak of it as the residence of the King of the Fleas, who should certainly be a great potentate in Palestine. We did not seek audience of his majesty, having already made acquaintance with many of his subjects, but took a boat to the upper end of the lake.

It seems remarkable to me that we are rowing away on the Sea of Galilee, and it requires all the discomfort of a cramped position in a not very roomy boat to prove to us that we are not dreaming. Our rowers are doing their utmost, for the dreaded "sharkia" is said to be coming, and against it we can make little way. But, for the present, nothing can be more delightful than the tranquil progress over the calm, solitary sea. Far away toward the part where the Jordan flows into the lake we can catch sight of one white sail, probably a fishing boat, but there is no sign of any living creature on land or sea as we make for the ruins of Tell Houm. It is strange to think that in the days of the history which gives life and interest to all these scenes, this coast was a centre of bustling life and commerce with the four cities of Capernaum, Bethsaida, Chorazin and that other unknown one whose ruins are yet to be found somewhere near Gennesaret where he had camped. I am told it took the name Dalmanoutha.

Stephen Kitsakos

Before we departed I had a dizzy spell, probably brought on by the heat which descended upon us rather oppressively one morning. The Reverend John Robertson couldn't decide whether to be disappointed at my unplanned disappearance, or relieved that I found my way back to the rest of the group. From the wife of a rector people expect a certain amount of reliability. And I believe, as untraveled as I have been, I have indeed risen to the occasion in accompanying him and our Holy Land companions from the Episcopal Diocese of Maryland.

Still, I couldn't explain what had happened in those hours when I lost track of the time. Honestly, I must have rested my head somewhere, collapsed into a peaceful reverie somewhere on that black shore. The Reverend John Robertson believed there were three or four hours I had been unaccounted for.

Indeed, I have been quite well since we started this long journey and other than a slight gastric incident shortly after we arrived at Haifa, I have been the picture of health. One must become acclimatized to the heat. The Baltimore sun was never as mighty as his Palestinian cousin. I shall continue to write to you of our journey, posting when I can seize the opportunity.

Your loving and faithful sister,
Rose Frances

When Rose read the next to last paragraph her skin almost jumped off her body. She couldn't quite comprehend what she was reading, couldn't process the words, connect the sentences. *"Still I couldn't explain what happened in those hours when I lost track of the time ... three or four hours I had been unaccounted for."* The words were like a blade slicing against her brain.

"Are you alright, Rose? You've gone all pale and pasty on me," Nkososana came around from her desk and put her hands on Rose's shoulder.

"Yes, yes. I'm fine. It's such a strange old letter and how odd a coincidence that it's turned up here and related to my query."

"You'd be amazed by what a little digging can often bring to the surface."

"May I have a copy of this please?" Rose asked.

Now, in the middle of a cold winter Sunday afternoon, with Simon ferrying Nathan to an all-youth orchestra rehearsal preparing for a spring concert, Rose was alone in the house. She picked up the phone to call Tel Aviv, dialing the long series of international codes. Seconds later she heard the series of beep-beeps on the phone. They repeated a half dozen times until a voice responded, "Allo."

"Umm, hello. This is Dr. Rose Strongin calling from Canada. For Noah, uh, for Dr. Chazon."

"Oh hello there," the voice responded in good English, "this is Shoshana Chazon."

Rose hesitated for a split second and then answered, "Shoshana, how nice to meet you, albeit on the telephone. Noah often talks about you."

"Oh, Rose, of course I know you who are. Noah has told me all about you and your work together. I'm so sorry we haven't been able to meet before. Living on separate continents makes that a bit inconvenient," she laughed a little. "We have the same name, you know."

"Oh? Do we?" Rose responded.

"Yes. Shoshana is the Hebrew word for *rose*."

"What an interesting coincidence." Pause. Brief silence. Rose felt awkward, but she didn't really understand why she should. It was a phone call she was placing to a colleague, not an invitation to dinner and a movie.

"You're calling from Canada?"

"Yes. Sorry. I wanted to discuss something with your husband, if he is available to talk."

"I'm sorry but he's up in the Kinneret," the woman explained, "on the boat project. You know about that, of course, don't you? It's incredibly exciting, especially for Noah."

"Yes, of course. I knew he had been contacted by the Department of Antiquities, but he was unsure what his actual involvement would be. I haven't talked to him since he said goodbye in Los Angeles a few weeks ago."

"It's quite close to the site of the harbor project you worked on, quite near the excavations at Migdal and Ilanot. In fact it's very possible this was a boat that had moored there," she explained. "You must know this has been Noah's special area of interest," but then she backed off. "Actually I'd better not tell you anymore," she laughed a little rigidly. "There's a veil of secrecy apparently around the project."

"Of course." More silence.

Rose thought that Shoshana had a pleasant, if deep, voice. Her English was near perfect, but she wasn't surprised. A psychiatrist, now in the employ of the Israeli government, Noah told her that they had met when they were doing their compulsory military service, *Tzahal,* the shortened Hebrew for Israeli Defense Forces.

Shoshana, he explained, had an orthodox upbringing in a rural kibbutz on the Mediterranean coast, while Noah was raised a secular Jew in Tel Aviv. Her training was in the field of transpersonal psychiatry, therapies that deal with individuals who have near-death, out of body and, especially, past-life experiences.

Rose didn't know much about this area. It was complex, controversial and miles off from her background and experience in studying the bio-acoustic attributes of marine mammals. But all scientists somehow are bonded in their desire to contemplate, analyze and ultimately understand the mechanism of life.

"If you like I can give you the telephone number where Noah is staying. He's actually back at Ginosar. Of course, you've been there before."

"Thank you, Shoshana. I'm not sure I want to disturb him."

"I think he will be quite pleased to hear from you," she lingered on the word pleased.

Rose was unsure what the woman meant by that. The tone was congenial, but there was something underneath she detected. As she jotted down the long telephone number Shoshana said rather spontaneously, "If you don't mind, may I tell you something about my husband?"

Rose hesitated a moment, her mind flashing to a myriad of possibilities before responding, "Well, yes, of course, though that sounds mysterious," followed by a short, awkward laugh.

"It's less a secret than a reality," Shoshana answered, "but I thought it is something you should know about. At least it's something I had hoped my husband would have confided in you before. Are you able to listen now?"

"Go on, please. I'm intrigued," Rose countered.

"Noah has dissociative amnesia." There. It was out in the open. Bluntly stated.

"I'm sorry, I don't understand."

"It's a neurological condition," Shoshana explained, "a psychogenic disorder in which a person cannot remember the details of a stressful event."

Rose was perplexed, "Oh, dear. I had no idea. Is this something that's ongoing?"

"It's mostly under control now. I assume Noah has never mentioned this to you? I didn't mean to drop it so suddenly on you, but you see I do have a reason."

"No, he has never said anything about it. We have an open relationship as colleagues but, honestly, our work together dominates our conversations," Rose answered back, though she knew this didn't fully or honestly illuminate her relationship with the Israeli.

"It is something that has dominated his life since he was a child. It was one of the things that drew us together before we married, and my work with him throughout the years of our marriage has grounded him," Shoshana explained.

She made clear that the condition was related to memory loss, predominantly over the blocking of a traumatic or stressful event, often something that occurred in childhood. The person realizes they are experiencing a form of amnesia but cannot do anything about it. For some it can be disabling but for others, depending on what type of dissociative subcategory they fall into, it could be used to channel energy, ambition and drive into something advantageous or remarkable.

In Noah's case his disassociation was categorized as *selective* amnesia, that is, he had a patchy and incomplete recollection of the distressing event but could recall sensations, impressions, even images.

"That's where you come in, Rose," Shoshana announced, "and I want you to take this in slowly. When Noah met you the first time, the first time he brought you onto the harbor project in the Galilee, he thought he recognized you."

"What? I don't quite understand," Rose was bewildered.

"He called me that first night. When you arrived with your family. He told me that he'd seen you before. Images of you, flashbacks, related to the event."

"I'm stunned," Rose responded, "but it's quite impossible. I'm sure he must have been mistaken. We had never met before. Perhaps I resembled someone he thought he recognized, but …"

Shoshana interrupted her, "No. It *was* you. But don't be alarmed. He didn't want to put any pressure on you. Not then, and certainly not now. I am sorry to drop this on you, but I wanted you to know because the actual dissociative event happened when he was a child, just five years old, and occurred somewhere near the site the two of you worked together. The same site he has now been deployed somewhere on the lakeshore between Ginosar and the ancient town of Magdala."

"What happened to him?" Rose asked, and Shoshana told her the story.

Noah and his family had been on a summer holiday in the western Galilee. His older brother, sister and his mother and father were boating on the lake and tethered their boat near one of the beaches somewhere between Tamar and Ilanot in order to go swimming. Noah had been running in and out of the lake and then suddenly he was nowhere to be found.

He was lost. Nobody could find him for hours. They searched and searched, and thought he had drowned. The police were called. He was only five. And just as swiftly as he had been lost, he walked out of the water. Right there in front of one group of volunteers who had been looking for him. He walked out of the lake as if he had been there all along, swimming and playing. As if nothing had happened. He had no memory, no recollection except that he was walking on the sand, and then he was walking out of the lake."

For Rose this was like a one-two punch. Her purpose in calling was to ask Noah about the letter she had been given by Nkososana, the reference to the writer's being lost and unaccounted for. To ask him more about Shatapattra and their odd encounter in the hotel lobby. But now there was another strange piece to the entire affair.

Did she actually bear a resemblance to someone who figured into Noah's boyhood trauma? How could that be? A psychic disturbance of an event he could not recall but which had haunted him for forty years. And why had he never mentioned this to her after they had worked together, side by side, for two months those twelve or so years ago, or over the years when she had met him in New York or as collaborators on a variety of marine archaeology and bio-acoustic projects they had abstracted, participated in and wrote about?

"I hope I haven't freaked-you out," Shoshana said, using the popular American idiom, "but I felt that you needed to know. Especially when I learned about the piece of wood with the, shall we say, odd chemistry."

"He told you about that?"

"Yes. He also had a sort of souvenir. A small copper bracelet, braided and fastened to his left wrist. He couldn't recall where he had found it. Nobody recognized it, and they just assumed he had picked it up somewhere or dug it up and put it on his wrist. But years later, after he had outgrown it, when he began to learn about scientific dating and methodologies for determining aging of specimen samples, he had it analyzed. He wears it around his neck now. I'm sure you can figure out where this is going."

Rose was stunned. What was this woman telling her? "I'm not sure I am following all of this, Shoshana."

"He believes there is a, how do you call it, supernatural explanation."

"But Noah is a scientist. Surely he knows that's impossible," she countered defensively.

"Sometimes there is no explanation using physical laws. None whatsoever. Look at your two-thousand year old piece of timber. It has defied a rational, scientific explanation. It exists in the open environment. Irrationally. Like the Shroud of Turin."

"But what does this have to do with Noah?" Rose asked.

"He believes that, like you, something unexplainable brought him somewhere and then returned him."

"But where did it bring him?" she asked again, already knowing the answer.

"From the beach at Ilanot to Dalmanoutha, a place that has been hidden away waiting to be found," she said with great resignation. "And he is determined to find it again."

Then there was a long and silent pause. Rose had put the phone down to catch her breath. Shoshana continued on, "I am sorry to blurt all this out to you on the telephone, Rose. Really, I am. But you see, if you call down there to the Kinneret without knowing what is really going on, you will be like Noah, years ago before he was able to convince me. Before I was able to …"

Rose interrupted her, "I'm sorry Shoshana but this is all too much for me to …."

But mid-sentence she was cut right off, "Don't you realize Rose, like Noah, you also have been visited by God."

"What?"

"*The day you and your family missed the plane home.*"

A strange buzzing noise started banging in the phone, an aural hiccup, and Rose thought the connection had been lost. "Hello, hello, Shoshana …are you there? Are you there?" but there was no voice on the other side. Her head was spinning. She clicked the receiver and began to dial again the long series of numbers starting with the international code. The call would cost a fortune, but she couldn't leave the conversation unfinished. She heard the phone ring again, beep-beep a few times, and then someone picked up the phone and a voice said, "Hallo."

"Oh, there you are, Shoshana. Sorry. We must have been disconnected."

"English?" the voice asked. Rose thought it sounded different.

"Yes. Isn't this Mrs. Chazon? I mean, Dr. Chazon's wife?" Rose quickly asked.

"My English not good. I am housekeeper for *mar marat* Chazon. She is not at home," came the housekeeper's response.

"I was just talking with her a few minutes ago," Rose said quizzically.

"No. She not here. She with Dr. Chazon. Away from Tel Aviv. She not here."

"But that's ridiculous," Rose was getting angry, "I was *just* having a conversation with her. She must be there."

"No. Sorry. *Ani mitstaer meod.* She away. I take message, please."

"No, no. No message. I have to go now." Rose hung the phone up as the housekeeper was saying, "*Yala bye, le'hit.*"

She stared out of the large bow living room window into a bleak, grey sky. It seemed to be closing in, encircling her, the clouds gathering to form strange, ominous shapes. She thought she saw the outline of a face emerge out of the distant vapor. A man with a large, broad smile. And a space between his two front teeth.

~~~

Later that afternoon Nathan broke the stillness of the house, "The string section makes my ears bleed," he said as he walked through the front door into the small vestibule carefully placing his clarinet case down on a small table in the hallway. Simon trailed behind him listening to his son's complaining.

"They are ridiculously out of tune and it is irritating," Nathan whined.

"Oh, come on, they weren't that bad," Simon answered.

"No offense, Daddy, but I'm not sure you know what you're listening to. You're too nice, and I think you just tolerate bad music. I'm hungry now. Where's Mama?" all of this coming out of him with rapid speed.

Simon called out a few times to Rose and then went in search of her. By now it was quite dark, and most of the lights in the house were out except for the chandelier in the dining room that hung over the long, rectangular table. That had been turned on to its minimal brightness.

"Where is everybody?" Nathan called out. "Are we having supper?"

Simon walked into the kitchen, assuming some sort of preparation was being undertaken for their evening meal, but it looked exactly the same as when he left it four hours ago. He switched on a light and could see that there were still dishes and some flatware in the sink from lunch waiting to be rinsed and washed.

Nathan started walking up the stairs to the second floor where his bedroom, his parents' bedroom and Rose's study was. Simon switched on some of the overhead lights from the hallway below, and the brass sconces at the top of the stairs came on to light the boy's way making half-oval shadows on the landing as he ascended. They could both see that the door to Rose's study was closed, but there was faint, pink light drifting out underneath the door's saddle.

Simon walked up to the door and knocked, "Rose. Are you in there?" There was no answer, but Nathan pushed the door open and walked in. His mother was seated upright in her desk chair. Sprawled in front of her were files, pages, papers, folders, an assortment of books, maps and other paraphernalia. Her head was down on the desk as if she had fallen asleep.

"Mama! Are you alright?" Nathan ran over to her and shook her. Simon's heart skipped a beat. Rose jerked, suddenly, lifting her head from the desk and jumping up.

"Oh, my God. I'm sorry. I just drifted off. I've been reading and must have lost track of the time. I didn't realize how dark it was." Her speech was sluggish. Not crisp or present.

Nathan put his arms around his mother, and she hugged him. Simon stood in the doorway and watched. The study was a mess. It looked like his wife had pulled out files and papers, books and baskets of material and randomly spread them out all over the desk and the floor.

"What's going on Rose?" he asked.

"What do you mean?" she answered defensively, "I'm just reviewing some material I need."

"Material? For what? It looks like a bomb was set off in here."

Just then the telephone on the desk rang. It startled her and she bounced up. It was an extension of the house's main residential number. "It might be for me," she said. "I'm waiting for a call. I think it might be." But as soon as she answered all three of them heard the sweet voice of young Cindi Beecher. Rose handed Nathan the phone.

"I'll pick it up downstairs," he shouted as he bolted into the hallway and bounded down the staircase, "We're going to gossip about the rehearsal." And then he hollered, "I've got it! You can hang up now!!"

When they were alone Simon looked at his wife and asked her if she had been drinking.

"Excuse me? No, I haven't." This was not the truth. He winced.

"Another diazepam, then? Your third or fourth since yesterday?"

"I took a half. I'm feeling anxious, okay."

"You're acting drunk," he told her, "and it is not very becoming to have your son see you like this."

She put her head in her hands and wiped her face. He went and kneeled in front of her placing his hands on her lap. "Rose, we'll get you through this. But you have to work with me."

"I'm confused Simon, scattered. I keep having thoughts, memories that float into my mind and unsettle me. I don't understand." She looked worn out. Tired and tattered. She never had dark circles under her eyes before but now he saw them making an attempt to form, puffy and bloated.

"What kind of thoughts?" he asked her.

"You know," she hesitated, "about when we were in Israel."

He tensed up. "Did being with Chazon bring all this up?" trying not to elevate the volume. "Is this why you have been a basket case?"

"No, no. But I think he knows something."

"Are you kidding? How could he …"

"I placed a call to him today. In Tel Aviv. I spoke to his wife. He's back where we all were together. Working with the discovery of that boat. At Ginosar," she tried to explain to him, but he swooped right in, cutting her off at the last syllable.

"Blah, blah, blah Rose. Goddamn it!! Can't we put this all behind us now? You know it was a freak thing. What the doctor called a "fugue state." It happens. Especially to people under a great deal of pressure. It was over twelve years ago. It hasn't happened again. And it won't. You've moved on. But it seems that every time you're in that man's company something happens to set you back again."

It was eerily silent except for the occasional high-pitched giggle coming from Nathan downstairs. They stayed together, studying each other's faces, contemplating each other's breath. This was an argument that neither wanted to elevate. They remained that way for a while until Rose said, "Simon, did you ever feel that you were hearing something? Not with your ears, from the outside. But from the inside?"

He got up, shook his head and said, "You're kidding? Take another valium. I'm sure you can have a chat with Moses about parting the Red Sea. Meanwhile, I'm getting a pizza for Nathan and me. Join us if you like. Or not. Your choice."

He walked out of the study closing the door behind him descending the stairs. At the bottom he saw Nathan standing there, his arms folded.

"What's going on?" the boy asked his father. "She's losing it, right?"

"I'm not sure I know."

"Is it because of you? Is it your fault?" he asked quietly.

Simon didn't know the answer.

CHAPTER THIRTEEN

Galilee, Israel - September, 2014

Nathan looked down the ladder that was placed midway on the main deck of the Sundancer. From the corner of his vision he saw Simon sitting quietly below. "There he is," Nathan thought. "My father is now in his early 70's, looking his age, lined and weary." He felt a pang of guilt. Why did he always find the need to think the worst of his father? Couldn't he be like his sisters and go with the flow, roll with the punches?

He had just the edge of a memory. A small boy being carried securely in his father's arms.

Barbara popped her head into the passage of the narrow ladder putting her index finger to her lips. "Sssh," she said.

"What's he doing down there, Barb?" Nathan whispered.

"His eyes are shut and he's sitting quietly. Let's just leave him be," she answered climbing up the ladder slowly to join her sister and brother. "What's going on up here?"

"I keep going back to that summer," Nathan answered, "when she had the breakdown. It still sticks with me."

"How could it not? I'm sorry we weren't around much," Sharon replied. It sounded guilty. "We didn't realize."

He had heard their apologies, their excuses before.

"Things were different then," they reminded him. "Surely you remember how it felt to finally be free, liberated from living at home," Sharon repeated. "Mama was in the dark then and she and Daddy forgot how to find any joy. I sure as hell didn't want to be around that."

But Nathan could only remember how difficult it was for him. He knew that his father thought his mother had betrayed him.

Ontario, Canada - Summer, 1986

Back then when Rose was engrossed in the discovery of the "Jesus Boat," everything else was put on hold. She found it all too consuming to focus on ordinary things, her mind wandering constantly, her waking hours filled with snippets of conversations, her dreams infused with surreal images. The only thing that could alleviate the anxiety was chemical and, consequently, she began to rely more heavily on anti-anxiety medications.

She had been through the gamut: antidepressants, selective serotonin inhibitors, antihistamines, beta blockers. It seemed like she was living in an age where physicians were ready to write prescriptions on a trial and error basis. "Here, try these for a bit Mrs. Strongin and call me in a few weeks."

Of course, no physician actually knew what to prescribe for an anxiety disorder that had been induced, apparently, by a *supernatural* event. At least that's what she had difficult admitting to herself. Such things did not really exist in medical science. The medications helped to steady her, but they were not a solution. It was also what drove Simon out.

The summer of 1986 split them in two with Simon moving into a house in downtown Toronto, and Nathan staying behind in the Ontario suburbs with his mother.

"That was a tough summer for me," Nathan remembered. He was lonely for his sisters, unaccustomed to being without his father in the house, and angry with him at the same time. But more importantly, having to negotiate the malleable ups and downs of his mother's peculiar mood swings frightened him in a way that was entirely incomprehensible to a young adult, no matter how precocious.

The entire episode was made more poignant because it was the summer he realized that he wanted Thom Beecher to be more than just his friend. The boys were both twelve years old and Nathan had made some observations about his own body he'd had a vague notion would happen. Growing up in a house with three women, he'd become accustomed to the sights and smells of feminine enterprises: the lotions and creams his mother and sisters would use, the long strands of hair accumulating in the bathtub or on the bathroom sink or behind the toilet. He was aware, of course, of the musky, heavy scent of his father, a marked contrast from that of his mother. And he'd had recollections of a gentle, satisfied feeling when he was a child and Simon would cradle him in his arms, or swing him around, his small limbs extended dangerously, but always drawing him back into safety.

In his mother's bosom he receded into the satisfied feeling you get when your belly has been filled, or you've awakened from a restful nap. But in Simon's embrace, the feeling was more complicated. Exciting, perhaps, if a little exposed. He didn't understand it, and the usually confident Nathan struggled to subjugate a force within him that was as natural and instinctive as his musical proficiency.

That summer he noticed that his testicles had grown larger; there was the beginning of a swelling in his chest, and he observed light hair beginning to grow on his legs, underneath his armpits and in his groin. Thom, too, had suddenly began to change. He seemed to be growing taller with each passing month and Nathan noticed that with each spurt in height, Thom grew sideways as well. Muscles started forming on the boy's upper arms and his neck became thicker. For Nathan, this too was exciting, but also confusing.

But the drama of Nathan's sexual awakening paled in comparison with the estrangement of his parents. Their separation happened with much more theatrics than anyone could have anticipated.

It's possible that his mother's breakdown and separation from her husband was the catalyst that propelled Nathan into extraordinary musicianship. He was reluctant to leave her on the weekends when Simon would come and pick him up to spend time with him in Toronto. Most of the time he didn't want to go. He thought he would come home and find his mother zonked out on antidepressants, or worse, alcohol. He thought his father tried too hard to insulate him from the reality of his mother's psychological and emotional problems, but that was unnecessary because he lived in the house with a woman who, as was apparent now, had been damaged. His education that summer was swift and intense.

He learned how to prepare meals, how to strip and change a bed, how to pre-soak delicate undergarments, reconcile a checkbook and pay a bill. With each of these tasks he harbored the twitch of an antagonism towards his father. But Rose enjoined him not to think that way.

"This isn't your father's fault, Nathan. It's mine. I will get better," she told her son, "but your father needs to be where he is. And I need to be where I am. You may not understand this now, but someday you will."

That summer, when mother and son lived together in the house during the week, the evenings would be filled with music. It was the one thing Nathan knew he could do, the one thing he felt called to do. Music was a powerful healer so he studied and practiced, played and performed Bach, Paganini,

Debussy, Gershwin and Faure. Warm Thursday nights in July were devoted to concertizing for his mother and himself with *Three Pieces* by Stravinsky, followed by the *Andante* movement from the Copland *Clarinet Concerto* that he had been struggling with for the past year.

Rose sat in a lounge chair on a small patio that had been inlaid with flat fieldstone. Nathan sat across from her with his music stand holding a three-ring binder that held his books, treasures from G. Schirmer and Boosey Hawkes. When dusk was beginning to fall he would turn on miniature fairy lights that had been strung in the backyard trees, blinking on and off like fireflies. He would make his entrance by coming out from the sliding glass door that separated the living room from the patio and take a dramatic bow. Then he would announce the piece he was playing, sit down to tune and begin.

Sometimes he would watch his mother drift off into a reverie. He would see her looking at him, studying him, considering his face. Of course, Nathan had no idea that what she was actually looking at. He could not know about the images that both confused and haunted her simultaneously. How could he have known that she was flipping through a psychedelic nickelodeon?

"No'ach," she called to him one time. "Come and stay by me." But Nathan thought she was just tripping on the pronunciation of his name, blurring her words. How could he know that his mother was recording Simon's smiling face, his arms reaching out to pull her onto the bed in the Ben Gurion Airport Hotel room where they had spent the night the day they were returning from Israel. And then look up again to see Noah's face, his wide mouth grinning, his tongue playing in the space between his gums and his teeth. And then the mask of another man. Dark and brown, bearded and furrowed from the sun.

That face would move in and out of her consciousness over that summer, superimposing itself into her visions until she would snap out of it, awaken, or jump up so it would vanish. Until one day she knew that she was ready to understand who it was and why he appeared to her.

Time passed quickly, but moved slowly. By mid-August Nathan began to notice the change in his mother. By summer's end Rose slowly began to return to her old self. In small ways she lifted herself up and began to move on. She planted an autumn garden, started baking her own bread, took the train to Montreal to visit Sharon and Barbara and even went sailing one weekend on Lake Ontario with some former students of hers who had organized an outing.

She and Simon had started having supper regularly and then, while Nathan was away at a three-week music camp, the two of them decided to take a weekend out in Halifax and St. John, a reconciliation holiday. By the time Nathan returned from the Interlochen Arts Camp in Michigan, a world-class summer music and arts colony, his father had moved back home to their house, and life resumed its normal course as much as that was possible. It seemed to Nathan that everyone had awoken from a long, burdensome dream.

Still, Nathan kept his father at a distance. Regardless of Simon's devotion, his affection, his encouragement, father and son strained to make conversation, especially when Rose was absent. Their intimacy was predicated on familial proximity but, emotionally they seemed to be disconnected, to be unaware of each other's needs.

"Nathan always seems to be angry with me," Simon complained to Rose.

"I don't think so," she answered. "He's at that ghastly age and I'm afraid the last six months haven't exactly been comforting to him. He's more like you than you think he is."

But Simon couldn't help noticing that as Nathan began to grow and develop into maturity, he took on a physical form that was totally unlike his own. Where Simon was broad in the shoulders and on the shorter side, Nathan grew taller and more lanky.

The pattern of hair on a man's arms, legs and chest follows his father. But Simon noticed that Nathan's had sprouted differently. Even the hair on the top of their heads was different. Simon's long, straight hair, which started to turn to salt and pepper when he was only in his thirties, defined his crown. Nathan had been given a wild mop of curly, unmanageable locks.

Then there was the eye color. Both Simon and Rose had blue eyes, Sharon's were also blue and Barbara's were a blueish-green. But Nathan's were brown. Dark brown. Almost milk chocolate. It is, of course, possible for two blue-eyed parents to make a brown-eyed child. It happens, but it is uncommon. Predicting eye-color isn't quite as straightforward as a Mendelian matrix.

None of this was particularly important to Simon for that matter. There was enough of the father in the son to dispel any issue of paternity. But sometimes a slight itch that remains unscratched starts to radiate and proliferate. And eventually, no matter how hard one tries not to move their fingernails up and down on it, the physical overtakes the psychological and the body needs relief.

By the end of the summer the breach between Simon and Rose was mended. There would not be any more mention of Noah Chazon or the "Jesus Boat" for many years to come. Rose dedicated herself to her profession, publishing in many journals, writing chapters for a textbook, co-authoring a Canadian government sponsored oceanographic study. Simon mentored a number of young men in the fishery until he sold his shares in the mid-1990's.

Nathan, for his part, had sailed through high school with great popularity and, eventually he had gone off to study at the esteemed Conservatory of Music at Oberlin College in Ohio where doors began to open for him. Though he visited his parents regularly, once he had left his house there was, practically speaking, no returning.

Simon and Rose stayed in that house in Mississauga for another twenty years. It's where Sharon and her husband had their wedding, where Michele spent many summers with her grandparents, where Barbara, who spent a great deal of time in New York, flew up for holidays and weekends when she could get away.

Galilee, Israel - September, 2014

But now, after what seemed miles and years away from their life growing up together in Ontario, the three siblings stood leaning against the boat's railing, looking out wistfully into the water. They looked like a stage tableau from a Chekhov play. Two sisters and their brother, as different from each other, as they were the same. And the one thing they all shared was their father, elderly now and drooping as he ascended the narrow stairs to come back up onto the deck of the Sundancer.

With their mother's remains disposed of there was nothing onerous left for them to do except turn the boat around, comfort their father and return to their separate lives back home.

"Nathan, would you please turn the ignition back on and head for the dock at Nof Ginosar," Simon asked his son. The long wooden dock could now be seen clearly in the distance.

"We have to pay a visit to the Museum and see the ancient boat," he explained, "the 'Jesus Boat.' I'm told it's a fascinating exhibit."

Without knowing it, each of the siblings thought to themselves, "So there's more. That's what we're doing. So that's what this is all about."

Nathan stepped up to the control panel, turned the key and the engine roared on. He adjusted the navigational instruments, turned the wheel slightly and began to steer slowly towards the shore, slowing down the speed as he approached the dock at Nof Ginosar. It was a short but silent trip.

With Barbara's help Nathan docked the boat carefully at the end of the pier where they tied it securely to the large iron anchor weights that kept the Sundancer steady in its bay. There weren't any other boats in proximity, so they had an easy time negotiating a space. They lined up the large vessel with the forward and aft spring lines so it was parallel to the wooden dock platform while Nathan prepared a cleat hitch for the bow and stern lines. It was something he was already accustomed to doing with Barbara's help. Sharon, never particularly interested in boating, knew the procedure but would only help if she was asked. They both made sure to check to see if the knots were tied securely, crosschecked the remaining closing procedures and waited for their father.

Meanwhile, Simon had gone back below deck and opened the wooden box he had brought on board. He removed the small package that had been in there, sitting alongside the urn filled with Rose's ashes. The package was compact enough to place inside the pocket of his jacket. He closed the lid of the now empty box, looked around, adjusted his green windbreaker and disembarked.

By now the afternoon sun had transitioned from yellow to a rich orange, and against the backdrop of the monumental edifice called the Yigal Allon Museum, it looked like a large theatrical spotlight illuminating a stage set.

There were many people, mostly tourists, who had come to see the remnants of the famous boat that now, twenty-eight years later, resided in the museum. A group of tourists surrounded the periphery of the exhibit, some carrying I-Phones for clicking photos or sporting compact digital cameras clinging to their necks.

The crowd seemed to be a mixture of Americans and a few Europeans although it seemed to Simon that the rise and fall of American English inflections permeated what was audible or at least could be comprehended. And there was an appreciable sense of mystery, quiet and powerful, that infiltrated the viewing.

Maybe because from the very beginning of the discovery there had been the implied association of this artifact with Jesus and his Apostles. Perhaps. But speculation or not, the assembled structure of the boat's remains, noble but frangible, was a tribute to the sensitive and intelligent strategy of the scientific restoration. Only the most skilled restorers, archaeologists and scientists were called on to preserve this unique specimen.

Simon, of course, had been skeptical from the beginning. Especially when Rose became fascinated and then obsessed, by the discovery. And now faced with actually seeing the remains of the boat on display fifty yards or so away from him, Simon had to seriously take into account that the relic of the twenty-seven foot boat had indeed survived at all given its position stuck in the mud, in fresh water and subject to the power of marine bacteria.

Logically these should have digested the fibers in the pelvic-shaped wooden frame leaving it shredded, beaten and dissolved. But it didn't. There should have been very little chance of finding it after two-thousand years. But there it was. And even if there wasn't a carbon date-able fragment to analyze, a cooking pot and lamp found inside were enough to successfully place it on the right page in the ancient history timeline. A modern miracle.

Simon had known for years that Rose did not believe in miracles. She said they were assumed to be caused by the intervention of God. Since there was no God then miracles were merely hallucinations, unrepeatable and imaginary.

There was an expedition Rose had participated in sometime in the late 1960's, a few years into her study at the University at St. John. The students had all gone on an excursion to the northeast corner of Lake Ontario off of Amherst Island to delve into sound source localization by fish. Their mission was to record vocal activity for marine life inhabiting the shipwreck of the *George A. Marsh*, a three-masted schooner that had gone down in a violent storm in 1917. The idea was to compare vocal attributes to other shipwrecks and see if any conclusions could be drawn about sounds surrounding underwater wooden structures.

The *Marsh* had gone down in about eighty feet in Lake Ontario and could be seen upright in the water. The students were all required to perform due diligence by researching the history of the shipwreck.

"The newspaper accounts of the day are just ridiculous," Rose claimed, as she was describing the assignment to Simon.

"What do you mean?" he asked.

"They say it was a "miracle" that there were two survivors out of the fourteen who were sailing to Kingston that day. Miracles had nothing to do with that. There were five men, two women and seven children. Twelve dead out of fourteen. Sounds just tragic to me. If you read between the lines you can see that the so-called survivors were the Captain's brother and the chief deckhand. Both young, strong men. Miraculous?"

"So you're saying they were just interested in saving themselves?"

"I'm saying the boat foundered in a heavy gale. The seams gave way and the pumps just forfeited. Who would you put your money on to survive? The kids and their mothers? Any of them? There's nothing miraculous about survival. It's instinctual."

"That's really skeptical, Rose," Simon said.

"It's there in the accounts. In black and white. The two men lowered the yawl and made it to Amherst Island. They fought through black rain. It's not like God plucked them out and shepherded them to safety."

"But those poor children. Could they have even had a chance of survival?" he asked.

"Probably not. If they hadn't drowned they would have died from exposure. I read an excessively detailed account of the Anglican memorial service. You know what the congregants sang? *'What a friend we have in Jesus.'* Some friend."

~~~

But miracles notwithstanding, here was Simon now. Back in Israel, back at the Ginosar kibbutz, following in Rose's footsteps. She had returned here one more time, in 1986 without him, confused but determined to see Chazon and view the remains of the ancient boat. It was the start of the crack in their marriage. But if she had not come, she would have sunk faster than any of the shipwrecks she had explored. Only at the time there was no way for him to know it.

CHAPTER FOURTEEN

Ontario, Canada - March, 1986

The phone rang in the Strongin house a few days after a strung out Rose had tried to contact Noah. The day Shoshana Chazon had explained the mysterious circumstances of her husband's dissociative amnesia. That odd, supernatural connection seemed to bind disparate lives on two different sides of the world, one that was divided by great and powerful waters yet simultaneously held together by them.

"Hello, this is the Strongin residence," Simon answered the phone that morning, still quite chilly despite what the calendar said.

A slight hesitation, "Oh, is this Simon? Simon Strongin?" the caller asked. A deep, masculine voice. The slightest trace of an accent.

"Yes, may I ask who is calling please?" Simon said firmly although he was aware, from the first breath of sound, who was on the line.

"It's Noah. Noah Chazon. I'm calling from Israel. It's been quite a while since we have spoken, Simon."

"Yes, many years. I know you and Rose have continued to do some work together," he answered, and then added, "Off and on. I mean. Here and there." He would have said, "I know you and Rose have been close," but that would have not been as effective over the telephone as in person.

"Yes," Noah continued, "I am a great admirer of your wife's research abilities, as well as her, how shall we say, scientific mind. We have always been somewhat compatible." Pause.

"Well, I will get her for you. I'm not sure you want to use up your dime talking to me, eh? Or your shekel. I guess," he laughed at his own joke. "Hold please, and I'll get her."

Simon hung back while Rose talked. A lot of "*um hmm*" and "*I see*" from her side of the conversation. She hung up the telephone, turned to Simon and said, "He needs me to help him," as rational and emotionless as possible. But Simon could sense there was something more powerful, almost ominous, underlying their conversation.

"Help him? Doing what? You've got a full time teaching load. Not to mention *us*."

"Just some data he needs. It's no big deal," she answered. "Look I'm going to be late, so I'll fill you in on all of this later, okay." She had taken a quarter tab of alprazolam earlier, and it was starting to even things out. She collected her things and headed for the door, turning at the last minute to remind him, "You're doing taxi today for Nathan, right?" Simon nodded and then Rose was out the door.

Later that afternoon, when Simon had returned to the house after dropping Nathan off at his friends' house, he walked into the front vestibule and could see through the archway in front of him that Rose was sitting in the dining room drinking a glass of wine.

"4:00PM calls for tea not Chardonnay," he thought. She was dressed for travel in a two-piece suit. In the hallway was a suitcase and a documents purse; her coat was draped over the top of the luggage.

"There's a taxicab waiting in front of the house. Are you going somewhere?" Simon asked her, more than a bit rattled.

She pushed out a large amount air from her mouth, her lips pursed. She was nervous. "Simon, I need to go back to Israel," she told him.

"Are you kidding me? What for?"

"Noah needs me there. I can't explain. It's too complicated. Please, I'll be back in a few days. I've got a flight out at seven o'clock," she informed him.

"I'm not believing this. It's not happening, Rose. How can you just pick yourself up and leave? What about Nathan? What about your classes?"

"They will be covered for me. I made arrangements. It's not the end of the world. I am senior faculty and my students can work independently. I just need to go."

"Yeah, I know. And what about our son?" he asked with acquiescence.

"Nathan is busy with school and the orchestra. You know how self-sufficient he is."

A slow burn, and then he knew she had pressed the button, "Goddamn it. You're driving me fucking crazy. Please just tell me. Just tell me. Is there something between the two of you, *please* tell me," Simon pleaded with her. "I don't want to lose you."

Rose looked at him dead on. "He is not my lover, Simon. I've told you that before, but you don't believe me." There was no anger, hardly any emotion. Just resignation.

"How can I believe you when you won't be truthful with me?"

She paused a moment. "Honestly, I don't know what the truth is. I need to find out. But it will help me, and it will help us."

"You talk to me in puzzles. Cryptic. Ambiguous. What's happened to you? You aren't the woman I married. You are not! You want to find out the truth? Figure out who you are first and let me know when you've worked it out," he barked angrily.

She rose from the table and walked into the hallway telling him calmly she would be staying at a hotel in Tiberias, that Noah's wife had made arrangements. Shoshana Chazon would be there as well.

"I'll be back in a few days. The girls won't even know I am gone. Please tell Nathan I will try to call tomorrow. Even if it is late. Explain that this came up suddenly. That I didn't have time to tell him. Because of the time difference. The distance. Please Simon do this for *him*," she asked her husband with a trace of desperation. Then she picked up the suitcase and documents, flung her coat over her arm, and closed the front door behind her.

"Well, I cannot stop you from leaving, but when you return, that is if you decide to return, I'm not sure I will be able to stay here." The words were like darts being thrown into her back, each one stinging. She knew she had no choice but to succumb to their pain, and climbed into the waiting taxicab knowing she had to press on.

Galilee, Israel - March, 1986

Rose had not been back to Israel for almost twelve years, but she couldn't really tell any difference. Other than the fact that she saw many more dark-skinned faces working at the airport and in Tel Aviv than she had before. A few years earlier the so-called Operation Moses had attempted to covertly bring as many as eight thousand Ethiopian Jews into Israel.

After getting off the plane she still felt that same sensation that she was in another world, on another planet, an exotic sensibility that was only enhanced by signs in a language she could not read. Her English was perfectly understood by the majority of people she had come into contact with. Still the colorful junction of Arab, Jew, European and African lent itself to a kaleidoscope of sights, sounds and smells that told her she was no longer in North America. She came through customs without a hitch and saw a sign with her name on it waiting at the exit where a myriad of limousine, and taxi drivers and other travelers had congregated.

"Shoshana? Shalom. Hi. It's so nice of you to meet me here," Rose told her. Shoshana put the sign down, hugged her firmly, kissing her on both cheeks.

Rose sized her up, in a friendly way, thinking she was cute but noting that she was much shorter than Noah. Rose pictured the two of them together, in a split second, and thought they were an odd combination.

She assumed they were likely the same age, or close to it, early forties. The same as Noah and Simon. The woman wore large, tortoise-shell glasses whose frames touched the bottom of the bangs of a boyish haircut. She was dressed in bluejeans and a powder blue cotton sweater that covered a trim and efficient body. Around her neck hung around amber pendant with a double strand brown silk cord.

"I'm betting you're exhausted?" she asked Rose.

"Well, a little. It was a bit tense leaving home and then the long flight and …."

Shoshana cut her off, "You're looking beautiful, nonetheless. I've seen your photograph, but I never imagined how captivating you would look in person."

Rose blushed a little. "You're very kind. I think right now I must look like a train wreck."

Shoshana laughed, "You have a mother's beauty. That's what I see in your face," and then, "It's a little less than a two hour drive to Tiberias. Mostly highway driving. But I thought, if you like, we could go back to our flat for a few hours and you could have a nap and wash up. That is, if you want to. Noah is occupied most of the day and not expecting us until evening anyway," Shoshana rattled on. Her English was quite good though once in a while Rose detected a guttural "r" coming from the back of the throat.

Rose thought about that offer for a moment and decided it would be a good thing. Her head was spinning a bit from the flight and the valium she had taken to help her sleep. She assented, and they drove the short distance from the airport to Sheinkin Street in a quiet, residential neighborhood populated with Bauhaus architecture and upscale restaurants and boutiques.

Inside Rose put her head on the pillow in the guest room, more to try it out rather than sleep, but found herself totally succumbing, and an hour later, she awoke, washed quickly and walked out into the living room where Shoshana was reading.

"Shall we get on the road?" she asked. Shortly afterward, Rose found herself back in the sporty BMW and on the coastal road heading north to just below Haifa where they would turn sharply right and head towards the Galilee. The sun was setting to the left of them, and Rose found herself lulled into a pleasant rhythm as they climbed and descended on their way to Tiberias. It was just starting to get dark as they arrived, the busy city's suburbs reaching out with garish neon lights and traffic even before they had headed to the central district.

It was mostly a quiet ride interspersed with Shoshana asking questions about Rose's three children. She and Noah had no children. It was a deliberate decision and one they had discussed many times before and during their marriage. Shoshana had come from a large family. She had six siblings, four of whom were still alive. But she never wanted to have any of her own children. She thought Noah had mixed feelings about it but now, fifteen years into their marriage; they were so driven by their vocations they didn't know how they would be able to fit in children.

"You'd be surprised what a person is able to juggle when they have kids," Rose told her. "Sometimes I didn't think I'd even have the energy to cook breakfast, but somehow you just do it. Somehow it sorts itself out." She explained that both she and Simon had been single children and how they had always wanted to make sure their children had siblings.

Afterwards Shoshana pulled the BMW into the car park of a small hotel off of the Yigal Allon Promenade and helped Rose with her suitcase.

"I've been staying here when I can," she said, "on the weekends. It's too crazy up at the kibbutz where the rest of the expedition is. Noah is meeting us here. I'll let you settle in, and then we will come collect you?"

"Sounds good," Rose agreed, and the two women parted, Rose carrying her own suitcase to the elevator and up to the fourth floor where she had a room with a view of the lake. It was just as alluring as she had remembered. Twilight had set in and lights were coming on along the serpentine shoreline. In a little while the sun would completely vanish, and the waters would dissolve into blackness.

She stretched a bit and massaged the small of her back, a casualty from sitting on a long flight, followed a few hours later by a car ride. Then she looked away back into the room and reached for the telephone to call home. She knew Simon and Nathan wouldn't be home during the daytime, but she wanted to hear Simon's voice on the answering machine and, at least, leave a message. Yet as soon as she grabbed the phone's receiver she was distracted by something.

A blinking light. A whirring sound coming from the lake. She turned sharply around and looked out the window, and she heard the voice. It pleaded, "*Ima! Ha'av!*"

She recognized neither the sound of the voice nor the words it called out, but there was something about it that scraped the edge of her memory.

In the distance she saw a fluttering light somewhere out in the middle of the lake. Each second caused the waters to get darker and darker and the light, at first a pinpoint, began to grow brighter. Through it she saw the lake water pick itself up in the long curve of a wave like a giant flat hand stretching itself up out of the foamy caps.

"*Ima! Ima!*" she heard it calling out again.

It sounded like a child. Like the voice of a child, but she couldn't be certain. She could have sworn it was coming from somewhere outside behind the windows. She blinked a few times, put the phone receiver down and rubbed her eyes. When she looked again all seemed fine, and she decided that she must just be physically and emotionally exhausted. But something about the apparition and the sound of the frightened voice still seemed to gnaw at her.

The phone call would have to wait. She opened her handbag, unscrewed a small plastic vial and swallowed a pill, washing it down with a warm bottle of Coca Cola that had greeted her on a table, along with drinking glasses and an ashtray, in the vestibule of the room.

A moment later there was a firm knock at her door, and thinking it was Shoshana come to collect her she opened it. But it was Noah who unexpectedly walked in. He looked frazzled.

"The last time we met was also in a hotel room, Rose," he said suggestively.

Rose was surprised by her reaction. "Noah, I'm not finding that funny. I've had a rough few weeks. Rougher since it appears that you have known more about what I've been going through than you've let on. I feel foolish."

He extended his two arms out to her and she hesitated, "We should not have had any secrets. I am sorry for that," he explained. "I was never absolutely sure I wanted to burden you until Los Angeles. Then I knew for sure. But it was Shoshana who interceded on your behalf."

"Why should she need to do that?"

"She has seen first-hand what damage the dissociative condition can cause," he said.

Rose turned away from him, taking a cigarette out of her handbag and lighting it. She sat down in a chair set up next to the window.

"The dissociative condition?" she asked watching him as he remained standing by the door. Studying him silently, she wondered where Shoshana was. Even now, Noah looking a bit worn out, his clothes dusty, his face free from a few days of shaving, there was something undeniably appealing about him. It was the nucleus of an attraction that had bewitched her from the very beginning.

"I think you'd better start from the beginning. I need some answers. It's been twelve years since we were here together and I disappeared. I thought I had moved on, but since Los Angeles, I've been experiencing flashbacks, sensations that are confusing me. Simon and I are at odds with each other and you are upsetting me," she went on.

The Israeli walked over to the large windows of the hotel room. The shoreline had by now been lit by lamps on the promenade, and the reflections that were generated by neon and fluorescence bounced and refracted their illumination into a giant light show below.

"Rose, I never meant to deceive you. It's just that I was never sure. Never certain what I was feeling," he began.

"Feeling? What are you talking about?"

"Between us. The chemistry, the flirting. The attraction. Surely you felt it when we met. It was electric. But somehow it didn't seem right. I wanted to be close to you, but I couldn't seem to put into motion what would read as intimate. Sexual intimacy. It was something else altogether."

"Is that what all this is about," she asked, but he was shaking his head "no" before the words came out. "Noah, you already know I cannot deny being attracted to you. But is that why we are here? Is that what this is all about?" she demanded to know.

He paused a moment and then turned away from the window to face her, "Don't you think it's odd that we never made love?"

Rose was stunned. Is this what Simon meant? Is this what Simon had been afraid of?

"Goddamn it, Noah. What on earth are you saying? What are you asking?" she responded with astonishment. "Are we talking about us?"

"Have we never come close, Rose?"

"Noah, I have been faithful in my marriage, but I never assumed the same about you," she exclaimed. There. She had said it. How could he have not been unfaithful with his looks and authority, surrounded by women, students, colleagues?

"Regardless of my desire, of what I may have thought or fantasized about," she went on, "I have always been able to measure it and put it in perspective. Tell me what is going on here, Noah? Tell me what is going on?" she demanded as she stood up to face him.

"I've had to fight it. The attraction. I've always had to fight it because ... because when I saw you that first time, at the bottom of the stairs in the kibbutz, I realized I had known you. From the past. We were already connected. But not in the way a man and woman might be. I realized I had found my *mother*," he blurted out.

"Your mother? Noah we are practically the same age ..."

"My other mother, Rose. The woman I experienced as my mother. When I disappeared as a young boy. Shoshana told you about my disappearance, but she didn't tell you that you are the woman whose face was etched into my brain after I disappeared. After I started to remember. Little by little. The thoughts. The shadows. The faces. You pulled me out of the water. You carried me home."

"Carried you home? But from where?"

"From the beach to Dalmanoutha," he said quietly, "it was a real place."

There was no turning back now. It all poured out of him. He repeated the story of his own disappearance, the same story Shoshana had told her. He explained why he had always been drawn to explore the archaeology of the Galilee and the mysteries of the lake. Why he was impassioned about scientists authenticating scripture, how he was prepared to accept a metaphysical explanation for events that science could not substantiate.

He told her that the morning she returned to the kibbutz common room, unaware of where she had been for hours, he knew instinctively what had happened.

"You'll think I'm a madman at first. And then you will gradually see. Believe me, Rose, trust me. This is how it will happen," he began to explain. "You will start to remember. Little by little. You will see images, hear voices. And then it will become part of your present."

"Noah, if the brain has experienced some sort of memory lapse, then it is possible that there are still things stored in it, like a computer."

He shook his head. "No, Rose. No! Don't you see? The land that embodies Israel has a special pull. There are places in this world that defy time and dimension, windows that open through an energy, a power that is manifested unknowingly by certain individuals. It is unexplainable. Wanderers who are five years old or twenty-five or fifty years old pass through a curtain on the physical plane and arrive in the same place at a different point in time. They are infiltrated into that moment."

"You expect me to believe this ludicrous science fiction account you're describing? Are you for real?"

"This is what happened to me," he confessed softly. "And that is what happened to you. We were destined to intersect with each other before, during and after our journey."

Rose sat down on the bed. "I can't even imagine ... Dalmanoutha. Is that a real place? Is that where you think I was?"

"There is no other explanation," Noah told her. "I was there and I know you have been there, too. It existed somewhere between the Tamar and Ilanot beaches. I've been trying to locate it since I was a boy and started to remember. We *were* there, and now we have just been recycled into the present."

She put her head in her hands and wiped the perspiration from her forehead. "That's the part that's the most blatantly ludicrous to me," she responded. And then a beat later, "Look, I can understand that there might be a town, a village, whatever, that had been hidden away for centuries. Buried as so many other ancient sites under the rubble of time, but I cannot get behind your assertion that I had been actually transported somewhere physically. Yes, I got high with you the night before I disappeared. Yes, marijuana or peyote or a hundred other entheogens with psychoactive properties might have induced a transcendent effect. Yes, this has been documented over the centuries and for those who believe that the power of God is apart from the material laws of nature, it would be quite believable that some form of transport has occurred. But not in the cold, stone soberness of the next morning."

Noah started to grin broadly, "This is your gift, Rose. What makes you a discerning scientist. But you know as well as I do that our theories, our laws, assumptions, arguments and our hypotheses only tell us what is possible. They don't have to reveal to us what is impossible."

"I've heard this argument before."

He sat down next to her on the bed. "Why must time only flow in one direction?" he asked. "Einstein changed our understanding of time and space a mere fraction of a second ago. We do everything we can as archaeologists, as scientists, to turn back the clock so we can comprehend where we are now. But why shouldn't we be able to jump backwards, guided by something that we are not quite ready to comprehend? Would the men who worked the ship we found have ever imagined us riding in an elevator or flying in an airplane?"

"So we traveled through a tunnel?" she responded curtly.

"I don't know. There may be a name for it. A wormhole maybe. Gravitational waves from a planetary alignment. Or a supernova. But there was definitely a disturbance in some form. Maybe the ancient astronomers were right and the modern ones still have their heads stuck up their asses …"

"What are you talking about, Noah?"

"Science is about the state of knowing," he went on and then turned, looked out at twinkling lights on the lake and said, "You don't need any scientific argument for believing rationally in God. You only need the *sensus deitatis.*"

"The what?"

"The awareness of God," he said tenderly.

She turned away from him and flashed quickly on the lobby of the Los Angeles Biltmore. She saw Shatapattra throwing her head back and laughing. "You have the awareness of God already," the Indian woman told her. "That's all that is needed to begin."

There was dead silence for what seemed like minutes. Noah kept his eyes focused on Rose trying to get her to look directly at him, but she wouldn't turn around and look into his face. Instead, she picked up the package of cigarettes and pulled out another one. She felt beaten down, drugged and tired. Finally, she confronted him. "How do I know you're not a raving psychopath?" she asked.

"You already know what I am telling you is the truth. And now I am even more certain."

"And why is that?"

"First of all it saved your life. And the life of your husband and children. And then, of course, there is the reason you are here now. The ancient boat."

"What?"

"The "Jesus Boat." Don't you get it? I've seen it before. I've been on it." He paused and took a deep breath, "You must know this is all true. It belonged to my father. *You have a piece of it.*"

~~~

The two of them sat in the room quietly for a long time, Rose on the bed and Noah in the chair by the window.

"May I see the boat?" she asked.

"Yes. Tomorrow. It's still submerged in the mud. It will take a long time to figure out how to dredge it up and conserve it so it doesn't disintegrate in the open air. Could be years. But they will figure out how to do it."

"What a relief it would be for me to think this is what happened. But you and I know that, deep down, there must be another explanation. As natural as a solar eclipse, or an electric blue sea."

"I was where you are now. But you will get there, Rose, believe me."

Eventually Shoshana arrived, pushing the door open and entering assuredly. She went directly over to Rose, put her hand under her chin and brought their lips together.

"You came to Israel the first time to follow a calling to your vocation," she told her. "You didn't know then that you were taking a pilgrim's journey."

Later that night, after the three of them had dinner, Rose told Noah and Shoshana about the letter from the archive, the one from the Baltimore minister's wife. Neither of them was surprised. Noah disclosed that over the years he had discovered there were others who had experienced Dalmanoutha. He tried to find them, and he met a few, but knew there were bound to be more. The town had a population of at least five hundred men, women and children.

And later that year when Rose finally remembered what happened, when the voices and images merged into a lucid memory just the way Noah was able to fully recover his memory, she made her own discoveries as well.

She found out that Dalmanoutha connected her in more ways than one with the distinguished explorer, Sir Edmund Hillary, whose research on the Yeti pointed Rose to Dr. Annabel Winters and the University at Brunswick back when she was applying to graduate schools. She discovered that in 1960, Hillary had been scheduled to board TWA Flight 266 in Columbus, Ohio, one of those two ill-fated planes that crashed midair over Brooklyn, New York close to her house. But just like Rose and her family, he missed the lethal flight. He wasn't meant to die then.

Diaries published after his death in 2008 revealed that in 1968 he was visiting the Galilee when he became separated from his wife, Louise Mary Rose, and daughter, Belinda. Eventually he was discovered many hours later wandering the beach just above the Tamar shore near Ilanot where the Nahal Tslalman river dumps itself into the lake. He claimed he had been meditating. He never talked about his experience to anyone though he left instruction for a passage from *The Gospel of Mark*, Chapter 8, to be read at his funeral service after his passing.

And it was obvious that Anne Malik, the inscrutable Indian woman, had been there as well. She and Noah had found each other in London a few years before she worked on the harbor project with him. Before she joined his project in 1974, she had been assigned to a dig near ancient Magdala. She, too, had an unexplained disappearance on the beach near Ginosar.

Noah had not known that she would be in Los Angeles at the same time he and Rose were there, but he confessed he had completely deceived Rose about Anne's demise. She did not die in a plane crash as he told her. She avoided it completely. She was scheduled to board a British Airways Trident 3B from London to Athens in September 1976 when it was involved in a mid-air collision near Zagreb, Yugoslavia. But a road accident on the M4 to Heathrow had backed up traffic for hours causing her to miss the flight. Anne Malik may have gone missing, but Shatapattra was very much alive.

CHAPTER FIFTEEN

Ontario, Canada - July, 2012

Rose had not thought about the Indian woman for many years. It was the nurse at Toronto General who had been drawing Rose's blood that made her think of her. Not that the woman, middle-aged, chunky and of a presumed Caribbean ancestry looked anything like Shatapattra. It was the nurse's unusual tattoo that Rose noticed.

For the past few months Rose had been having her blood drawn regularly. It was a methodology to chart the progression of her disease. She had already been diagnosed with a Stage 3C breast cancer. Her oncologist explained that her condition was inoperable, but it wasn't untreatable. There were a number of options to consider, many opinions to wade through and a series of decisions to be made about moving forward. Now, almost six months after the original diagnosis had been made, Rose was seated comfortably on a high-backed chair as the nurse fussed over her.

Though blood tests could not reveal everything, the calculable levels of a variety of markers pointed to her slow downslide. The late stage breast cancer had snuck up on her, a consequence of an unknowing Ashkenazi ancestor who had passed on a faulty version of a mutated gene. Although enormous progress had been made in battling the disease, her options were limited and pointed mainly to massive infusions of chemicals into her veins.

Though she had sought alternate viewpoints at the time, her background as a scientist and her knowledge of the uncertainties of medical treatment led her to seize control of her own future. She would go about the business of living for as long as it was possible. After that she would ask for pain relief and that nothing extraordinary be done for her. She certainly was not interested in a surgeon slicing off one or both of her breasts nor enduring the constant battle her body would undergo from the inevitable consequences of chemotherapy.

She didn't tell Simon right away. In fact, she waited against the advice of her physicians to bring him the news. Every time she'd had an appointment with a doctor she would tell him, "It's just a follow up. You don't need to waste your time. I can handle it." Simon, knowing her lifelong streak of independence, didn't get in her way. When he did find out his reaction was confusion.

"Rose, why won't you fight this?" he asked her when she finally revealed the extent of her illness. "You *can* be treated," he insisted.

"Yes, I know Simon, but what's the price?" she answered with anything but despondent resignation. "You who have adored my hair from the day we met. Do you want to see it fall out on the floor until I'm left with a spindly pate of wisps? I don't think so."

Rose's lustrous blonde hair had eventually turned a silvery white and though she continued to dye it throughout her forties and fifties, when she reached sixty-two she decided she would stop and let it settle into whatever color her genes had pre-determined.

"It doesn't look like you anymore, Rose," he had said, "You look like an old woman."

"And Simon, in case you haven't passed a mirror lately, you're looking like an old man."

Simon, who had been remarkably healthy all of his life, still managed to retain his dignified, handsome appearance. Though he began to develop slight heart irregularities as he approached his sixties, this was nothing extraordinary for someone his age. He had slowed down little by little, but spent as much time as he could with Michelle, his only grandchild whom he visited on a regular basis in Montreal where her mother still had her practice.

Rose, after a career in teaching and research where she had developed an estimable reputation in the field of bioacoustics, just wanted to stay put and read, spending quiet time alone with Simon, her children and granddaughter. She had no more interest in travel. Her projects in Lake Ontario, the Bay of Fundy and in Israel brought her recognition in her field. She looked forward to peaceful days with Lake Ontario in her backyard, good food, music, reading and conversation. Now, in her late sixties, she faced the possibility of a life that would be truncated.

Simon had reacted badly once he recognized the degree of Rose's disease and the magnitude of her reluctance to pursue a remedy. But faced with limited treatment choices, Rose told him, "My treatment of choice is no treatment at all," and from her perspective that was that.

He had called his daughter Barbara in New York, "Your mother is not well. You need to come up here as soon as possible."

"Oh, my God, Daddy. What's the matter? What's going on?" she had asked, her heart palpitating as the weight of his words repeated themselves in her mind.

"She has a cancer diagnosis. I'm sorry to have to tell you this on the telephone."

A brief silence and then. "How serious?"

"Quite," Simon responded, "it's a late stage. But it's more complicated. After all, this is your mother we are dealing with. Why wouldn't she make things complicated?"

"What do you mean, Daddy?" Barbara detected a strange tone coming from her father. "Can it not be treated?"

"Selfish. That's all," his voice started to break up. "I've got to go. Please come up here."

"Put Mama on the phone. Please, Daddy. Is she there? Where is she? Give her the phone."

After that there was a flurry of phone calls. People to be notified. Calls and texts and emails flying back and forth. But Rose, the center of such turmoil, remained tranquil and resolute. Even when Simon told her he needed to get away to clear his head, to reconcile with the overwhelming knowledge that he would survive his wife.

She, above all people, understood and told him to go. She would be fine. Barbara traveled from New York, and Sharon and Michelle came west from Montreal while a forlorn Simon headed east. Back to Halifax needing to put his feet down on the Nova Scotia soil of his youth. His daughters were equally sympathetic to him, as they were to their mother and gave their father the distance they believed he needed.

Only Nathan responded badly to Simon's departure. Out in Vancouver with the orchestra he attempted to get back to Ontario, but his mother and his sisters had entreated him to stay where he was. He would be back soon enough. As would Simon also.

Now today Rose was weary, but not in any particular pain. She extended her own arm out to the nurse and said, "I like your tattoo. That's quite an accomplished work of art. May I see it close up?"

The nurse beamed. "I designed it myself. You see there are five rings. One for each of my children," she explained in a flat Canadian accent." And they are separated by small geometric shapes." It looked like a bracelet with loops and fasteners that wrapped around the nurse's left wrist. She also wore large hoop earrings that set off her broad features.

"The geometric shapes are symbols of the spirits of my ancient ancestors. The triangle is the hierarchy of the family, the squares are the natural elements, and the circle means the continuation of life."

"All those shapes. Was it painful?" Rose asked her.

"No. Not at all. Tattooing is a real art. He did it quickly and cleanly."

"Have you ever seen a tattoo of a Jewish star?" Rose wanted to know.

"You mean the Star of David?" the nurse followed quickly. "Well, yes, I have seen them. I mean in movies and in photos. The Holocaust, you know. I heard that the Nazis put them on the Jews when they threw them in the camps. But I thought those tattoos were just a bunch of numbers. Sick people *they* were."

"Sometimes they would ink on a triangle as well," she said as the nurse pulled out the small butterfly needle used for the venipuncture, the standard for drawing blood. Rose studied her own wrinkled, loosening skin for a moment. Now that she was in her late sixties, it reminded her of her own grandmother, the fiercely independent Fanny, who helped finance Rose's way up to Canada that summer of 1963.

"Yes, the triangle," the nurse repeated. "Well, that was even more nasty. I always thought that the Jewish people weren't supposed to have tattoos on their bodies anyway. Against their religion," she said closing up the small puncture mark with an adhesive plaster. "Leave this on for thirty minutes."

"You're right. It's straight out of Leviticus. A proscription against idolatry. Do you know the Old Testament, dear?"

"We are a spiritual people, Mrs. Strongin," she disclosed. "Both my mother's and father's people came from Barbados where they yoked their dignity to their religion. But honestly, I gave up on that book a long time ago. That God was always jealous of something!"

She reached for a plastic clipboard from an adjacent countertop and started to write some notes. It was quiet for a few moments and then Rose blurted out the question, "So what do you think happens to us when we die?"

The nurse looked up from her notes with a puzzled expression on her face.

"That's a tough question. I could give you the answer I learned in my organic chemistry classes. But I'm not sure that's the response you are looking for."

Rose puckered her lips like a jaunty little girl, "Nope. That's not what I am asking."

"I thought so," the nurse said. "You're talking heaven and hell, right?"

"Well, that depends," Rose answered back, starting to shift in the chair and prop herself out of it, "if it's the afterlife you're referring to, we Jews have a rather bleak vision of it."

The nurse thought for a moment and then said, "It's quite unclear to me what the next world is. If there is such a thing."

"Do you think there is?" Rose wanted to know.

"Isn't the obligation on those who believe there is, to prove it to those who do not?"

"If indeed proof is something that is needed," Rose answered.

The nurse put the clipboard and pen down. The question now felt like a challenge. She went over and put her arm around Rose's waist helping her out of the chair and supporting her back while she stood up.

She spoke plainly and directly, "When I was a child I used to roll down the car window and stick out my hand to feel the force of the wind against it. A silly game I played by myself. It made me feel good. And maybe a little powerful. I didn't understand how something I couldn't see could touch me. Just plain air. Clear and still. I would pull my hand back into the car quickly and feel nothing, and then I would put it out the window again and *whoosh*. It made my meager hand quiver like I was arm wrestling with the wind."

Then she took both of Rose's hands into her own and said to her, "Of course, now I could give you an explanation. The physics. An acceptable answer. But honestly, all I can remember is thinking that the force of the air against the back of my hand was God. Pushing up against me." She paused for a moment and then said, "You're a very brave woman, Mrs. Strongin."

Simon was waiting for her outside in the busy corridor. He had been sitting in a small waiting area separated from the series of endless doors that contained windowless rooms holding clusters of machines, equipment and other medical contraptions used to prod and poke their patients. When he finally saw Rose walking cautiously out of one of them he stood and waited, keeping his eyes fixed on her as she approached.

"Everything go okay?" he asked.

"Nothing has changed. It is what it is."

Later in the car as they were driving back to their townhouse, Rose asked Simon to pull into the miniature park that had been carved out as part of the gated community of town-homes they lived in. The park was set against a small strip on Lake Ontario, and the developers had landscaped it with indigenous shrubbery, a few paved paths and some scattered benches that looked out over the water. The park was kept tidy and the black, red and sugar maple trees that were lined up, like well-behaved sentries, provided ample shade from a warm July day.

"Do you feel like a walk?" Rose asked her husband.

"You're well enough, I presume, otherwise you wouldn't ask, right?"

Rose threw her head back and laughed, "Simon, nobody knows me the way you do."

"And vice versa," he admitted.

"It's extraordinary, isn't it? After all this time. It gives me such comfort. Do you feel that way too?"

"Of course. How could it not? I've spent almost fifty years inside your head."

They parked the car, and Simon went round to open her door.

"Are you hungry?" he asked

"A little. Yes. But let's sit on that bench for a few minutes." She pointed towards a scenic bench sitting isolated at the edge of the path. "I have something important to tell you, Simon. It's something I have wanted to tell you for the longest time, but I was afraid. Now, it seems, is the right time."

Simon's eyes got large and watery. "What, Rose?"

"And I have something to show you. It's upstairs in the house. In a purple velvet sack. In a box where I've kept it hidden for close to thirty-eight years."

CHAPTER SIXTEEN

Galilee, Israel - September, 2014

Simon patted the lined pocket in his jacket, feeling for the small package he had put in there a short while ago. It's not that he thought it had disappeared. No, it was just assurance that he would see this all through to the very end. And it took on even more gravity as he got closer to the Museum exhibit that displayed the "Jesus Boat." It was almost over. Everything Rose had thought about, everything she had planned.

He was finally there, at Nof Ginosar standing at the railing studying the ends of the boat's wooden frame, examining from afar the color and texture of the curved ribs that looked like the skeletal bones of an ancient stegosaurus turned on its back.

Still, what could one really expect from a hunk of wood that had been built by the hands of early Galileans sometime in the early first century. The boat's remains had been placed in a solid metal frame that helped stabilize its structure. The armature looked like a giant spoon for dishing out spaghetti. It was separated from its viewers by a long guard rail, about three feet high, separated by protective panels of clear glass, to keep gawkers at a safe distance.

Behind the railing in the foreground preceding the boat was a strangely beautiful sculpture of plexiglass and plastic, round discs of green: tea, mint, and fern. It looked like the stage set for an avant-garde opera. It had been assembled abstractly, but with precision, to create the illusion of a lake. No human being could reach his hand over the railing and touch what nature and science had preserved together. Beyond the boat, projected onto a blank wall, were LED images of computer renderings and mosaics of what the boat might have looked like intact.

It was mid-afternoon and there were about two dozen or so people milling about the large, expansive exhibit hall, lined up alongside Simon to study the boat intensely. Sharon and Barbara were at the far end of the long barrier looking a bit bored.

Nathan, however, had taken his time entering into the building. He loitered outside for a bit, not really understanding his reluctance. "This must be the last and final piece of this," he thought to himself. Perhaps he knew that after this was over and they returned to the boat, sailed into the southern sky back to Tiberias and departed the next morning, it would be the last of Rose Strongin.

Finally, he decided he would go inside and find his father. As he started to walk through the front glass doors he caught a sideways glimpse of someone he thought he knew, someone he recognized, who was pacing outside the entrance. He was going to go back and get a better look, but he spotted Simon right away, standing by the exhibit and then he became distracted by a small group that had gathered in a corner of the exhibit hall.

"*Israel is the only nation everybody will be looking to at the end of days,*" announced a middle-aged man loudly, standing close to the display with a few tourist disciples hanging on his every word. The speaker was clearly an American wearing a short-sleeved madras shirt, Bermuda shorts and donning a cream-colored bucket hat. He had just the slightest American regional accent and Nathan, who had always been interested in deciphering inflected speech, placed it in California. He noticed that his father kept looking at his wristwatch.

"Bible prophecies are being fulfilled all the time. Every week there's another event that ratifies the accuracy of the Bible," the man continued. "The end of history can be confirmed. It's written down for all of us."

"Are these people serious?" thought Nathan. "This boat only confirms one thing. That people in the first century went fishing on boats." He remembered when he was younger that his mother had been inordinately interested in this boat. Something to do with her research. But that was when she and Simon had separated, and he endured their short period of estrangement. He rubbed his temples fearing a slight headache had come on and reasoned it must be from the sun, the wine, the emotional stress of the day's activities.

"Science has authenticated the Bible overwhelmingly through the science of archaeology. It confirms the written record of the Bible," the unofficial tour guide went on. "This boat is just more proof that the Bible is our real history. A boat large enough to accommodate the twelve apostles. This boat validates the Gospel accounts."

"*Amen*," one of the members of the group said in a conversational voice. After all, this wasn't a revival or a church service. It was a museum. Still, there was a palpable sense that visitors were in the presence of something sacred.

Nathan immediately spotted his two sisters and noticed they continued to mill about, but he decided to walk a bit closer to his father at the exhibit. By this time he'd had enough and wanted to know when they would be leaving. He noticed that Simon checked his watch again.

The proselytizing man went on, "Was Jesus in this boat? Can we say for sure whether His bare feet touched these planks? Are we required to have an answer? No. Isn't it enough to say that our Lord *was* in a boat like this when he was out on the Sea of Galilee. Just outside that door my friends. That's where He was. We have all the evidence we need."

Some of the other tourists seemed to be annoyed by the man's proclamations, but nobody had quite the nerve to tell him to shut up. After all, this type of exhibit was meant to stimulate, not dissuade. Still, there were appropriate rules of behavior.

"We know that Jesus had control over nature. Matthew tells us. Mark and John tell us as well. He walked on this water. Down that stone path just one hundred feet from here. He went fishing with Peter. He told a nasty storm to take a hike," the American laughed loudly, "and then when He reappeared after He died, He taught his apostles how to fish!"

"Will someone shut this man up," Nathan began to quietly wish. There didn't seem to be any type of security around. No guards. Docents. Nobody he could appeal to. He'd already been through enough turmoil today and this man's voice was heightening his anxiety. He looked over again at Simon who seemed to be fixated on the boat.

The man continued, "One day. One staggering, bewildering day in 1986, all was changed forever when this ancient artifact, this revelation was uncovered. The moment that changed everything. To reveal the truth. To announce to the world with unvarnished certainty. To disclose for all time that Jesus is Lord. To ….."

"Will you shut the *fuck* up," Nathan screamed.

Astonishingly, at precisely the same time, the large glass doors to the exhibit room flew open and another young man started screaming in Hebrew, "רופפת באה סירה. עזרה. עזרה. זרהע." loudly and precise, as if on cue. All the heads in the room turned and looked towards the open door, away from the exhibit. All except for Simon.

It appeared that he had expected the interruption. The young man repeated urgently, "רופפת באה סירה. עזרה. עזרה.". At the same time Simon reached into his inside jacket pocket and took out the parcel, the purple velvet bag that had been covered with the small tassel and began to unwrap it.

"What is that man saying?" asked one of the American tourists. "We don't speak Hebrew. Is he in trouble?" There was a hubbub and a lot of uncomfortable shifting. The loud American evangelist had stopped talking and started walking over to the young man. "What's going on?" he asked.

Barbara recognized him immediately. "It's Arkin. The porter from the Hotel," she announced out loud. "Sharon, isn't it him? That's him," she called out. She rushed over to the young Russian.

"*It is your boat miss. It is slip from dock,*" he repeated, "*it is slip from dock.*"

"How did you get here? What are you saying?" she asked quickly. Sharon looked perplexed in the confusion. It seemed surreal – an odd juxtaposition of people and sounds. She found Nathan's eyes across the room.

While this was happening Simon took out the object that had been wrapped so carefully and held it up. It was the ancient piece of wood, Rose's souvenir, about seven inches in length, shaped like a pencil and dappled like the mottled skin of a horse. Brown and matte, an exact rival for the ribs of the "Jesus Boat" that was on display.

"Oh, no. Nathan and I tied the boat securely. Let's get out of here," Barbara yelled. "Nathan …"

Simon looked around over his shoulder. Nobody was looking his way. He took the wooden fragment in his left hand, and assessing the distance between the guard rail and the empty shell before him, threw the object over his head watching it glide in the slowest of motion until it landed gently inside the vessel. The final fulfillment of his late wife's wishes.

No alarms were rung. No warning lights flickered on and off. No announcements rang out. There was a deafening silence inside Simon's head. The kind of silence encountered when you put your head underwater and yield to the still vibrations of silence. And then the sense you get when you awaken from a dream, not knowing what world you are really in.

His corruption of the remains of the boat did not go unnoticed though. As Simon turned around to proceed out, he noticed Nathan staring directly at him, dazed and perplexed. He realized his son had been watching him. The old man felt a sudden twinge in his left arm. He thought it might have been from the arm retracting after the throw. He began to walk towards the exit, shuffling his feet and breathing heavily; he felt strange, uncomfortable. Nathan ran over and grabbed onto his right arm to hold him steady.

"Go, Barbara. Get out of here," Nathan shouted. "Take Sharon and see what's going on with the boat. I'll stay here with Simon. There's something wrong with him."

Barbara looked back and forth at Nathan and Simon and at Arkin urging her, "Come, Miss. Rope not good." Sharon rushed up and pushed her sister out of the door with him. They ran out of the Museum onto the path down towards the dock.

"Daddy, what's wrong? What's the matter. What did you do? What did you throw in there?" Nathan questioned, his voice rising in alarm. "Let's go sit down. Get you some water." Simon slipped to the ground as Nathan's arm gave way. He was crumpled on the floor. Some of the tourists looked over at them not knowing what to do, or where to go.

"I had to do it, Nathan," Simon's voice was raspy. "It was a gift from your mother. She told me. It came from your father. It had to be returned to where it came from," he said.

"What? Simon, what are you saying?"

"I asked that young Russian man to come here. To create a diversion so I could return it."

"What's going on? I don't know what's happening."

"A gift from God. That's what your name means, Nathan. It had to go back to its home. She couldn't take it with her. It's what your mother wanted."

"I don't understand," he started to shake. "I don't know what you mean." His eyes filled up with tears. Simon looked into his face. Nathan could see specks of red start to inhabit the whites around the pale, watery blue.

"My left arm hurts. My jaw," Simon said.

Suddenly, Nathan shouted out, "Call an ambulance. Get a doctor. My father is having a heart attack. Help us. Please. Help us."

The loud American with the white hat ran over. "Let me look at him. I'm a doctor. I can help." He shouted out to one of his flock, "See if there's a defibrillator somewhere on the premises." He called out, "Does someone have an aspirin? I need an aspirin and some water right now." Someone else ran out and flagged down one of the museum officials.

But at this point there was nothing anyone could really do. Simon had lost consciousness. His entire body pushed up in one sharp spasm, and his heart stopped. The American doctor, the fervent evangelical, tried to resuscitate him, but it was too late. The oxygen stopped flowing to the brain, the organs began to shut down, and the air and gases slipped out of his body as ordered and as natural as his breath had been fifteen minutes ago.

It turned out that the evangelizing doctor was indeed from California. He had been born and raised in San Diego, went to medical school in Oklahoma, and served his country as a medic in the first Gulf War. He rode in the ambulance with them to the hospital back in Tiberias.

~~~

Later that day, when they were collecting Simon's clothes and making arrangements to fly his body back to Canada, Sharon found a letter folded in three in one of the inside pockets of her father's jacket. It had been dated a little more than one year earlier, and it packed a powerful punch.

CHAPTER SEVENTEEN

Toronto, July, 2013

My darling children, this is a handwritten letter I've asked your father to read aloud to you after you return from the sad enterprise of disposing of your mother's remains. It's so odd for me to be using a pen and paper when, for years and years, my fingers have tapped out words on keyboards, both fixed and virtual. But there is something elegant about writing things down in the penmanship one practiced torturously in grammar school. I remember how excited I was when, as a girl, I "graduated" from printing to cursive writing. It was similar to that grown-up feeling I later felt being old enough to smoke a cigarette. Well, we all know what that did to my lungs. Your father's too from breathing in all that second-hand smoke. Thank goodness I finally put that behind me years ago.

But I can still write now. I am strong enough. I have a cancer that will kill me sooner than later. For now I can breathe on my own, recall my own thoughts and lift a pen. So think of this letter as a record of my final instructions and an affirmation of my love for each of you.

I'm told a mother should stand ready to die for her children. At least that's what my mother and grandmother believed. This was during those ugly years in America when I lived in Brooklyn, geographically, but metaphorically on the edge of destruction. We looked to the skies each day to see if the Russians were sending over their bombs to blow us to smithereens. We were the faithful Americans who were free to believe whatever we wanted to. But we were also free to shout out "God is dead!" to whoever wanted to listen to such ramblings. Versus the Russians. They worshipped a god who sat on the top of a tractor. We worried ourselves sick, but they never dropped their bombs and, as of today, they never came to our shores.

    You never knew your grandmother or great-grandmother. I've thought about them more often in the last month than I have in the last twenty years – they both passed out of this world when they were younger than I am now. But they also passed along some miserable genes that point their ugly chromosomes at Jewish women. In my case the Ashkenazi and the Sephardic schmushed together to form me, back in the days when you just got cancer and died. Not now. When you can test your DNA. Reduce your risk factors. (Mind you, Sharon and Barbara, you're not condemned to this.) But, as you already know, forewarned is forearmed and with the right knowledge you can choose how you want to live your life.

    I chose nothing. No infusions of drugs. No chemical cocktails. None of it is necessary. I've spent my life listening to voices in the oceans, for almost forty years attending to the blackest sounds of silence. I'm going to be 70 soon and I know that there really is water for us to cleanse ourselves. God is not dead. He reinvents us. Like the billions of tons of seawater that flow in and out of Fundy during one mighty tide.

Please listen to your father. He will explain it all to you. I've asked him to do some very specific things in order to bring order and completion to my life. He has loved me since the day we met on that ferryboat out on the Bay almost fifty years ago.

I've asked him to return something that had come into my possession many years ago when I was here in Israel to meet Noah Chazon. Noah helped me to understand what it was that I had. He said this to me: "The world is filled with travelers who hesitate to find the truth when everything they have done leads them to it."

He helped me to accept what had happened that day when you, my darling daughters Sharon and Barbara, and your father, were frantically trying to find me at Nof Ginosar. The day we missed that fateful flight back home. The same day, my sweet Nathan, you were conceived.

Your loving mother,

Rose

CHAPTER EIGHTEEN

Galilee, Israel- September 8, 1974

It was a few minutes past 7:00 AM. It was her last day on the expedition in Israel and Rose was unsure of where she was. She thought she might have walked out further along the reedy shore a bit more vigorously than she had done before. Though she could still make out some of the familiar markings of the landscape that had previously guided her, some of what she observed seemed unusual or misplaced. The craggy brown hill, which hugged the side of the lake as it turned sharply south, looked more barren. A graveled road which created a switchback zigzag pattern now appeared like a dusty, dirt road. She didn't see how she could have missed seeing the odd-shaped buildings that dotted the shore in the distance. Still, there was something distinctly familiar about it all.

A few minutes earlier she had slipped out quietly, making sure not to wake Simon and the girls. She grabbed a cup of coffee and a piece of bread downstairs in the common room, walked out the kibbutz's front gate and down towards the beach. The morning air was delightful, and she sipped the coffee, holding the cup with two hands, as her nostrils took in the warm, clean air.

She flashed back to the little "pot" party they had last night, to celebrate the end of the harbor project, when it seemed that Noah had walked dreamlike out of the water. A short distance later she passed the point where they had parked themselves, silly stoners celebrating the end of a successful expedition. She spotted the scraggly boulder that she sat on with Noah, but somehow in the buttery light of mid-morning it seemed different. It was as if the environment had been rearranged, somehow. Though the morning was quite balmy, she shuddered a bit, wrapping her hands around the warm mug of coffee.

Suddenly, a strange sensation started to overtake her. A climbing pressure began to mount in her ears, a pressing inward, as if her head was being squeezed, not painfully, but steadily. She felt her breathing accelerate.

"Must be the coffee," she thought and poured the remains out onto the sand, sallow and hot. But no sooner had she done that there came a fluttering sound, a motor reverberating, wings beating, perhaps, or the sound of the wind whipping through a sail. She sat down on the rock to catch her breath. A warm feeling overtook her, penetrating her limbs, and then a quiet roar which got louder and louder until she had to put her palms over her ears to block out the sound. She held her head between her two hands, closing her eyes tightly, holding her breath. And then, as suddenly as the roar began, it ceased.

When she opened her eyes she saw the man standing there, about three feet from the boulder where she sat. He was looking directly at her, and she gasped loudly.

"What are you doing there? Are you sick?" he asked roughly.

She jumped up quickly, "What? Who are you? Where did you come from?"

"I called out to you, Rosi," the man started to explain, "but you didn't hear me. And then you put your hands up to your head. What's the matter my *pehrakh yahfeh*?"

He was a large stocky man, heavily built, with deeply tanned skin, black eyes, long dark black hair and a full beard. He was oddly dressed in baggy drawstring pants that looked as if they were sewn from a sack. They were rolled up to his calves. On top he wore a white cotton tunic shirt, unbuttoned. He was barefoot, and she saw how brown the feet were as well.

She looked around, assessing where she was, seeing if anyone else was around, either walking on the beach, or between the tall, tawny reeds that punctuated the shoreline, but it was desolate. She felt her heart pump rapidly, her pulse quickening.

"I've been out with Nechunya and Calev," the man said. "We've been fishing all night. I pulled the boat onto the beach. I have some repairs to make. Did you come down to meet me, Rosi? Where's the boy?"

He grinned broadly. Large teeth with a small space between the front two.

"I must be hallucinating," she thought to herself. "The marijuana must have been laced."

"Who *are* you?" she shouted out.

"Who am I? You're just being silly now, Rosi," he answered, "Did you bump your head? It's Simeon. Simeon-Peter. Your *husband*."

With a puzzled expression she looked down and noticed she was wearing sandals with a wooden sole and leather straps. Not the shoes she had put on her feet that morning. And she had on a flesh colored tunic hanging loosely with a long seam at the top of her arms. Her breasts felt tight, and she could feel the binding that kept them in place. A long scarf covered her hair.

But these discoveries were fleeting, because within seconds she began to feel faint, and the strange man, the shoreline and all that surrounded her seemed to be spinning like a top out of control. She started to lose her balance when he suddenly reached out for her hand to steady her. She saw it coming and was about to cry out, but as soon as his thick, leathery fingers touched the top of her hand all fear abated, and she experienced a moment of complete serenity.

In a flash Rose remembered the difficulty she'd had giving birth to her second daughter, and the swift shot of morphine given that, in the course of a second, entered her veins and crushed her pain. After that there was no remembering. Just an empty chamber of time and space.

Dalmanoutha, Galilee - September, 32 c.e.

"Well, now that you're here you can help me," Simeon-Peter told his wife. The sun was up fully, and other fishermen with their boats were coming to shore, dragging their vessels as far as they could upon the beach the locals called Ilanot. Beyond them, heading west, was the small ancient village of Dalmanoutha where Simeon-Peter lived with his wife, young son No'ach, and mother-in-law, Dvorah. The village was populated with working families, fishermen who sailed the Galilee by night, hauling their catches to shore at daybreak, and farmers who cultivated the rich, alluvial brown clay between the coastline of the lake and, further west, the Roman road.

Dalmanoutha had sprung up because it was ideally suited for maritime commerce and the larger families who had commercial interests along the western coastline had financed an artificial stone harbor. It was here that Simeon-Peter had carved out his own modest place, the location where he anchored the boat he had brought with him five-years ago from Capernaum.

He had come down to Dalmanoutha after he had married. His father, Jonah, had arranged the marriage with Rosi's mother, Dvorah, a widow who lived with her only daughter in Capernaum. Simeon-Peter was Jonah's eldest son, and they operated a bustling fishing business in Capernaum with a fleet of three boats. Simeon afforded his father every respect a first-born son must bestow, according to the laws of Hebrew patrimony. Thus, when Jonah and Dvorah had made a match for him, Simon was more than agreeable. Of course, it didn't hurt that Rosi was not only beautiful, but he suspected she was also smart, something he desired in a lifelong companion.

Once Simeon had married he asked for his father's blessing to begin his own business, and he and his brothers went to work constructing the flat-bottomed boat that would be the start of his enterprise. With its cutwater bow the boat had a central mast with a large, single square sail. It could be oared or sailed, depending on conditions, and was large enough to accommodate at least a half-dozen, if not more, fishermen.

Simeon sailed along the western shore of the Galilee looking for the ideal spot to open his business and settled in Dalmanoutha. He found his crew shortly thereafter, two brothers, Nechunya and Calev, who were honest and hard-working.

Rosi was kept busy all the time with the chores that were required to run even a modest household. Milling flour, baking bread, cleaning and salting fish, curing olives, drying spices, purifying and trying to insert herself into the small, but cliquish community of Jewish women in Dalmanoutha. No'ach, their son, arrived shortly after they all found themselves in their new home. That was five years ago and no more children had, at least yet, come forth alive.

The boy was devoted to his father and followed him everywhere he could, even trekking behind him in the early evening as he journeyed down the dirt road less than a quarter of a mile from the beachhead where Simeon's boat was anchored. Simeon had already taught the boy how to repair patches in the nets and restore sections of the sail. But as much as he wanted to go out with his father, the boy was too young to be out in the dark stillness of the waters.

"Come with me, Rosi, and give me a hand with a plank," Simeon requested. "Are you feeling any better now?" he asked his wife.

"Oh, yes, Simeon. I think I may have just needed some air and came down to get some water," she answered, getting up from the boulder.

"See over here?" he led her eye. "One of the ribs near the boat's aft has cracked and is coming loose," he told his wife. "I may be able to glue it back together, save the wood, and put it back in place. Hand me that small plane tool over there."

Rosi reached down and gave him the tool. He carefully extracted the faulty plank and worked the plane down, bit by bit, little by little, until all the nails had been extracted. With a strong tug he pulled it away from the boat's wooden frame a little more vigorously than he had anticipated and, as it was released, a small, narrow piece of wood, about seven inches in length, cracked off the timber rib and flew out into the air like a missile.

Rosi was in a direct line to the flying chunk and she held up her hands to stop the projectile and protect her face. But as quickly as the brown and mottled piece of wood flew into the air and towards her, Rosi's right hand clenched itself around it, and she caught it in mid-air.

"*Rosi, Rosi. Are you alright?*" Simeon dropped the plank and ran over to her. "*You could have lost your eye!*"

"Oh, no, I'm fine," she laughed a little clasping the fragment. "I guess you'll need to replace the whole thing now?" She turned the small object in her hand around to look at it and, without thinking, placed it in the pouch of the woolen tunic she was wearing.

By now the beach was bustling with more than a dozen small fishermen and their boats, nets, fishhooks and spears scattered on the shore, the debris of a successful night. The atmosphere of the beach had the appearance of being disorderly but, in reality, there was a regular, predictable rhythm to the hustling enterprise. God had furnished the lake to nourish and sustain his transcendent creation.

They headed away from the splashing and clatter, walking uphill through the henna-colored reeds to the narrow path that turned into the central square in Dalmanoutha, a short distance at the top of the chalky trail.

Two neighbors, Timothea and Gaia, were trudging down in the opposite direction, towards the beach, going to bathe. The women weren't Jews like Rosi and Simeon-Peter but Rosi smiled politely. There was no reason to engage in a conversation, but neither was it necessary to be unfriendly. Everyone needed the water, and there was more than enough for all. Timothea and Gaia, like many of their kind, had distinctive markings on their bodies. Tattoos on their eyelids and mystical symbols inked into the underside of their forearms. One, she noticed, was a distinctive hexagram with two triangles laying upside down on top of each other.

In no time the disorganized stone walls of Dalmanoutha appeared, and after a turn in the road they entered the large wooden door that was opened to the courtyard. No'ach spotted his father first and then his mother walking a few steps behind and ran out to greet them.

"*Ha'av! Ha'av,*" he cried

"Oh, there you are children. No'ach come back in here now and leave your mother and father be," his grandmother scolded. Her white hair was pulled back and kept in place with a hijab that wrapped over her head and forehead and tied under the chin.

"Your *ha'av* is tired," Rosi called out to her young son. "We are going to give him something to eat, and then he is going to sleep." Simeon and Rosi unloaded their baggage and the women began to lay out a meal.

"Is your head any better?" Dvorah asked her daughter.

"Yes, mother, I think so. I don't know what came over me. I was up early, as usual, and then I felt my eye begin to twitch."

"It's the smoke from the ovens," she told her. "It's very close in this courtyard with so many fires. It's good that you went down to the water to clear your head."

Simeon took his young son outside, and they sat on the floor underneath a square canopy that hung off the side of the house. He took out a small paring knife and a piece of oak and began to scrape gently. He took the boy's hand, placing the knife in it, and traced his own movements. His son was enthralled.

"May I come out with you tonight father?" the young boy asked.

"Silly boy. You know you have to stay here with your mother and grandmother. But soon enough you will be with me. You'll see. Wait long enough and it will happen," his father confided in him.

Later, when the sun was higher, after Dvorah had taken the boy down with her to the lakeshore to bathe and soak some of her son-in-law's garments in the still water, husband and wife were left alone in the small house. He brought her over to the corner where a straw mat, assembled from reeds that had been gathered and dried, was laid on the dirt floor. Rosi removed the headscarf that covered her hair, and now she untied the cord that gathered her long, lustrous hair in place.

Simeon-Peter enjoyed removing his wife's clothing. He placed her beneath him on the mat spreading her hair out like a fan. He lifted her tunic, rolling it beyond her waist and pulled off the thin, triangular linen undergarment that she wore around her pelvis. Then he raised her legs up and wordlessly entered her.

"This is a good day," he thought to himself. "I feel lucky. We will make another son together."

The rest of the day passed quietly. Rosi let Simeon-Peter sleep for many hours knowing that by the time the sun began to set he would have to rise, go down to the lakeshore and drag the boat out into the lake for another evening. By nightfall the Dalmanoutha fleet had been dropped into the lake some sailing north, some northeast out into the vast open waters of the Galilee, oared by robust arms or danced by sails propelled by the fragrant wind that rose up reliably to guide the sailors into the tranquil night.

It came up suddenly and unexpectedly. The *sharkia*. There were no indications, no warnings. It had been placid water. The nets had been flung out. Simeon-Peter, Nechunya and Calev were resting in the boat, their heads leaning against the starboard side. Three oil lamps that had been fluttering now were fighting to stop from being extinguished by the wind. When a squall whips itself up into a frenzy there is never time to prepare either on land or on the water. And so the three men bolted what they could, pulled the nets back into the boat, lowered the sail and grabbed the oars furiously to push their way back to the western shore and try to anchor the boat safely on the beach against a blanket of hard, black rain.

The lightning woke the boy, and he jumped up urgently. It lit up the house for a split second, and then it was quiet. He could hear his grandmother snoring in the far corner of the large room. Rosi was closer, just a few feet away on a pallet, but she, too, was sleeping tightly. There was no rain, just the cold smell of dampness. Then more thunder and lightning.

The boy threw his tunic over his head and ran out. The courtyard was empty, and he started walking, trancelike, out of the courtyard. When the lightning flashed No'ach could see the outline of the route. A few minutes later he was pushing his way through the reeds and was on the deserted beach. A few fires had been burning earlier and there were embers still glowing. Suddenly there was a giant roar and a huge gust of wind almost knocked the boy to the ground, but he ran up to the waterline, soaking his bare feet and legs.

Then he saw it. Out in the distant lake, backlit by a bolt of lightning, an angry cloud hovering over a boat, tossing and flinging a vessel in its mouth like a triumphant cat who has finally caught up with a rat she'd been stalking.

"It's my *ha'av*. It's his boat," the little boy shrieked, "*Ha'av!! Ha'av!!*" he screamed into the empty air. There were some others now on the beach. A few men who had heard the coming storm ran down to check the moorings of the boats that had not taken the journey over the dark waters that night.

"Who are you boy?" one screamed from a distance. "Go back home. It isn't safe here."

But No'ach did not hear them. He was transfixed by the boat that floundered out in the lake. With each lightning strike he glimpsed the three men bouncing, holding onto the center mast to keep them upright as rain poured down on them soaking them to the bone. And then the boy started to walk into the water, the waves swirling up savagely then flattening themselves onto the broad sand.

"Where is he going?" one of the men called out, now running closer. "Get out of the water boy. Get out of there."

But No'ach could not hear anything. He was hypnotized by the sight of his father's boat rocking back and forth just beyond the reach of the shore. A wave came up abruptly, tossed his small body into the air and then knocked him down, rolling him back onto the beach. Water enveloped him, shut his eyes, ears and nose off from reality. Then he was swallowing the lake. It entered his nostrils and his mouth. "Father! Father!" he tried to scream, but the sound would not come out. Then no more air, no more breath, just empty space and silence.

Two strong hands pulled his short legs back, turning him over and pushing on his chest. Shaking him awake. "Wake up, No'ach. Wake up!" Rosi was saying. "You've had a bad dream."

Dvorah was next to him and the two women were holding him, wiping his brow, gently caressing his cheeks.

"The storm. I saw *ha'av*. He was going to drown. They were all going to drown, Nechunya and Calev and father," he cried out.

"Everything is alright son. There is no storm. Just some distant lightning and thunder. It has cleared up. It will be morning soon. Your *ha'av* will be home. All will be fine."

The boy was dripping with sweat. His heart was racing, and his pulse had quickened. He opened his eyes wide looking around the room and then wiped them. "I'm home? Here with you?" he asked as she brushed her hand over his forehead.

"Yes," Rosi answered. "Where did you think you were, little monkey?"

~~~

It was before daybreak that Rosi heard the voices shouting. "Come quickly. Something has happened to your husband." Rosi looked up and saw one of her neighbors, the wife of another fisherman.

"Zacchus is back from last night. He said Simon-Peter had gone overboard," the woman hollered.

"Overboard? Why? There was no storm?" Rosi cried out.

"Exactly, it was a calm night, but something happened out on the lake."

A wave of anxiety flooded her. "Is he … is he drowned?"

"No, no, Rosi. But hurry."

She arrived a few minutes later to see a small commotion. Nechunya and Calev were securing the boat into its position. Simeon-Peter was on the ground, splayed on the sand, his white kufiya unraveled, his long shirt shredded and torn. Calev spied her first.

"He's going to be okay. He is. It was a miracle!"

"What happened?" she ran over to him and knelt beside him. He was drained but breathing steadily.

"I've had the wind knocked out of me, Rosi," he started to whisper with some effort.

"Don't talk, Simeon. We will get a cart and carry you home."

"I'll be fine. Just let me lie here," he said panting. She took his hand in hers and squeezed it. Nechunya came over with a flask and lifted Simeon up slightly. "Here my friend, drink from this."

Then Nechunya explained what had happened. They were out only a short distance from the shore. It had been an unproductive evening, and they had not caught much. Without warning a brisk wind erupted blowing down on them with a cold spray. They could see the curved outline of the shore fifty strokes away and calculated they weren't too far from the beach. There were a few fishermen who had pulled into the harbor, their small lanterns dotting the coast.

"All of a sudden Simeon-Peter looks out and says, *'There's my son!! There's my No'ach. What's he doing there?'*"

Calev joined in. "Where? I asked him. I don't see anybody."

Neither of the other two men saw the boy on the shore. Then there was a quick strike of lightning which lit up the sky, and in that illumination Simeon-Peter saw his son walk into the violent waters.

"NO, NO!" he cried out, "*What are you doing? Where are you going?*' And then Simeon-Peter jumped off of the boat into the rough waves of the lake.

"It was so dark, a black cloud passed overhead," Nechunya added. "He began swimming to the shore calling out to No'ach as best he could. We oared the ship as quickly as we could to the shoreline and were calling for Simeon-Peter. But we couldn't find him anywhere."

"And then," Calev said, "and then, both of us saw him."

"Saw who?" Rosi asked.

"The stranger. A man we had never seen before," Nechunya told her.

"A stranger? From around here?"

"We don't know. He was kneeling over Simeon's body. It looked like he had pulled him out of the water. His two hands were pressed again Simeon's forehead."

"Did this man say anything?" Rosi asked.

"It was odd," Calev related. "He said, 'I cannot let this man drown,' and then he was gone."

But by then the first rays of the sunrise began to bubble up on the eastern horizon. Simeon had regained some of his strength and was breathing freely and steadily. Nechunya and Calev gathered up their nets and started walking through the grassy reeds.

"Let's go home," Simeon said to Rosi, and they followed close behind the two fishermen until the narrow brown dirt path emerged, the one that led them up the dune to the flat stone walls of Dalmanoutha.

EPILOGUE

Simeon-Peter never did take his son out fishing at Ilanot. A few months after the stranger pulled him from the water, he heard the news that his father Jonah had passed away. He and No'ach, his pregnant wife Rosi and his mother-in-law, returned to Capernaum. The boat that had served him well was mortgaged to Nechunya and Calev. It lasted for another twenty years undergoing extensive repairs and restoration until it outlived its usefulness and was abandoned.

Simeon returned twice more to Dalmanoutha. He had fallen under the spell of a Galilean rabbi, a man who had been brought to him by *Ammo* Andreas, his youngest brother. Simeon and Andreas decided to leave their families and travel with the rabbi, a charismatic man who gathered many followers. They traveled often along the western shore of the lake and on one occasion, when the rabbi needed some rest, Simeon-Peter suggested they sail to the beach at Ilanot and take the rabbi up the dirt road to the village where he had lived for five years.

The second time was three years later, just before Simeon-Peter returned to his wife and family. The rabbi had stirred up a great deal of trouble in Jerusalem and was arrested, imprisoned and executed. Afterward rumors abounded that this man had escaped death, that somehow he was able to stay alive. But the men who had followed him for those three years were not convinced. They were depressed and dejected and a few of them decided, on Simeon-Peter's recommendation, to travel up to the western Galilee and see if they could start anew as fishermen.

They settled on the beach at Ilanot, just south of where a traveler would now find Ginosar. Simeon eventually sent for his wife. Rosi joined him with their second son who had just turned six. She lived with Simeon and traveled all over with him. Even as far as Rome where she died in his arms many years later.

Acknowledgments

I am grateful to many who have helped me by reading early drafts of the manuscript, discussing the characters or providing me with information and suggestions for research. These include Stephanie Blacksmith, George Burger, Barry Canner, Russell Dembin, David Denniston, Maureen Herlehy, Yoav Kaddar, Daniel Kempton, Christopher Lavin, Laura Liebman, The Rev. Canon Thomas P. Miller, Michael P. O'Connor, Robert Travers, Prof. John Rayburn and Prof. Eric Meyers in the School of Science and Engineering at SUNY New Paltz, and the Rev. Ellen C. O'Hara. My editor, Andrew J. Daniels, supported me immensely and I thank him for his steady, close reading of the drafts I submitted to him. I very much appreciate the encouragement of my husband, John DeWald, my brother, Paul Kitsakos and my sister Bonnie Menicucci.

The letter from Rose Frances Albertson in Chapter Twelve was adapted from a 19th century travel journal archived in the New York Times.

CPSIA information can be obtained
at www.ICGtesting.com
Printed in the USA
FFOW02n1847200315
12039FF